BONES AND LIES BETWEEN US

BONES AND LIES BETWEEN US

MARCY MCKAY

SkipJack Publishing

Burton, Texas

Enjoy Sunday Canyon.
This story came to
me while visiting a
cemetery years ago—
Marcy McKay

For Mark, Mason and Luke

Always.

"The most terrible poverty is loneliness, and the feeling of being unloved."

—Mother Teresa

Accolades

"Don't expect to walk away from Marcy McKay's stories unaffected ... expect to be touched and enlightened."

– A.G. Howard, *New York Times* Bestselling Author of the *Splintered* Series

"Marcy McKay has a God-given talent for creating gripping stories and unforgettable characters."

– Linda Broday *New York Times* Bestselling Author

"*Bones and Lies Between Us* is packed with action and emotion. Marcy McKay's voice leaps off the page."

– Pamela Fagan Hutchins, *USA Today*-bestselling author of *Saving Grace*

"*Pennies from Burger Heaven* is a fun, wild read that grabs your heart strings and never lets go."

– Ken Oder, author of *The Closing* and *The Judas Murders*

CHAPTER 1

In my dreams, Mama still haunts me. I'm usually chasing her down endless hallways or dark alleys. I always reach out for her, desperate to touch her long black hair or that dingy rabbit fur jacket she wore like a queen.

I never catch her, though. Didn't in real life, either. I just wake up, covered in sweat and sometimes screaming, while the truth socks me in the gut.

I *hate* her.

Snickers yank me from my thoughts. The cafeteria at Remington Elementary School roars all around where it smells like Mexican food and floor wax. I don't look back to Brittney and her Bowheads giggling at me from their table.

The mean girl loud-whispers to her friends, "She's doing it again."

My face turns stop-sign red. Out of habit, I'm rubbing my hand over my buzz cut shaved extra close to my skull. Those crazy red curls are long gone.

I ignore the Bowheads 'til I hear Brittney calling Mama a bag lady, then I turn around and look at her dead-on. "Don't laugh. I'm in summer school 'cause I was homeless my whole life. What's *your* excuse?"

Her eyes widen, then fill with tears. She scoots back and hurries through the lunchroom. The others stumble over themselves trying to keep up with her. I refocus on my food, taking another bite of burrito. The mystery meat squishes in my mouth. The refried beans aren't too bad, though they could use more cheese.

Me and Mama used to be hungry all the time, but I've got a whole new life now. A bedroom all to myself. I bathe every day. I haven't missed a single meal in almost four months.

It's awful.

School is as rough as the streets of Paradise—it's just a different kind of bad. Most kids laugh, joke and eat, while I sit at this table by myself for Lonely Lunch. I got in trouble for telling Stan Donaldson I'd knock his balls up to his boogers if he touched my backpack again. I was always better in math than reading, but Mama pushed me hard at both. It's one of the few things she did right. I'm smarter than the rest of these obliviots and don't belong here.

I eat a spoonful of beans and glance at the boy with black hair, alone at the table in front of me. You can't see 'cause of the back of his head, but he's wearing glasses, too. That's Walter Anderson. He has no friends and likes it that way. Walter makes weird noises and croaks a lot. Lunch is his favorite part of the day 'cause he can build forts out of tortilla chips and no one bugs him about it. We have different teachers and classes, but still know each other.

Freckles cover my pale legs. I'm wearing brand new everything: jean shorts, a purple T-shirt and orange sneakers. No more hand-me-downs for me. My Mickey Mouse watch says it's 11:50. Forty-five more minutes 'til today's torture is over. I miss my old friends. From my old life.

Uh-oh. Dusty Hamlyn and his goons carry their lunch trays toward us. He's the one with dirty-blond hair and hazel eyes, standing between Tyler and Kyler Robinson. He's also the oldest boy here—almost thirteen, but still in fifth grade. It must be the twins' jobs to laugh at everything he says, 'cause that's pretty much all they do. The trio walks down the aisle between me and Walter.

Dusty doesn't look at him or slow down as he pops Walter upside the head, sending him crashing into his guacamole. They chuckle and move on.

I skid my chair back and shove Dusty from behind hard enough his tray clatters to the floor. He topples some chairs over with a loud clang. The cafeteria falls silent as Dusty turns to see who dared to touch him. I hook his nose with a hard left and blood splatters all over me. Before he drops, he pops my right eye.

Pain explodes inside. I'm dizzy but manage to dive onto Dusty and pin him down. The past four months bleed from my fists as I whale on his ugly mug. His misery makes me hungry for more. Stupid Dusty's got a mama and a daddy. I know 'cause I've seen 'em holler at him at the grocery store. I'm sure he deserved his daddy slapping him near the Cap'n Crunch.

He's the one crying now. His goons scream from the sidelines for me to stop, but I push away the noise and keep punching. It's all that matter now. Dusty shouldn't—

Someone tugs me off him.

It's Mr. Allen, the fourth-grade teacher. He's bald and usually likes to tell knock-knock jokes, though his goatee twitches now as he demands, "What's going on here?"

The kids all watch with their usual disgust. The teachers look more disappointed. A blush heats me up while I press a paper napkin against my nose.

Dusty spits blood and stands. "She started it! Scab Face!"

We lunge for each other, but Mr. Allen stops us.

The long, thin scar across my left cheek throbs beneath these stares. My voice trembles. "Dusty hit Walter for no reason."

"Liar," Dusty says.

Walter croaks from his chair, guac dripping from his glasses. "It's truuuuuuuuuuuuuuuuuuuuuuuuuuuuuuue."

"Dusty steals his lunch money every morning," I add.

"Nuh-uh." He wipes his palms on his ratty shorts.

"Check his pockets. Walter draws blue stars on all his cash."

"How does he eat, then?"

"I buy most of his meals for him."

Mr. Allen pokes out his palm like a tray, then Dusty sighs and fishes out a wad of dollar bills. It's like the teacher's holding the night sky with so many blue stars there. He scolds Dusty, then asks Miz Shelton to please clean up Walter. The boy squawks as she leads him away.

"Let's go." Mr. Allen tells us.

I grab my Dallas Cowboys backpack, sure to stay on the right side of the teacher, far from that bully. I hold my head high through the whispers and stares. These Somebodies think they're so much better than me, but I can take whatever punishment they dole out.

It's all I've ever done.

My eye throbs worse with each step to the principal's office. We pass a poster on the wall with a hand spread out wide that says, "Bullying STOPS here!"

Up ahead, Walter sits on a bench. Miz Shelton has wiped off most of the guacamole, so he looks Walter-ish again. His giant toad eyes shine at me behind his glasses as we pass by. He croaks to me, "You're myyyyyyyy friennnnnnnnnnnnnnnnnnnnnnnnnnnd."

I mumble, "I don't have friends."

"What's that?" Mr. Allen asks.

"Nothing."

The office at Remington Elementary School has huge windows that overlook the main hall. Most folks walk straight to the big counter up front for what they want, but if they take you back into the work area, then you're in trouble.

Big trouble.

Mr. Allen knows to sit Dusty across the room by the copy-machine chair, then he parks me on the bench outside Miz Simpson's door. He leans so far into my face I tilt back.

"Knock-knock," he says.

I sigh. "Who's there?"

"Wooden shoe."

"Wooden shoe who?"

"Wooden shoe like to hear another joke?"

Mr. Allen breaks into such a silly grin that I might smile the teensiest bit, but no more. He taps my nose. "You did the right thing. You just handled it the wrong way."

He salutes the secretary before leaving. "They're all yours, Mrs. Taylor."

"Thank you, Mr. Allen."

Blood speckles my clothes and skin. Uncle P bought me this Mickey Mouse watch at Disneyland over spring break. We had the worst time there. Somebodies are so snooty they take vacations from their already perfect lives. A few classmates went to the beach or skiing, while others visited grandparents. Some had what they call "staycations" right here in Remington. None of 'em told me any of this, but I've got ears.

Through the hall windows, I watch Mr. Allen give Walter back his money. They high-five each other and walk away together. I smile 'til Dusty oinks like a pig at me, then I give him the O'Dell finger—the middle one that'll make cops drop their donuts and chase you for twelve blocks.

Trust me on this. Dusty deserves my one-way salute and so much worse.

"Mizzzzz Taylor," he whines to the secretary.

"He started it," I say.

The lady sighs extra loud, so we shut up. I hate being alone with these thoughts, but people irritate me worse. I've gone over the days, the weeks and the minutes leading up to February 15 a bazillion times, so the past four months should make more sense by now.

Nothing makes sense.

Movement through the hall windows scoots me to the edge of my chair. I sit up straighter. That mountain of a man stops in the doorway in jeans and a brown polo shirt. Tall, broad shoulders, dark hair, walnut brown eyes, hands on his hips and wide-legged. Patrick Noblitt. I bet he stood like that back when he was still a detective for the Remington Police Department.

Now, he's just my uncle, though I don't want or need him.

A twitch on his face. Something's off. He must be extra mad. He's shaking his head at me. "Copper Daniels . . ." is all he says.

I gulp. He's Mama's older brother. I never even knew we were family 'til she was already dead. I thought she was an only child.

I wish it'd stayed that way. I've got a jailbird daddy who was a TV preacher, too, but at least he's behind bars. I've never visited him there and don't plan to, thank you very little.

Dusty hollers from his chair. "Scab Face attacked me. My dad will sue your ass."

"Quiet," my uncle barks back.

That stuns Dusty. I grin 'til Uncle P moves in on me.

The school secretary swoons as he passes by, even though she's old enough to be his mom. "Hello, Officer Noblitt."

He seems surprised to see her. She tells him how nice he looks, and he just nods his thanks. Everyone thinks he's so great.

They're wrong.

Dead wrong.

His belt buckle's extra sharp. He stands over me and whispers, "What happened?"

Principal Simpson's door swings open. Her gray hair's cut into a bob, and she always wears those pearl earrings. Everything about her is nice, neat and no nonsense. She's one of the few women who doesn't fan-girl over him.

No smile. "Mr. Noblitt. Copper. Please come in."

Her office is small, with every paper clip in place. I bet she's read all the books on these shelves. Me and Uncle P sit in the two big chairs in front of her desk. He glances at his phone, then shoves it into his pocket.

I can't figure out what's off with him. I keep my backpack close, and he folds his ginormous hands on his lap. We're about to get a talkin'-to. Miz Simpson stares at me, drumming her pale pink fingernails on her desk. I watch her with my one good eye. She doesn't look away, so I don't either. My palms break into a sweat and this black eye twitches, but I can't let her know she's winning. My whole school life depends on this moment.

"Copper . . . this is your fourth trip to my office this week."

Uncle P sits up more.

She opens a folder and reads from a piece of paper. "We've tested you. You're quite bright, but your grades don't reflect it."

"I was never in school."

"I understand you came from challenging circumstances, but that doesn't justify your conduct. Citizenship is just as important as your education."

Not again. Citizenship sounds like a cool party boat, but it's how you treat other people. I scoot forward. "Dusty wouldn't know citizenship if it bit him on the butt. He's a total bully and you never stop him."

"We'll tend to Dusty."

"That's what you said about Brittney and the Bowheads."

"Copper," Uncle P scolds me, then nods for Miz Simpson to continue.

She closes the folder, her lips pursed tight. "We may have no choice but for you to repeat fifth grade."

"I don't want to. I'm not stupid. Send me on to middle school."

"Your grades tell me you're not trying. Your behavior says the same thing. This is all up to you."

"If I don't cause any more trouble in summer school, can I go on to sixth?"

"We'll see."

"That means no." The room swims out of focus. My chest tightens. It's harder to breathe and I'm covered in sweat. Tears rush up my throat, though I'll drop dead before I bawl in front of these two. "I just wish . . ." My voice disappears.

Uncle P stands. "We're done here."

Miz Simpson flinches like he slapped her. They normally take turns lecturing me. Her gaze questions him as she stands. "Actually, I need to speak to you privately."

He sighs impatient.

After I step outside, the door closes behind me and I press my ear against the wood. They're talking about last week. I may or may not have stuffed paper towels in the girls bathroom sinks, then left the water running.

Dusty yells, "Mrs. Taylor, look!"

"Shhh," I tell him as the secretary tries to get off a call. They're making it impossible to hear, but catch one word from my uncle — *juvie*.

Juvenile detention center.

There's no way I'm going there. My heart catches fire. Miz Taylor puts her hand on my shoulder as the principal door swings open.

My uncle storms out without so much as a thank-you or goodbye. That's so not him. He stomps down the empty hallway, staring at his phone.

I grab my backpack, then follow behind him. The principal ushers Dusty into her office. He sticks his tongue out at me, so I give it right back. The other kids have gone for the day.

My sneakers squeak as I catch up to Uncle P in the hall. "What's my punishment?"

No answer.

That means *Wait for your beating*.

His phone's buzzing so much it almost falls from his hand. Texts and voicemails keep pinging through. He grumbles a cussword I've never heard him say.

"What's wrong?" I ask.

He hurries through the exit to the parking lot. The June sun blinds me. There's not a cloud in the sky, so the heat presses down extra hard. It's the kind of day me and Mama worried about melting like popsicles. The weather irritates my Diablo scar from that horrible terrible night. It's throbbing on my right cheek now. I can still smell the burritos from lunch.

Uncle P moves in angry silence. He owns the nice new truck on the end—the dark gray one. We could pile six to eight people in to go to the movies if I had any friends. That's not even a real parking spot. He just slammed to a stop. Johnny Law never does that. His phone rings with a new call, but he just grumbles and sends it to voicemail.

"What's wrong?" I repeat.

He opens my door, then holds it for me. "We need to talk about your mother."

"You know I don't want to—"

"It's important."

I climb inside with my pack, then groan at the bundle of white tulips between our seats.

"We're not visiting her. I was on my way to the cemetery when the school called." He doesn't move.

The empty playground stands behind him. He keeps his grip on my door, watching me with that dark puppy-dog look. Mama's eyes were leafy green. Besides the color difference, that's her staring at me now. My heart pangs so much I glance away.

It doesn't stop the pain.

"Your mom . . ." Uncle P says.

"I told you—"

"Please let me finish. You're going to see this on TV, and the other kids may tease you."

His face and tone scare me. I hold my backpack, then nod him on.

"Your mother has been accused of murder. It's in today's paper."

An invisible fist rams me in the gut and my breath catches. "What? How?"

"Before your mom died that night . . . she killed a cop."

CHAPTER 2

My world turns topsy-turvy. Down is up and up is down. I'm too stunned to speak. I stare at Uncle P still standing at the truck doorway like a pale ghost. He looks as awful as I feel. I try to absorb his words, though I can't stop shaking. Nothing makes sense. Mama's dead, but somehow hurting me even worse.

Uncle P takes my hand. "Are you all right?"

"You're lying." I pull away and press my face against the Dallas Cowboys star on my backpack.

He shows me his phone screen. It's the headline from the *Remington Daily Herald*:

PROSTITUTE ACCUSED OF KILLING COP

My breath quickens. I stare at a zoomed-in picture of Mama. It's just the side of her face, but she looks mad. Her mouth's open like she's arguing with someone. They're cropped out, so I can't see who. She's wearing her dingy fur jacket and the macaroni necklace I gave her for Valentine's Day. I made that at the library, so I know she wore it less than a day before she died.

I gulp. It's been over four months since Mama held me. She loved playing with my crazy curls. She whistled as we walked all those miles to and from Paradise. She called me her Copper Penny.

Memories brush up against me again and again, like a pair of eyes always watching.

I want nothing to do with the past. Truth is, she also left me sleeping a lot, then sneaked off to do bad stuff.

Like killing a cop.

That can't be.

Can it?

My uncle holds his phone out again. "Do you know who took this photograph?"

I shake my head.

A few seconds tick by. "What about a police officer named Felix Riker? He was the victim."

"No."

Uncle P falls silent. I'm struggling for words. I feel him searching me for answers. He says, "It happened –"

"She didn't do it." I can't believe I'm saying that.

He blinks a few times, then runs his hand over his chin. "The evidence says otherwise. Her blood is on the murder weapon. It doesn't look good."

"I don't care. She didn't do it."

My uncle puts his phone back in his pocket. "It happened inside the courtyard of St. Columba's Church in Paradise."

"City Cemetery?" I cringe. "Mama hated that place. We avoided it as much as possible." I don't want to, but my mind pictures all the creepy wooden crosses outside that church:

++++++++++++++++++++++++++++++

++++++++++++++++++++

++++++++++

My legs feel so wobbly I'm glad I'm sitting down.

"Someone smashed in Officer Riker's head with a brick."

I feel sicker. "Mama wasn't that strong."

"You know that's not true."

"I want to go home."

"I don't think we can. I'm sure the media's swarming the house."

"I don't mean there." I stare behind him into the distance. You can't see Eternal Peace cemetery from the school, but me and Mama lived just seven blocks from here. We slept beneath the stars under the Warrior Angel statue for protection.

Different girl.

Different life.

I hate that place, too. Watching my uncle, he's got that same worry brow across his forehead Mama always had. I ask him, "When'd you find out?"

"Right before Mrs. Simpson's meeting."

"Why didn't any of your cop friends tell you?"

"I keep asking myself that."

He's on vacation to take care of me, though I don't want or need him. His phone rings again. Uncle P cusses, mutes it, then jams it into his pocket.

A white van parks behind us in the parking lot. *News Action 4* is painted red across the side. A woman with long blonde hair and baby blue eyes hops out from the front seat. She's wearing a suit jacket and jeans.

That's Gigi Carlisle, their star reporter. Me and Mama used to watch her on TV in between clients. The camera dude is skinny with a no-name face. Definitely not a reporter. He's filming me and Uncle P with his video camera now. Gigi's even prettier in person and gives us her full TV smile.

"Stop that," Uncle P tells the cameraman.

She whispers something to her coworker, then he returns to the van.

"You should've told me about this." My uncle glares at her.

"I called and texted you the second I found out. Check your phone." Her eyes sparkle as she sticks out her hand to me. "Hi, Copper. I'm Gigi Carlisle."

Uncle P says, "You're not talking to either one of us."

"Let me tell your side of the story, Patrick. Give me an exclusive. I'll treat the girl well."

The girl.

"Move now, or I'll smash down your van."

"Be reasonable."

His keys jangle as he rushes around to the driver's side.

The reporter leaves, too. My uncle revs the engine. He backs up and pauses at the van, then hauls forward. We whip a U in the empty school playground. I watch the grassy tire tracks from my side mirror. Mama would've bulldozed over Gigi ten times already.

We roar onto the street, with the *News Action 4* van close behind. We speed up, then they do, too. The tulip smell fills the truck. I want to puke but buckle up instead. A banana-yellow umbrella sits on the floorboard on my side since thinks he's Mr. Prepared.

I ask him, "How do you know Gigi?"

"Our jobs."

"She likes you."

He drives faster.

"Where are we going?"

"I'm not sure. I didn't have time to pack."

Seconds tick by. Up ahead, I see the black iron fence of Eternal Peace and my chest hitches. He's not thinking today. We usually drive out of the way to avoid the cemetery. I haven't been back *once* since Mama's funeral.

He says, "Sorry, I forgot."

When I was little, I thought the fence tips looked like little pointy soldiers to keep the goodness in and the badness out. They failed her, then failed me worse. All I've got left is that horrible terrible night.

We speed along the backside of the graveyard where weeds and brown grass cover the Nobody Section. The boy who stole my heart is buried there. I look away, Tommy Tucker sadness seeping through me. My Diablo scar pulses so hard my whole cheek aches.

Gigi's van stays glued to us. We pass the open gates with the golden EP across 'em.

It's not home.

Never was.

Not really.

I'm sweating. I close my eyes, but still feel every blade of grass, each headstone, and all the pretty bones buried beneath 'em. I grip the door handle; certain I'll have a whack attack any second.

My uncle slams on the brakes at a four-way stop. Gigi's van skids behind us.

Another white van pauses at the cross street. It's the *Eyewitness 12* news team. Every TV station must be out looking for us. The guy reporter sees Uncle P and barrels this way.

"Vultures." We blow through the intersection.

Gigi powers on, too. It's about to be a three-way crash 'til we swerve around at the last sec.

I shout, "Go to your house!"

"You sure? It'll be a zoo."

"At least we can hide there."

Even six feet under, Mama's still causing trouble. We blaze through my uncle's neighborhood of nice, normal houses. I don't say a word when we pass the little white house with red shutters.

That's where him and Mama grew up—2613 S. Hilltop Street. My people were Somebodies. He grew up to be a cop. She grew up to be a crack whore. I used to know the Irish setter named Sugar that lived there long after 'em. Now . . .

Mama's dead.

Tommy's dead.

Sugar's dead.

There's a trail of blood and bones I can't escape. Doom

spreads deeper inside, so I count my breaths like Dr. Vasquez taught me, trying to leave freak-out mode. One, two, three.

It works some, though my thoughts stay so scrambled. Our truck rounds the corner. I hear the noise before I see the craziness.

Uncle P stops at the edge of our block. He whispers, "Oh my God."

News vans line the entire street. Several reporters stand on the sidewalk in front of his house—that small brown one in the middle on the right. Men and women hold microphones and talk to TV cameras. Others snap pictures of the yard. Some are from local television stations, while tons are newspapers from out of town.

My jailbird daddy's sort of famous, so this is even bigger news. His wife murdered Mama at Eternal Peace cemetery on February 15, 2010. Now they're saying Mama killed a cop earlier that night. I'm dizzy.

Uncle P's house seems so far away. I stare at all the people in the yard, demanding juicy details about me and Mama. I grip my backpack, trying not to lose my mind. This can't be happening.

But it is.

Uncle P says, "Don't talk to anyone. Not a word. You got that?"

I nod.

It takes a while for us to work our way down the street. We can't just whip into the driveway 'cause too many people block it. Pink, purple and yellow pansies line the flower bed along the porch. He keeps a pretty yard to hide all the ugliness inside.

In the middle of all the madness, I recognize the brown piece-of-crap truck parked in front of the house. That belongs to Eugene "Butt Munch" O'Dell. He was the cemetery groundskeeper who always tried to run me and Mama off. He was there that horrible terrible night.

Now he's Uncle P's yard boy. He mows every Friday.

Not today.

A reporter shouts. "They're here!"

Everyone swarms so close they jostle our pickup. I yelp as cameras flash, and they hurl questions through my window. "How do you feel about the accusations against your mother? Do you think she's guilty? Did you know Officer Riker? What was your favorite Dumpster find? Why'd you cut off all your hair?"

My uncle sees it the same time as me, then he turns even paler. One word is spray-painted in black across the front window of his house:

TRAITOR

CHAPTER 3

The media catches us staring at the graffiti, so more cameras flash. My uncle blasts the horn long and hard, revving the engine. The mob parts for us, still shouting questions and taking pictures. We inch our way into the garage. He closes the door the second we're inside.

The mechanical hum lets me sigh for the first time. The last thing I need is to have a whack attack in front of the world. Mama's news is bad enough. The ruckus outside roars on so much I focus on my blue bike in the corner to stay calm. I never even had training wheels. It took a whole afternoon, but Uncle P taught me how to ride and I just did it. Pedaling through the neighborhood is one of my favorite things to do.

Was.

He may never let me outside again. His tools and garden equipment hang in a perfect line on the wall. Patrick Noblitt likes his life in order.

He got the wrong niece here.

My uncle turns off the house alarm in the small kitchen, then he resets the code as soon as I'm behind him. Dark cabinets and hardwood floors, a framed photo of us in mouse ears at Disneyland sits on a shelf.

There are no pictures of me and Mama. 'Cept that one of her in today's paper with the ugly headline:

PROSTITUTE ACCUSED OF KILLING COP

My heart twinges again. I smell the bacon and eggs from this morning, even though there's not a dirty dish in the sink. This house is two bedrooms, one bath, a kitchen and a tiny living room. It's the kind of place me and Mama would've killed to live in.

Uncle P cusses, drops his keys in a bowl on the counter, then paces.

"Why'd they write 'traitor' out there?"

"I guess since my sister killed a police officer that somehow makes me a traitor at the station."

"She didn't do it."

"Please don't start."

"She didn't. Let me see the article again."

"I'm not sure you should."

"Seriously?" I listen to the buzz of reporters out front. The Shangri-La motel has forty-two free channels, so me and Mama watched a lot of shows in between clients. I understand our dirty laundry makes for good TV. My jailbird daddy just adds to the scandal.

An irritated meow rattles the walls as Princess the Evil Cat wanders into the kitchen.

"Hey, girl." Uncle P scoops up the gray Manx into his arms. Manx should mean a worthless bag of fur, but it's the name for her nub tail. He nuzzles that hairball. "Sorry about all this."

"I like how you apologize to the cat, but not to me."

"What'd I do?"

"You don't believe in your own family." I plop into a chair at the round table. "How do we help Mama?"

"We don't. She's guilty."

"She's not. Besides, it's not like there can be a trial. She's dead. He's dead."

"I think they're making a statement since he was an officer of the law."

"Instead of helping the homeless, they're wasting time and money on this crap."

"A dead policeman isn't crap."

The doorbell rings. Uncle P locks his jaw tighter. Uh-oh. With Mama, that face always meant trouble. He hurries across the hardwood floor, muttering, "Sonova—"

I expect him to go all Johnny Law on some reporter, but he checks the peephole, then lets O'Dell in and resets the alarm. "Sorry. I should've invited you in sooner."

"No problem." O'Dell wipes his forehead under his ball cap. "I can't get any work done. It's nuts out there."

"It's going to get worse." Uncle P stares at TRAITOR reflecting backward at us from the large window.

No one talks. O'Dell's still beanpole skinny with pale blue eyes, but his shaggy brown hair's been chopped into a normal boy cut. Those cargo shorts and worn Rolling Stones shirt are his uniform now. I wonder if Mama would still be alive if O'Dell had run us off from the cemetery like he always tried. He's the closest thing I've got to a friend.

Doesn't say much.

He clears his throat, then tells my uncle, "I saw some kid vandalizing your house as the media showed up. I chased after him, but he got away."

"What did he look like?"

"Short black hair, Dallas Cowboys T-shirt. Teenager."

I say, "Sounds like the Barrio Brothers."

My uncle looks away. His phone rings, and he answers it. "About time. What the hell?" He storms into the kitchen, then turns on the faucet to drown out his conversation.

O'Dell gives my beat-up face a once-over. "You look like shit."

"You are a shit."

"Who waylaid you?"

"I won, so shut up." I lower my voice. "Take me to Paradise so I can prove Mama's innocent."

"Are you kidding me?"

"Does this seem funny?"

"I don't have time for your nonsense. Besides, I've got plans."

"Pah-lease."

My uncle walks back to us. "You're not going anywhere, young lady."

"Watch me." I rush by, grab my pack, then answer 'em both with a door slam.

Uncle P painted my bedroom sunny yellow before I moved in here, thinking I wanted to be reminded of the sunrise at Eternal Peace. Like the scar Diablo carved into my face isn't enough. I hate the color. He also bought me this froofy canopy bed, all these prissy dolls and stuffed animals.

Does any of this look like me?

I dump my backpack onto my purple comforter. Pencils, pens, a homework folder and a copy of *A Little Princess* spill onto the bedspread. It's a story about a super-rich girl who becomes orphaned. I won't be at summer school to return this to the library tomorrow.

Doesn't matter. It's mine now. I shove the book into the bag again. Fifth grade sucked anyhow.

A full water bottle sits on my nightstand, so I pack it, along with a tiny flashlight. My stomach growls. Stupid Dusty interrupted my lunch. I'll grab something on the run. I'm sad about missing guaranteed meals, but I push the thought away. Food isn't reason enough to live with a traitor. He's betraying his own sister. With all the bad Mama did, she's no cop-killer.

I think.

Ripping off my T-shirt, I go to the closet. Uncle P bought me this training bra even though I still just have two pancakes. Tons of clothes hang here, but I slip on a Dallas Cowboys T-shirt. Blue and silver are the Barrio Brothers' gang colors, so everyone else has to wear 'em, too. It's like school spirit, but with life or death.

I never thought I'd go back to Paradise, and didn't want to, though I miss my friends more than anything—Salt, Pepper and Mai Wong. They're all I've got left from my old life, though I haven't seen or talked to anyone since February.

It's not like they've got phones there. Summer is crazy hot, so I keep my shorts on. I glance at the framed photo of Mama sitting on my dresser. That teen in a white dress. It was her favorite color. White's for purity, which is funny 'cause it's so not her. I found this picture taped to my uncle's dash in his cop car and that's how I learned we were family.

Now I know it was taken in the backyard of their little white house with red shutters. I've always wondered if she was pregnant with me there, so I'm sort of in the picture, too. I've never asked him, and she's not around for questions.

In the bottom drawer of my dresser, I fiddle under the stacks of jeans and grab Tommy Tucker's Dallas Cowboys ski hat. It fits looser with no hair. I used to call him Turdmouth, but he didn't like it and told me to stop.

When a guy dies for you, you do what he says. I take out his rusty pocketknife. Uncle P lets me keep it since it was Tommy's. They were both there that horrible terrible night.

I flip open the dull blade and ask, "You hear about Mama?"

Of course, he doesn't answer. Heaven's not real. Neither is God or the Warrior Angel.

The only thing that's real is hell on earth and I'm already living it 24/7.

That's about to change. I'll prove she's innocent, then CPS will find me a better home and school somewhere else. If not, I'll run away and do it myself. I'm not staying with a traitor. Especially since he's part of why she's dead.

I close the knife and slip it into my shorts pocket. Next, I pick up the taped-up cardboard sign Mama made for us years ago:

NEED MONEY FOR FOOD
GOD BLESS

It feels weird holding this again. I hated standing on corners like street beggars while cars whizzed by us without a second look. Mama should've never made me do that, but she was too busy thinking of herself. I stuff the sign into my pack, hoping I don't have to use it.

Am I sure Mama's innocent?

"What are you doing?" Uncle P says behind me.

I squeal and spin around. He's standing in the doorway. Arms crossed, wide-legged and wounded look. I'm not sure how much he saw, but I zip my pack shut. "You already know what I'm doing."

"I said no."

"You're not my mama."

You wouldn't think you can hurt a man that big, but he looks like he might cry. I go back to packing. "Somebody's got to take up for her 'cause flowers on a grave don't mean jack. A partial print doesn't mean she killed him."

"How'd you know about that?"

"I saw it in that article on your phone."

"You shouldn't understand that at eleven." He sits on my bed and holds a no-name teddy bear. "You shouldn't know the difference between crack and crank. You should be playing with dolls and having lemonade stands."

"Eleven is just a number, and I hate dolls."

"All we do is fight."

"There's no 'we' here. There's a reason Mama didn't want you in our lives."

"We've talked about this. Your mother was afraid I was going to take you away from her."

"That's 'cause you were."

"Only temporarily. I was just trying to get her attention."

"Instead, you got her killed." He says nothing, so I bring it up. "Heard you and Miz Simpson talking about juvie."

"You shouldn't eavesdrop."

"You shouldn't betray your own sister. Traitor." I double down on my glare.

The doorbell rings. Uncle P doesn't move or even blink. He just watches me with her eyes. The seconds tick by. The doorbell sounds again. I feel myself sweating.

O'Dell hollers from up front. "Want me to answer that?"

"No, I need to turn off the alarm. Be right there." Uncle P sets the stuffed animal down and stands. "I'm sorry, but you're not going to Paradise and that's final." He takes my backpack, then leaves.

I'm not sure what the noise is from the other side of the door, then realize he jammed a chair under the knob. CPS won't let him put a lock in my room, but he's still treating me like a prisoner.

Screaming, I kick the door and call him every name in the book, including the ones that'd make Mama wash my mouth out with soap. Wait 'til CPS hears about this! I'm *not* going to juvie. I'm so out of here now.

Gigi Carlisle sweet-talks those two fools up front. Should've guessed it was her. She still wants that exclusive with *the girl*. Add her to the list of women who've probably offered him their monkey pie on a silver platter. I'm just not sure they've done the Sweaty Betty yet or not.

Gag.

I jiggle the handle. There's no secret passage to the attic, or invisible cloaks like in books. I pace around, then notice I'm doing like my uncle did earlier and stop. I wish I could drain every bit of him, Mama, and my jailbird daddy from my blood, but I'm stuck with this crazy family cocktail.

Pulling back the curtains, I stare into the backyard. A barbecue grill, table and chairs sit on the deck that Uncle P says he laid the wood himself, but it's probably a lie. O'Dell hasn't mowed back here today. Lazy Butt Munch.

Forget it. The window's sealed shut (another CPS rule). I can't grab my bike from the garage, so I'll have to move fast. I set a T-shirt under each foot of the dresser, take out all the drawers, then scoot it across to block the door.

He locked me in. I'll lock him out.

Next, I sneak my baseball bat from the closet. Uncle P took me to watch the Texas Rangers play at home. Grown men with gloves chasing a little white ball. So dumb. I'm woozy. Guess Dusty hit me harder than I thought.

A glint through the window startles me, then I spot a head peeking over the fence at me. A black lady with a monster 'fro points a camera this way. She's snapping pics like I'm a supermodel or something. I'm surprised there's not more media back here.

I'm not sure I can do this. Paradise is hell on a good day, but there are no good days. Plus, I'm not sure Mama's worth it. We saw how much I meant to her. I glance at her framed photo and ask her teenage self, "Why am I helping you?"

Of course, she doesn't answer. We both already know the truth.

Taking care of her is all I've ever done.

I close my eyes and swing the bat.

CHAPTER 4

My bedroom window shatters. The house alarm screams. A few pieces of glass fall inside, though most shoot onto the patio. It takes a couple more taps to knock out all the strays. I'm already crawling through when I hear Uncle P jiggle my door handle.

He pushes against the barricade, then knocks. "What are you doing? What's wrong?"

That startles me. I shriek and cut my thigh on some glass, then hobble on across the yard. He'll be here any second. The lady photographer acts like it's a Hollywood premiere, she's taking so many pictures over the fence.

"You got a car?" I holler. My head hurts from Dusty's punch.

"Standing on my van now. Give me an exclusive, and I'll give you a ride."

"Deal."

As I open our wooden gate, my uncle shouts my name from the back porch. O'Dell's with him, and they're zooming this way.

I slam the gate behind me so hard the whole fence rattles. I grab a stick and cram it through the latch hole like a lock. That'll slow 'em down some. The van engine's running. Uncle P will sue this lady and the news station for kidnapping me.

Not my problem.

I leap into the front seat and we speed away. Glancing back at the guys in the alley, I feel a little better. They stand there several seconds, probably memorizing the license plate, then disappear back into the yard. Probably headed for my uncle's truck.

The cut on my thigh burns. I feel woozy. Dusty must've hit me harder than I thought. The van barrels down the tight space and hits a plastic trash can. It flips high in the air, then spills garbage everywhere. The neighbors won't be happy. Somebodies are weird about citizenship.

"Oops." The photographer giggles, then drives faster.

I like this chick but buckle up just in case. At the end of the backstreet, I tell her, "Stay away from the media. Turn right."

She does. Hmmm, a grown-up who listens to me. She's even better than I thought. Uncle P's neighborhood is so boring with its perfect lawns and pretty flowers. These people could use a few mobile homes, cars on cinderblocks, or good ol' fist fights.

The house with a concrete gnome in the front is where Walter from school lives. I hope he's forgotten all about Dusty and is home building tortilla-chip forts right now.

The photographer studies me. "Why'd you run away?"

I open my mouth to explain, but too much of Mama sticks in my throat. I've promised this woman an exclusive, so I swallow hard then tell her a different truth. "I hate living with my uncle."

"How come?"

I shrug.

"Think yo' mama killed that cop?"

"No."

"Why?"

"'Cause even at her worst, she'd never do that."

"You ever gonna forgive her?"

Her gaze bores into me so hard I squirm in my seat. "How do you know I haven't?"

"You never visit her."

My stomach turns over. I was right. Someone *has* been watching me.

When I glance back at her knowing eyes, she winks and picks up her camera one-handed. "This sees all."

I shiver, imagining everything behind the scenes she's caught on film. My fights. My whack attacks. Who knows what else? My breath quickens and I feel seasick. I try counting, but it doesn't work.

She asks, "Who wrote 'traitor' on your house?"

"What's your name?"

"'Chele."

"Never heard of that."

"It's like a seashell from the ocean."

"'Chele," I say. Me and Mama were supposed to escape to California together. We wanted to live right on the water in a little white house with red shutters and a dog named Sugar.

We pass a tiny one-story house. It's just a few blocks from Uncle P's, but a whole 'nother world away. There's no flowers and the yard's almost brown from all the dead grass. A black Trans Am sits in the driveway.

It's Dusty Hamlyn's house—Walter's cash-stealing bully. I don't want that punk anywhere near me but think it's smart to keep tabs on him. Dr. Vasquez says I shouldn't have an Enemy List anymore.

What does that headshrinker know?

'Chele says, "How'd you get your black eye?"

"You tell me."

The photographer grins a blinding smile. I'm surprised she doesn't ask about juvie, and I sure don't offer any answers. I've got to decide what's next.

I'm lost in thought when I realize we're slowing through the cemetery gates and grab the armrest. "Wait. What are you doing?"

"Tell me about yo' mama."

"Turn around. I can't do this!" My palms break into a sweat

and I fidget, my heart hammering. I don't even hear what 'Chele says next. I can't have a whack attack in front of this photographer, though she may already have pics.

She heads extra slow toward the Warrior Angel. I scream and jump from the van, leaving the door open. At least it'll be harder for her to maneuver on this path.

"Come back," she hollers.

No dice. I tug Tommy's ski hat farther over my forehead and pass a stone bench. They water so much to keep the grass this green for all the Somebodies buried here. I could go back to the main street, but Uncle P might be there.

Endless graves stretch out in every direction. The sun's shining bright, but that horrible terrible night storms inside again. *Raining. Running. Death.* Diablo and Miz Jesus both chased me for different reasons. Mama stole his drugs and Miz Jesus was insane. He slashed my face. She held me prisoner. They weren't working together, but it felt like an army of evil out there.

I remind myself all the bad guys are dead. That doesn't give me much comfort as I sprint through the cemetery, tapping on my chest like Dr. Vasquez taught me, hoping my body will listen for a change. "I'mokayI'm okayI'mokay . . ."

'Chele's van still follows behind. At least she can't leave the road. My gaze lands on the Vanderhausen Mausoleum. The stone door looks locked tight now.

Sunny-yellow CAUTION tape roped off the crime scene that horrible terrible night. I found Mama's body mangled inside the bottom right drawer . . . the hint of her blue angel wings tattooed across her back . . . her mouth caught in the forever O from her final scream.

I hobble faster, sure to steer clear of Mama's grave and Tommy Tucker back in the Nobody Section, too. Can't go near the Warrior Angel. I head toward the fence straight ahead in the Garden of Friends. My legs zigzag through the headstones, bushes and trees. I accidentally knock over some plastic flowers, but don't bother to pick 'em up or say I'm sorry.

I glance back. 'Chele's van is gone. I'm not sure if she gave up or will try to stop me on the street. I zoom past the pine trees and crunch over pinecones, then come up on the crystal blue water of the pond in the Garden of Friends. It makes me think of Tommy.

I hurry to the fence and slip through the bars—

No, I don't. I've fattened up so much I don't fit anymore. Not sure what to do, I look all around.

There's just one way. I pull myself to the top bar. It takes two tries to climb up and it's hard to balance, but I hook my leg over the railing, then jump down. The grass makes for a soft landing.

No uncles or photographers around here.

Mission accomplished.

He says people have patterns. Routines and habits that they live by. It's true for criminals and honest folks alike. Figure out those and you can nab 'em. He'll expect me to take University Drive into downtown, then on into Paradise, so I'll take a different route.

His pattern is to wake up and spend too much time stinking up the bathroom every morning. Then he eats breakfast, but I'm not sure what he does while I'm at school. I overheard his cop-friend Lydia say how much he misses being a detective.

I don't want or need him taking care of me. As I'm hurrying through the neighborhood, I open Tommy's dull knife. "Remind me not to ride with strangers."

He'd laugh if he was here.

"Sorry I didn't visit you today. It's still too . . . much."

He understands.

"Did Mama really kill that cop?"

I listen, then nod. "I didn't think so—wait, stop lecturing me. So, what if I got into that van? It turned out fine. You're as bossy as O'Dell. Shut up. Mama's innocent . . . Says who? Says me. Oh, just drop dead, *Turdmouth*."

Closing the blade, I stuff him back into my pocket and hope he's mad.

The digital sign at Walgreens says it's one hundred six degrees. They say it's the hottest June in over a decade. I believe it. We've had triple digits every day this month. I bet people are dropping like flies in Paradise. I stagger on, wishing Uncle P hadn't stolen my backpack. I'm thirsty.

My feet feel like bricks, and I scold myself for turning soft. Me and Mama made this trek at least twice every single day, morning and night. That's twenty-four miles round-trip. She thought living in Paradise was too dangerous.

Nowhere is safe. My thoughts scatter. It was iffy there for a while, but I somehow managed to hold it together with 'Chele. I wish I knew how to stop these whack attacks forever.

At the corner of Stratton Boulevard and Washington, I look left to the Burger Heaven restaurant on the interstate. It's shaped like an actual hamburger. That's where me and Mama always stood with our sign. People ignored us, looked down on us, and even spit at us.

Doesn't matter. The money hardly ever went for food.

My stomach growls. I'd like to chow on a Cloud 9 Special right this second. A burger and fries would be perfect right now since stupid Dusty made me miss lunch. Uncle P brought me to eat here, and we sat in booths like regular Somebodies. That tasted better than the food.

One block over, I ignore my sadness and head up the sidewalk to a two-story Victorian house. The green lawn at the downtown library is as nice as my uncle's yard. The US flag droops on the pole 'cause there's no wind today. Just heat. I almost feel Mama walking alongside me. Headed for Story Time. That was always my favorite part of the day. The last book we heard together was *Charlotte's Web*.

Wilbur lived.

Mama didn't.

I let Uncle P take me to Story Time all of once. He doesn't understand it's hard to believe in fairy tales after your life's become a nightmare.

The library rules are painted on the window entrance, but I know 'em by heart:

No bedrolls, blankets, duffel bags,
suitcases, or large plastic bags of
any kind in the building.

I need to learn the facts about that cop's death to prove Mama didn't do it, so I fix my sweaty ski cap, then go inside. I'm not one of *those people* anymore. I've got a library card and everything. It's in my backpack, but still counts. That's one of the only nice things Uncle P did for me. I can check out books all by myself now.

No worries. I've memorized my ID and PIN so I can still use their computers.

The air-conditioning hits my wet skin and I shiver. The smell of books and Mama memories hit me from all sides.

Tears spring to my eyes, but I wipe 'em away fast and remind myself: I hate her. At least Lizard Lady's not at the front desk. She didn't like us hanging out here. Me and Mama were usually upstairs in the kids' section, so I drag myself up the stairwell.

Flowers, rainbows and smiley-faced suns dangle from the ceiling of the second floor. Posters for the Summer Reading Club hang on the walls. The bathtub with the lion's paws sits empty in the center of the room. I'd like to crawl into that tub and finish reading *A Little Princess*, but Mama ruined that, too.

First, I stop by the bathroom to clean this nasty cut on my leg. Every stall is empty, so I've got the place all to myself. I can't just shove my thigh under the faucet, so I dampen a paper towel and dab the cut beneath my shorts. It stings so bad I growl. A mom walks in with her little boy, sees me, then spins right around and leaves. I snarl louder.

Time to get to work. I find a computer facing the steps and

elevator in case I need to bolt. It's the only way out, though I could jump out the window if need be. I did that once from the Shangri-La and don't recommend it.

The library's also not part of my pattern anymore, so I don't think Uncle P will show up, but I can't be sure. Outrunning him isn't easy. I tap the keyboard, then set Tommy Tucker's closed knife on my lap. People get jumpy when you leave the blade out in public. Trust me on this.

I've forgiven him for our tiff earlier. I take off his ski hat to let my sticky head breathe. After typing in my access info, I go to the *Remington Daily Herald*'s website. Mama's still the lead story, with the same pic and headline:

PROSTITUTE ACCUSED OF KILLING COP

It's like seeing a stranger. Twenty-seven is old, but still too young to die. That familiar hurt destroys me again, so I concentrate on Officer Felix Riker instead. His photo is like a school picture, with the US flag hanging in the background. His brown hair is graying at the temples. No smile. Navy-blue cop uniform and gold badge. Fifty-three years old, Riker served on the police force for thirty years. He had a wife and two sons, ages ten and eight.

Lots of other newspapers picked up the article: the *Dallas Morning News*, the *Houston Chronicle*, the *Austin American–Statesman*. A few California papers also ran it since my jailbird daddy and his whackjob wife were big-time TV preachers in LA. I wish they'd kept taping *The Lord's Power Hour* there, but his hooter-mcgrooter got him in enough trouble that they skipped town. He took his congregation's cash, too.

The news doesn't mention it, but I know he shipped underage girls into the country for the Barrio Brothers to sell as sex slaves. I asked Uncle P why they only nabbed him for the white-collar stuff.

He stared at his shoes, while the color left his face. "I, uhh, wasn't allowed in on the investigation."

"Why?"

"I've got a personal connection to the case through him and your mom."

Whatever.

It's library quiet around here. I grab a pen and notepad, then jot down the facts:

- *Two eyewitnesses saw Corrine Daniels Noblitt arguing with Officer Felix Riker in the courtyard of St. Columba Catholic Church early the morning of February 15, 2010.*

That's City Cemetery in Paradise with all the white crosses. Miz Jesus murdered Mama a few hours later at Eternal Peace graveyard. I sigh.

- *Mama's partial fingerprint was found on the murder weapon. Riker was smashed in the head with a brick. Mama's blood is 100% on there.*

Two eyewitnesses. Before I can read more, I notice someone staring at me over my computer. She says, "I thought that was you."

CHAPTER 5

Lizard Lady steps around the table, then moves closer my way. Her hair's still piled too high on her head, though her pointy cat-glasses are gone. I don't know if she's wearing contacts now, or maybe she had that special eye surgery.

She glances at my buzz cut, black eye and slashed cheek. Rocking on her heels, she tries to smile. "You probably won't believe this, but I miss seeing you and your mom here."

"You're right, I don't believe it." I turn off the computer screen, then slip my notes beneath Tommy's hat.

"I wasn't very nice to you two back then."

I hold her stare.

"I've thought a lot about you both since your mom . . ." Lizard Lady pauses extra-long, then mumbles, "Passed. I regret my behavior."

"You should."

"I—"

"You suck at apologizing."

She chuckles. "I do, and I'm so sorry for not treating you with more kindness, and I'm so sorry about your mother."

"Which? The dead part or cop-killing part?"

"Both. Her passing broke my heart."

"People can't say dead. Mama's not lost or gone or passed. She's d-e-a-d."

The librarian's grin tightens, staring beyond me. This is so hard for her and I'm glad.

When she looks my way again, her face softens. "I have a new angel book that I'd love to show you if you have time."

"Angels aren't my thing anymore."

"Oh." Lizard Lady keeps glancing at the elevator and stairwell.

I look over there. "You're going to call my uncle, aren't you?"

"No."

"Why not?"

She clears her throat. "Because he's already on his way. I knew you were here as soon as you logged in. He's worried sick about you, but . . ." she smiles, steps back, and floats her arm toward the elevator like a game show hostess. "I wanted to apologize and invite you back first. Please don't destroy anything on your way out, and please know you're always welcome here."

I brush past her and hobble toward the stairwell. My uncle chased me down these very steps four months ago. He knew I was his niece back then, but I didn't.

Neither of us realized Mama was already dead. Life's weird in the secrets it keeps or shares.

In the lobby, I knock over the magazine rack, just so Lizard Lady understands what I think of her and that lame apology. I don't miss Story Time one bit.

Outside, the heat shocks me first thing. I realize I left Tommy's ski hat and my notes upstairs but can't go get 'em. I don't see Uncle P, that photographer, or any cop cars nearby.

Still, I race around the back of the library and take several side streets. My mind flashes back to Valentine's Day night at the cemetery for the bazillionth time. It was my last night with Mama.

The wind blew through me as I pulled out our sleeping bags extra fast near the Warrior Angel to get Mama to bed. It'd been a drain of a day—working the corner at the Burger Heaven, the Valentine's Day lunch at Mission for Hope, a few customers at the Shangri-La, then partying with Mama's frenemy, Bird, and her sons, Salt and Pepper.

My tummy growled as Mama staggered around the statue, laughing and crying at the same time. She flung her arms out wide like a cross and shouted at the night like she was screaming to God himself. "Don't fall into temptation. The spirit is willing, but the body is weak. Save us from walking in lusts, excess of wine and abominable idolatries."

God shivered up my spine. I hated it when Mama did her Bible talk.

She laughed and stumbled around more, wagging her finger at me. "Asshole, thinks he can trick me, but I'll show him."

"Come to bed now, Mama." I tried and tried, but she didn't budge.

She took off running. The chilliness didn't wake me up much. I just straggled behind her. By the time I caught up to Mama, she'd dropped to her knees and hung there a few seconds. "Whoa, I don't feel so good."

Mama slumped onto all fours and hurled onto the ground. She burst into tears, globbing onto my knees so hard I almost tumbled over. She wailed like the wind. I felt every teardrop as she sobbed against me. "I've got to chaaaaaaaaaaaange."

She didn't change.

The memory fades, but not the sadness. Of all Mama's stunts, I sure didn't expect her to get murdered that night.

Or kill a cop.

I glance at Tommy's pocketknife. "I always thought she was complaining about my jailbird daddy, but did she mean Officer Riker instead? Was he the one trying to trick her? I didn't know him, but . . . who was Mama blackmailing?" I stare at the silver blade.

Tires squeal around the corner. I jump back as a black Trans Am barrels my way. It's Billy Hamlyn's car—Dusty's big brother. The windshield's tinted so dark I can't see inside. O'Dell says Billy's a total jackwagon.

Must be a family thing. The hot rod swerves across the wrong lane and rockets at me. I back up as Billy slams on the brakes and fishtails beside me. I shriek and dive out of the way. The front window cranks down, and that's not Billy Hamlyn behind the wheel at all.

It's Dusty.

I gasp. His beaten face looks so much worse than I remembered. Principal Simpson should've expelled me from school for that. I went berserko on him.

"Get in," he demands.

"I won't."

"Get in."

"You can't drive."

"You just saw me, Scab Face."

I'm exhausted and my feet ache. A siren wails in the distance, though it's coming closer. Lizard Lady called my uncle, but she might've called the cops, too. She's done it before. 'Chele's probably snapping pictures this sec. I can't decide what to do.

"Back seat," Dusty says. "Lie down."

The sirens will be here any minute. I yank the door open and climb in back. Dusty slams the car into gear, then punches the gas. Tires shriek. He laughs as we haul down the street, and my head snaps against the back seat.

Clouds and blue sky whiz above. I kick at him. "Slow down."

He laughs and speeds up. The car peels around a corner, and I brace myself since I've crawled into a coffin on wheels. That may be Dusty's plan for revenge. You couldn't fill up one pew for my funeral. I want to pull out Tommy's knife, but don't want Dusty to know about the boy who stole my heart. I notice Dusty watching me through his rearview mirror.

"What?" I wipe my nose for any boogers.

"What'd you look like with hair?"

"Shut up."

"I heard it was long and curly."

"I said shut up."

"That's cool about your mom. Murder."

"She didn't do it, stupid."

"How can you be sure?"

"I just am."

He shrugs. "Your dad sounds like a total baller, too. My parents are never in the paper. Well, except those DUIs." He pauses at a stop sign, then floors it again.

My whole body jerks. "Does your brother know you stole his car?"

He shrugs.

"Billy doesn't, does he?"

No response.

"He's going to kick your ass." I laugh. Dusty still doesn't say anything, so I ask, "How'd you find me?"

"Saw you drive by my house. I followed the van."

I mentally kick myself for such a rookie mistake. I've lost all my street smarts. Stupid 'Chele.

"Where am I taking you?" Dusty asks.

"Paradise."

He whistles low. "Is it as bad as they say?"

"Worse."

"You can sit up now."

I do but wish I hadn't since Dusty almost hits some construction cones on the street. I slip Tommy Tucker out and thumb the closed blade like I used to my lucky penny. I'm sure to keep it out of sight.

He's not helping.

I study the outline of Dusty's face. The bruises on his right eye are so much bigger than I thought. I didn't realize I hit the other one, too. I whipped up on him bad.

Wait. Those scrapes and cuts weren't there this morning. My

stomach turns when I realize . . . "Who gave you that other black eye?"

"You, Scab Face."

"Nuh-uh. I hit your left eye, your nose and chin." I gulp, then say, "Someone else hurt you."

He grunts and looks off.

I stare at the cherry-red floorboard of Billy's Trans Am. This is his car. "Why'd he hit you?"

Dusty fidgets in his seat, staring out his window. I'm not sure he'll answer, then his gaze meets mine in the rearview mirror. He doesn't blink. "'Cause I got my ass kicked by a girl."

Guilt socks me as hard as him punching the gas. I lurch against the speed, buckling the lap belt across me as I shrink smaller inside. I just wanted Dusty to leave Walter and his cash alone. I never meant to get anyone in trouble.

Not like that. A police siren screams right behind us. Dusty cusses under his breath. Looking back, I recognize the cop in the passenger seat. "Crap. That's my uncle's ex-partner, Lydia."

Busted.

"Don't—" I yell, but Dusty already gunned it and our tires *screeeeeech* around a corner. I steady myself against the back of the passenger seat. Death better kill me fast 'cause my uncle will torture me extra slow.

Dusty laughs, weaving in and out of traffic like it's a video game. I cringe. His crazy look scares me since Mama used to make that same face. We race through downtown, where more people might die 'cause of us. We speed by the Remington Police Department. They all think my uncle's a traitor.

Dusty runs a red light. I know it's not real, but I swear the sirens shriek louder. Two more cop cars bound up behind us from either side of the intersection. I wonder if they've figured out I'm in here. If so, they'll drag me back to Uncle P's house.

No way I'm going back there.

Folks watch us from the sidewalks as we zoom by. Dusty laughs 'til we hit a dip in the road and the nose of the Trans Am *cracks* against the street. I scream, surprised we don't flip over. Somehow, we keep hauling.

For the first time, Dusty's eyebrows knit together, worried. He cares more about his brother beating him up than going to juvie.

"Stop!" I don't know if he doesn't see it or doesn't care.

Two cop cars block the street up ahead. Four policemen stand in the road in that same stance Uncle P does all the time. Arms folded, legs wide, daring you to cross 'em. We're trapped. It doesn't faze Dusty.

"Look out!" I scream.

His laugh scatters through me. I shriek so loud and shrill it doesn't even sound like my voice. Officers dive out of our way.

Last second, Dusty slams on the brakes. I close my eyes, waiting for death to take us. The crash whips my body and shocks me with a thousand jolts. My head smashes against the passenger seat, then I collapse . . .

CHAPTER 6

Where am I?

I flutter my eyes open and look around the back of some car. It hurts to move. Dusty Hamlyn lies limp against the steering wheel. Why's he here? His forehead's bleeding. It takes me a few seconds to remember.

His brother's Trans Am.

Dusty driving like a maniac.

Our wreck.

I can't have been conked out long since we're still in the car. The cops stand outside Dusty's door. Steam rises from the crushed engine. I keep my head down, so it looks like I'm unconscious.

Dusty groans. He doesn't budge, but mumbles something I don't understand.

Cop #1 has wide eyes and a full belly, like a human pug. He taps on Dusty's window. "You okay, son?"

Cop #2 says from my side, "Is that Noblitt's niece?"

"Don't know," #1 hollers. "Hey, Lydia, I think we found the girl."

The girl.

I debate on whether to keep playing possum or bail. Dusty's

still slumped up front. The cops don't hear him whisper to me, "Run."

That snaps me to attention. I moan and notice Lydia peering into my window. She's lean and mean, with a long brown ponytail. She's my uncle's only cop friend who I like. She won't be easy to escape.

Lydia taps on the glass. "Copper, can you hear me? Are you hurt?"

"I want out."

"Wait. I want to make sure you're all right first. EMS is almost here."

Dusty doesn't move.

"I smell gasoline." I whip off the lap belt and push the seat forward before she can stop me. The pain's dizzying. Lydia opens my door and offers her arm for support, then eases me to the curb. I assure her I'm fine, though I do feel wonky.

She sits beside me. "Who's your friend?"

"Juan Valdez."

Her mouth stays flat-lined. She doesn't think I'm funny. "You're on your way to Paradise, aren't you?"

"No."

"Copper."

I double over and groan to distract her. It's not a full lie. My lap burns from the seatbelt yanking against me. Plus, Dusty got in one hard punch this morning. I can't believe that wreck didn't kill us. Everything plays out in slow motion.

"Breathe," Lydia says, just like Dr. Vasquez.

Another cop hollers to her, "Noblitt is 10-76."

That means he's on his way. "Why didn't you tell Uncle P about Mama?"

Her lips twist tighter. "Chief Lancaster didn't release the report until this morning. He's still furious with Patrick. I called as soon as I could."

"Why's he mad at him?"

Lydia turns stop-sign red. "I, uh . . . let's get you some water." She hollers for someone to bring me a drink, then changes the subject. I can't get her back there.

I'm panicked. Sounds like my uncle's in trouble with his boss. Plus, he'll ground me for the rest of my life for this, and that's just for starters. The clock's ticking faster. My thoughts scramble.

Moaning again, I keep my head on my knees and scan the accident. We crashed straight between two cop cars. I don't see anyone hurt besides me and Dusty, so that helps. Folks from the sidewalk are rubbernecking our accident. I want to be mad at him, but he's banged up way worse. I'm worried since he still hasn't moved.

It's not an act. The *News Action 4* van sits across the street and Gigi Carlisle's walk means all business. I'm not sure if she realizes it's me. She'll still want that exclusive with *the girl*.

Irritating her may be my new hobby. Lydia doesn't seem to care for her by the looks of that frown. The ambulance pulls up and the EMT guys take a stretcher around to Dusty's side and work to open his car door. I hope they haul him straight to juvie. He better be okay, or I'll punch him.

Guilt socks it to me. This is all my fault, even if I didn't mean to, but I need to get to Paradise for Mama. I don't want anyone playing hero, so I'll stay away from everyone. I spot a drainage pipe in the alley that's too small and gross for any of these Somebodies.

The old me is back. I don't like her, but this new one sucks, too. The cameraman's already filming the wreck, and 'Chele may be snapping pictures this sec. I don't see her but feel those knowing eyes.

Dusty's wearing an oxygen mask. I swear he nods at me, then his whole body jerks around on the stretcher. I don't know if he's faking a seizure or not, but EMS flocks around him.

While Lydia's watching it, I apologize to her in my head.

She'll get in trouble with my uncle for this. I hate that but gear up for the only real lesson Mama ever taught me.

Run.

Downtown, I pass mirrored buildings and folks dressed in business suits or jeans. Most of 'em sip lattes while talking on their phones. Everyone avoids me. I tell myself it's 'cause I smell like drainage pipe, but it's probably my bowling-ball head.

I think I lost the cops for good. My sides pinch, my feet pound and my lap burns from the seatbelt. Don't forget my black eye. If I'm already this bad off, there's no way I'll survive Paradise. Plus, I need to get to City Cemetery to check out the crime scene for Mama.

I collapse onto the empty wishing fountain where we used to rest. A couple sits holding hands on the edge nearby, but they let go of each other when they see my filthy clothes.

"What are you looking at, punk?" I hold up my wrist. "This Mickey Mouse watch came straight from Disneyland."

They almost trip over each other leaving. Whatever. The fountain is empty. No coins shimmer beneath the crystal blue water anymore. It's run dry. I left my lucky penny on Mama's grave to help her in the afterlife, but someone stole it right away.

Doesn't matter. Wishes and luck are hocus-pocus. Life's just one big con game and you better hope you make it without too many bites in the butt. That penny was broken, anyhow. It did nothing but get Mama and Tommy killed, then me stuck living with a stranger.

Now Mama's all over the news, and my jailbird daddy doesn't help. Ex–TV preacher, please. He's just a pain in the ass.

I pull out Tommy Tucker's closed knife. "I didn't think Dusty would crash . . . I need to stop climbing into cars with strangers . . . I know I've got work to do. Why are you always on my case?" I start walking.

The Church of the Living Water still stands on the street like a giant square box behind the fountain, luring people in with its fake

Jesus talk. The sign says they're building a new fellowship hall, so they're not really interested in healing the sick, feeding the hungry or helping the poor.

They just want your cold, hard cash. Worry knots up my gut. I hope I don't run into Eddie Loco. He was Diablo's second-in-command for the Barrio Brothers and is still alive. That guy's straight-up crazy and wants me dead for what I did to him.

Just a few blocks from all the boutiques and skyscrapers downtown, the buildings grow smaller. Dingier. Bars show up on all the windows, or garage doors get pulled down over the storefronts at night.

All that money there.

All this nothing here.

At the railroad tracks, I don't pause or make a wish or anything. I did that last time and it didn't make one bit of difference. I cross straight into hell.

Paradise is home of the freaks, the junkies, and the whores. There are folks here of every color of the rainbow in shorts, tank tops, or swimsuits. A few men go topless. Some women do, too. Other people wrap wet towels or shirts around their heads and sit in pockets of shade, desperate to beat the heat. They all look withered and worn.

The smell of human trash makes me gag. I breathe through my mouth like Darth Vader, and yes, I've seen *Star Wars*. Uncle P took me to a retro showing. I should march straight to City Cemetery, but I stagger along the street, wondering . . .

Do people really live like this?

Did Mama actually bring me here every day?

Was this actually our life?

My gut says *yes*, *yes* and *yes*. Paradise is a whole 'nother world, and the meanest, nastiest part of the city. This used to be my home away from home. It's so much worse than I remembered. I want to hop in a shower, but the stains of Paradise can never be washed clean. People like O'Dell don't understand this really exists in their hometown.

Wait . . . something's different. I watch the crowd again. Nobody's wearing blue and silver like the Dallas Cowboys. In fact, I don't see the Barrio Brothers anywhere. No Mexican guys have B-R-O-T-H-E-R-S tattooed across their knuckles.

Everyone's wearing red. That's the color of the Asian Assassins. Did the Chinese gang take over? I wonder if Zhi Peng Wong's still their leader. He's Mai Wong's older brother. Folks stare at my Dallas Cowboys T-shirt. It's like I've stepped into a foreign land and don't speak the language anymore. I need to change clothes before this gets me hurt.

Panic squashes my chest and I look around for somewhere to duck in and turn my T-shirt inside out. The Party Palace liquor store sign blinks from across the road.

That was Mama's candy store, so I head to the alley there. I can name more brands of booze than Uncle P knows flavors of ice cream. The fire hydrant outside the Party Palace is empty. Mai Wong used to leave a soda can on top there as a secret sign she'd sneak over from Chinatown to see me. We spent hours hanging out in our phone booth.

Me and Uncle P called Mai's house to check on her after Eddie Loco raped her. Mr. Wong answered the phone and his voice was soft but firm. "This is a family matter."

Click.

He hung up. The last time I saw Mai was when I poured her into O'Dell's truck after the attack. He took her to the hospital for me so I could keep searching for Mama and Tommy. O'Dell's not always such a Butt Munch.

'Cept he was today. *Mr. I've Got Plans* thinks Mama's guilty, so . . .

"That you, Copper?" a man calls out behind me.

My insides zing at his voice.

Yep, One-Leg Larry hobbles toward me. He's the father of the boy who died for me.

CHAPTER 7

One-Leg Larry wears a grimy red T-shirt and looks even worse, though he was no cupcake before. His beard hangs way past his belt and it's even grayer. He's super old, like almost forty. Sadness and booze line every wrinkle. His metal leg and PTSD came from the Gulf War, so he uses that brown bag from the Party Palace to deal with it all. Something about his Hershey Bar brown eyes reminds me of Tommy.

It hurts to watch him, but I don't let myself look away. I destroyed his family.

One-Leg sobs and throws out his arms. "Oh, Copper girl! My boy's gone! Tommy's gone!"

He buries me in a whiskey hug and bawls all over my bald head. One-Leg's another one who can't say "dead," but I don't correct him since I caused his loneliness. We're flipsides of the same coin.

A girl with no mama.

A father with no son.

One-Leg looked so out of place at Tommy's graveside service. Uncle P found him a suit and everything. There were just five of us at Eternal Peace—me, my uncle, One-Leg, O'Dell and the preacher.

I promised Tommy then and there I'd take care of his pops. That's what he called him—Pops.

I see I'm not doing so great.

One-Leg pulls back and gives me a scraggly smile. "Are you as crazy as you look with no hair?"

"Afraid so."

"You've grown."

I nod.

He laughs, sniffs, then glances down at his liquor bag.

I ask, "You heard about Mama and that cop?"

"Nonsense." One-Leg takes a drink.

"I know. Right?" I hug him again, knowing he'd understand. I'm careful to not snap his bony body in half. "She's not a killer, is she?"

"'Course not. She'd never do something like that."

"Then what's the deal?"

"The world needs a scapegoat." His finger twirls around the top of that liquor bottle. I wait for more, but One-Leg never liked talking deep. Him and Mama were always more interested in the party.

I watch some Asian Assassins shove a guy into the alley across the street, then they disappear behind him. He'll come out bloody—Asian Assassin red, if he lives at all. My insides seize up. I tell myself I'm okay. I'm safe here with One-Leg.

He pulls off his red T-shirt and gives it to me. He's somehow both flabby and skinny.

"You're going to need this."

"Thanks." I slip it on over my clothes. "Do you remember anything about the night that cop was murdered?"

"I, uh, was indisposed. Too much fun . . ." He waves his whiskey bag at me, then takes another nip.

"Oh yeah. I forgot." I don't mention how me and Tommy worried the Street Killer murdered both our parents back then. He even showed me the blood in their tent, but One-Leg had just gone off on a bender.

Mama didn't. Seems silly I ever believed there was a real Street Killer. It was a stunt pulled by Miz Jesus for her murder spree. She spray-painted *God hates the poor* on the streets of Paradise.

It's hard to argue, looking around here. Really, she just hated me 'cause Mama hooked up with her husband years before. Not that I had anything to do with it, but I got punished on all sides. I refocus on One-Leg. "What's the word on the streets about Officer Riker?"

"I think the Barrio Brothers did it. Probably Eddie Loco, since he's the most bloodthirsty."

That name scorches through me. Those devil horns inked over each of the gangbanger's eyebrows. He's covered in tattoos, but the worst is his wandering eye. One looks straight at you while the other goes off looking for more trouble. He held down Mai Wong and ruined her in our phone booth. Left purple choke marks on her neck.

He tried to do the same to me, but some Asian Assassins helped me escape him in Chinatown. I stare at the empty alley again where that gang just stood. I tell One-Leg about TRAITOR spray-painted across my uncle's house and who O'Dell said he saw.

One-Leg smooths his hand over his beard a few times. "Sounds like the Barrio Brothers, all right."

"Where are they now?"

"Haven't you heard? Your uncle put 'em all in jail."

"Really? When?"

"Right after your mom died. There were busts everywhere, with your uncle leading the charge."

"He never said. How'd they trash my uncle's house if the whole gang's in jail?"

"Spider's not. Eddie Loco's kid brother."

"That roly-poly punk?"

"That's him. I haven't seen your uncle here in months. Where's he been?"

"He, ummm." I stare at my orange sneakers. "He's on vacation to take care of me, but I heard his boss is mad at him."

"Hmmm, how is it living with a cop?"

"He locked me in my room today."

One-Leg nods likes he expected as much and drains the rest of his bottle. The fumes smell like gasoline and sting my eyes. I should feel better that Eddie Loco's behind bars, but don't. His glare said he'd pay me back someday. The Asian Assassins beat him up after I told 'em he hurt Mai Wong.

I scan the streets again, but just see shadows. I realize One-Leg's talking to me. "Hmmm?"

"I said, the Asian Assassins took over right away. They're just a different kind of bad."

"How so?"

"Even more violent."

"Zhi Peng's in charge?"

"Yep. Never thought I'd miss Diablo."

The silence ticks away between me and One-Leg. We don't know each other anymore, and we've run out of stories. He was one of Mama's few real friends and always one of my faves. Not a john, or a wasteoid loser. Just a true-blue drinking bud.

Death is what binds us since we both loved Tommy. I need to try harder to keep my promise. I take his pops by the hand. "I've missed you."

One-Leg's eyes are shiny wet. He clutches my palm to his heart. "I miss you and your mom so much. It's not the same."

The smile dribbles away from his face. He watches me a while longer, then whispers, "Go home, Copper."

"Why?"

"Your mama and Tommy are both dead. Go live your new life and be grateful you escaped. Do something your mother never could do."

"What's that?"

"Be happy."

One-Leg lets go, then tosses his brown bag into the trash and leaves. The bottle *clinks* against a bin full of other glass, then he staggers down the sidewalk with no shirt. He wobbles even when he's not drinking 'cause his metal leg's lighter than his real one. He tilts his head like Tommy.

Me and Uncle P had One-Leg over for burgers last month on the geezer's birthday. They even drank beer together, though my uncle just had one out of the six-pack. When we drove him home, Uncle P didn't go through Paradise to get to Tent City. He went through Chinatown. That man's hell-bent on keeping me off these streets.

Here I am again. Thanks, Mama.

Staring at the trash can, I realize I've dug through this very bin for food. Shame tastes so bitter. I should be at City Cemetery by now, but just . . . can't yet. Being back here's just too much.

I swear the sidewalk's hot enough to fry an egg. I'm burning up in these two T-shirts. I wipe my sweaty forehead and hustle down the alley to my phone booth to change clothes. I'll get back to work then.

Sandwiched between these two buildings, I realize I'm excited to see my hangout. I haven't been back since February. This phone booth was my escape, and Mama liked it being next to the liquor store.

Something above glints in the afternoon light. I look up to the apartment complex. The window's closed, with a Dallas Cowboys sticker on the glass. That's the kiss of death with the Asian Assassins in charge now.

Not my problem.

My phone booth still lies on its side in the corner of the alley, covered with so much graffiti you can't see inside. The hours I spent there. I can't help but smile. Me and Tommy were enemies then, so we never hung out there together. Sorry.

Outside the phone booth's double doors, I hear stirring inside. A giggle escapes and I freeze. I haven't heard her laugh in four months. I step closer.

She's talking to someone. It's hard to hear from the hushed tones, but I swear I recognize the other voice, too.

It can't be.

I yank apart the glass doors to discover Butt Munch O'Dell kissing *my* friend, Mai Wong.

CHAPTER 8

The lovebirds spring apart like I caught 'em butt-ass naked or something, but they both know they're busted. They don't realize I've heard much worse from under Mama's bed at the Shangri-La.

Still . . . I grip my hips and scold Eugene Butt Munch O'Dell. "*This* is why you couldn't bring me here? You were coming to Paradise anyway." I shoot 'em both a dirty look.

Mai hangs her head. Her long black ponytail's still up high, but now shaved on the sides and dyed purple. She's wearing a baggy red T-shirt over camo long shorts and combat boots. Her licorice eyes don't shine as bright anymore. I'm not sure who this girl is, but she's not my Mai Wong.

O'Dell's cleaned up from his mowing uniform into nice khaki shorts and a clean red T-shirt. He clears his throat. "Your uncle's worried sick. You should call him."

"Don't tell me what to do. Besides, you bailed on him for your *girlfriend*."

"Maybe I'll call him now. Tell him I found you."

"Listen, Yard Boy." I crawl in between 'em even though there's not enough room for us all inside. "Do that, and I'll tell Zhi Peng Wong about you two. I'm sure he'll be psyched that his only sister's hooking up with some pasty-white dude."

"It's not like that." O'Dell pats Mai's hand, beaming at her.

"Yet," I add.

The tension grows. I don't like it, but they started this fight with their secrets and lies. My eyes inspect the dark splatters on the phone booth glass. I don't think that's random brown paint. Is that Mai Wong's dried blood from Eddie Loco? How could she stand to be here, after what he did to her? The purple choke marks on her neck flash through my mind again.

Forget that. These two lied to me, so I don't back off my glare. She looks away.

I don't. "My mama *died*. I called to check on you, more than once, but you didn't bother to do the same. Now I see why."

Mai wrings her fists on her lap, her gaze stays down. She whispers, "It wasn't like that."

"Really? Then how was it?"

"Copper," O'Dell snaps.

Mai curls deeper into herself. I hate myself for hurting one of the few friends I have left, but I can't seem to stop. I try to soften my tone. "Why would you ever come back here after . . ."

She lifts her head high. Her eyes flash angry as she looks me straight-on for the first time. "I *won't* let him break me."

The bite in her voice says she means it. Her bruises are long gone, but Eddie Loco still left his damage. I know all about that. Invisible hurts are the hardest to heal.

My thoughts scatter a thousand different ways. I was the one who found Mai Wong wandering alone through Chinatown after Eddie Loco attacked her. She was scared, hurt and confused. Out of luck and out of time, I called the last person I ever thought would help me—Butt Munch O'Dell, the cemetery groundskeeper.

Lot of good that did. My two people are dead, while they're are all googly-eyed over each other now. I don't care that they're a couple. I don't. If she wants him, that's her problem.

Mai Wong says, "You're here about your mom, aren't you?"

"She didn't do it."

O'Dell says, "Bet you'd be rich if you had a nickel every time you said that."

"Shut up, Yard Boy." I turn back to Mai. "Do you think Mama killed that cop?"

She shrugs. "Zhi said the Barrio Brothers did it."

"That's what One-Leg just said, but I need proof."

The conversation drops again. I feel their stolen glances. After a few awkward seconds, Mai touches my orange sneakers. "You kept my shoes."

"No," I pull away. "My foot has grown two sizes since then. These are *mine*. I have all new clothes now. Probably more than you."

Her and O'Dell don't know what to do with that, and I don't care. The old Mai Wong once gave me the shoes right off her feet, though I'm not so sure this new girl would. She wipes away a tear, then another one splashes onto her lap.

Great. Her crying should make me feel better, but I just feel worse.

Her voice breaks. "I'm sorry I didn't call."

O'Dell adds, "We should've told you about us sooner. Sorry."

I shrug. "I just hate secrets. You both know that, but you did it anyway."

He shoots Mai a look that makes me think he wanted to tell me, but she wears the pants in their relationship, so they didn't.

O'Dell gives her a side hug. "I need to get back to Copper's house before Patrick realizes I'm gone."

"Whatever. Does he know about you two?"

"You stay here and catch up." He scoots by me. "Can we talk?"

"Oh, goody." I follow him outside to the nearby Dumpster. The sun's blocked back here, but it still feels blistering. O'Dell stuffs his hands into his pockets. "I really like her."

"I can tell."

"No, I mean it." He pulls out a silver necklace with a round black stone dangling at the end of the chain.

"It's onyx," he says so proud.

I know why he picked the color. It matches her black licorice eyes. My throat lumps up, but I manage to say, "It's pretty."

"Don't tell her."

"Then keep your mouth shut with Uncle P."

"All right, but he'll kick my ass when he finds out I left you alone in Paradise."

"He won't hear it from me."

"That's not reassuring and no, I haven't told him about Mai." O'Dell backs up and gives me the O'Dell finger. "You still look like shit."

"You're always a shit."

"Be careful."

I stay to make sure he gets out of the alley safe and sound, then crawl back inside to Mai Wong. Her knees are pulled to her chest. The red bandanna she used to wear around her neck to fly her brother's colors is now wrapped around her wrist like a bracelet.

Her voice sounds so soft I almost don't hear her. "Can we start over?"

"I'd like that." I take off both T-shirts, then put the red one back on. I'll leave the other here for someone else in Paradise.

"I'm really sorry I didn't tell you about O'Dell," she says.

"It's okay."

Mai gives me a sad smile, then touches my black eye. "You're as banged up now as last time I saw you. Why'd you cut off all your hair?"

I shrug.

Mai lies down, so I do, too. Side by side, I stare at the new graffiti on the glass. Most of it's not repeatable. I hate how others have taken over our hangout, but that's how Paradise works. One gang goes to jail, then another rules the streets by sundown.

Mai takes my hand. It feels weird, but I let her. I've missed this.

She says, "What's it like since your mom . . ."

"Say it."

". . . Died."

"It bugs me people are too scared to say that. They act like I somehow forgot."

"I know what you mean." She nods. "People aren't sure how to act around me, so they avoid me altogether or pretend it never happened. That just makes me lonelier."

"Yep."

"I'm sorry about Turdmouth, too."

I chuckle. "I don't call him that anymore. His real name was Tommy."

My heart thuds louder and she squeezes my hand. I'm not sure I have the courage to say it, then I tell her the truth, "I don't have friends anymore."

"I bet that's not true."

"It is."

"O'Dell said you don't like living with your uncle."

"That's an understatement." The seconds tick on and I realize I'm stalling. "I need to get to City Cemetery to the crime scene. Want to come with me since you're allowed here now?"

"Can't. I need to get home before my parents do."

I follow her outside. I'm surprised when Mai throws her arms around me and she squeezes me tight. We're sticky, sweaty and gross, but it's the best feeling I've had in a long time. I hug her back.

She mumbles, "I've missed you."

"I've missed you, too."

"I really am sorry about everything."

"Me, too."

Her warm tears on my shoulder say she means it. For a moment, my old friend is back. Yeah, Mai Wong hurt me, though I understand what it's like to drown in pain. I wonder if she has whack attacks, too, but am too happy right now to ask. If I could bottle up this feeling, I'd stay drunk on it forever.

I stare at the bandanna on her wrist. It's Asian Assassin red. "Tell me one of Grandmother Wong's kooky sayings."

"The way of the dragon knows all."

"What's that mean?"

"I don't remember and my NaiNai died two months ago. Did you notice I said it?"

"I did. You miss her?"

"So much." Mai pulls away from me. She smiles, then hurries down the alley.

It reminds me of all those years Mai was forbidden in Paradise. She had to hide her colors back then. She's probably still not welcomed here, but folks can't say that to Zhi Peng Wong's only sister. She's a princess, even if it's just royalty on the streets.

A gray mouse runs by me. I squeal and jump back as he scurries behind the Dumpster.

"Hey, little fella. Where'd you go?" I check all around but can't find my new friend. I wonder if he's hungry.

Oh well, time to get to City Cemetery. The sunshine crushes me as I step back out onto the main road by the Party Palace. The liquor sign flashes, then someone slams me against the building's brick wall.

His low voice growls. "You should've never come back, Ghost Girl."

CHAPTER 9

Bricks burn against my arms as I gasp for air. A bulky Chinese guy dressed in all red grips me tighter. His ball cap is on backwards over short black hair. I recognize him.

The Asian Assassin's red dragon tattoo sleeve flexes clutching me. "*You're* why Mai got hurt." I struggle to speak, but he smashes me against the wall again. "It's your fault Eddie Loco—"

Someone else yells in Chinese and pulls him off me, then stands between us. The teen's hair is shaved on the sides and longer on top, and the same dragon tattoo covers his arm. I saw him follow this bully when their gang hauled off that poor man earlier.

The boy with the kind eyes argues in Chinese with the bulky one, though I only catch the tiniest bits of their argument. ". . . Mai . . . Zhi . . . Paradise."

I don't recognize these two from just today. They're the ones who saved me from Eddie Loco four months ago in Chinatown. They beat him up for attacking Mai Wong, but it sounds like some of 'em blame me for her visiting Paradise at all.

More dragon tattoos show up 'til I'm surrounded by the gang. They've all got pistols or knives tucked into the bands of their shorts. They're divided between Bulky and the boy with the kind eyes. I guess *blame me* vs. *don't blame me*. I'm not sure what to do.

Bulky slams me against the building again, and several others crowd in closer. My body's shaking. I'm about to die.

A car horn blasts from across the street. The bickering stops. They all look to a thirty-something guy sitting in the back of a black Mercedes SUV with his window down. He's got black cropped hair and cold eyes watching me.

I don't think it's Zhi Peng Wong. That's not how I remember him looking. Whoever this dude is, his silence screams loud and clear. They're all afraid of him.

Bulky tells me, "You lucked out, Ghost Girl. Don't let me see you again." He spits at my feet. "Or else."

Why's he calling me that? The others follow him away, though they all avoid the guy in the Mercedes. Still watching. The gang spreads to different corners nearby, and they go back to slinging weed, ghetto coffee and anything else that'll hook you. Just like the Barrio Brothers used to do here.

'Cept the boy with the kind eyes. He hangs back with me. His smile brightens when it's just the two of us.

"What . . . just happened?" I ask.

"Drago blames you for Mai."

"I got that, though her brother's the whole reason she ever sneaked here in the first place. She always wanted to make sure Zhi was safe."

"Yeah, but you're why she kept coming back."

"It's not my fault Eddie Loco did what he did."

"Yeah, but it's easier to blame the cop's niece. They don't like your uncle, either."

"Join the club."

"Just steer clear of Drago."

"I plan on it. That's not Zhi Peng in the car, is it?"

"No, that's Koi. Zhi's right-hand man."

"Koi," I repeat. "Why do I know that name?"

"I dunno."

"Hmmm, so what does Zhi think of me?"

"He blames you, too, but he appreciates you killing Diablo for him."

My heartbeat quickens. "I didn't touch him."

"No, but you were there. You're the whole reason he died."

I remember Diablo's blood splattering all over me after Miz Jesus sliced his neck in the cemetery chapel. That horrible terrible night tightens my chest.

Raining. Running. Death.

I realize the boy with the kind eyes is grinning at me. He says, "I didn't think I'd ever see you again."

I'm not sure what to say to that and switch topics. "Who murdered that cop?"

"Zhi says it was Eddie Loco."

"That's what I keep hearing, but nobody says why."

"If you weren't white, Riker didn't like you. He hassled us all."

"Why'd Drago call me Ghost Girl?"

"He doesn't like white people."

The Mercedes honks again. That Koi guy stares like he knows me, which gives me the willies.

"I better go. They think I'm weak." My guy trots away, then calls back, "Stay away from Zhi and Koi, too."

"What's your name?" I yell.

"Chao-Chao." He winks at me. "I like your hair."

Watching him run away, my insides flutter in a twisty-tumbly feeling. Nobody has *ever* said they like this buzz cut. For a few yummy seconds, I'm just a regular girl. His smile. The eyes. I hope to see him again.

Koi ends my lovefest. He's still watching from across the road. We lock eyes 'til his tinted backseat window rolls up and he's gone. His car chauffeurs him away, probably back to Chinatown.

"Koi," I say to no one. "Drago and Chao-Chao."

I take the long way to City Cemetery to avoid the Asian Assassins I just saw. Half their homies hate me, and whatever Barrio Brothers are left in Paradise do, too. That's not good. I wish I had Tommy's ski cap to cover my face more.

There's warring graffiti everywhere between rival gangs—on walls, buildings and billboards. This group says *We're the best*, then another says *No, dude, we are*. Meanwhile, the rest of us get caught in the crossfire.

So far, Eddie Loco is Suspect #1, but I need proof. It bugs me I'm getting used to the stink of Paradise again. A bus passes by with Gigi Carlisle's TV face plastered on the side. At least she didn't get her exclusive with *the girl*.

Her shiny smile used to be the faces of Mr. and Miz Jesus on all the buses—my jailbird daddy and his wife. Now I understand why Mama never let me watch *The Lord's Power Hour*. Their theme song replays in my head: *"What a friend we have in Jeeeeeeeeeeeeeeesus, all our sins and griefs to bear."*

Miz Jesus sang that while she hunted me down that horrible terrible night at the cemetery. She changed me forever. I bite my lip and hobble on. Most stores are still run-down or closed, but a few have been redone—a vape shop, a massage parlor.

Two little girls sit on the curb, playing with sticks and talking in high, squeaky voices.

I smile and the years peel away. Me and my best friend, Egypt, were both three when we built rock forts in these same gutters. She was my first buddy, long before I met Mai Wong. Salt and Pepper weren't even born yet.

Me and Egypt had a blast 'til the day her mama picked her up off the sidewalk, then sold her to that businessman in the white BMW. I can still hear her bawling in the back seat of his car. Mama hurried us the other direction. She bought me bubble gum and a cherry Slurpee to make it all better.

I never forgot and sweets didn't make it better.

Egypt's Mama did it again. And again.

'Til one day Paradise swallowed 'em whole.

They disappeared and I spent years missing Egypt, worrying what happened to her . . . 'til the day we collided on the streets of Chinatown, when I was searching for Mama. Egypt kicked my butt. We aren't friends anymore.

I always thought I had a good mama 'cause she didn't sell me for crack, but you can hurt someone without ever raising a finger. Must be a family thing. Uncle P likes to leave me black and blue.

City Cemetery's right around the corner, but I pause at the end of the street and look left. That abandoned hotel at the end of the block was the Barrio Brothers' headquarters, though I'm not sure if the Asian Assassins took it over, too. I wonder if I'd find any Eddie Loco clues there. I've never been inside, and sure won't go in today.

Moving on, I wipe my sweaty palms on my shorts. I'm such a coward. Mama's not worth all this trouble, but here I am.

Five minutes later, I stop at City Cemetery at St. Columba Catholic Church. The building's got stained-glass windows and a pointy roof with a cross on top like you'd expect and not some blank box like the Church of the Living Water. The side courtyard used to have a picnic table where me and Mama liked to stop and rest.

It's not a *real* cemetery. There are no marble headstones, mausoleums or statues like at Eternal Peace. The new priest turned this into a political statement a year or two ago. Almost one hundred white wooden crosses brighten the green grass. The sign out front says it all:

THESE CROSSES REPRESENT THOSE
KILLED BY HOMICIDE IN OUR CITY THIS YEAR

++++++++++++++++++++++++++++++

++++++++++++++++++++

++++++++++

I turn wobbly and numb. Each one has the murdered person's

last name and age on it: ALONZO—28, SMITH—17, YANG—61. At night, these crosses hover over the lawn like little ghosts.

The sunny-yellow CAUTION tape from the crime scene that winter's night is long gone. You can't tell someone picked up a brick and smashed that cop in the head. More than once. His sign is closest to me: RIKER—53.

Felix Riker was beyond old. I picture his photo from all the newspaper articles. No smile. No nonsense. A storm behind his green eyes. Chao-Chao says he didn't like minorities. Are there other clues here?

Scanning the rows, I spot Mama's name in the far corner: DANIELS—27. Didn't expect that. My chest squeezes and my thoughts clamber. Sweat trickles down my back. The heat swelters around me. I fight these feelings, but the ground feels shaky and unstable. My heart races. I try to calm myself down like I did earlier. *I'mokayI'm—*

Panic ramps up and I double over, struggling for air. Every muscle twitches. The shrieks inside my head are so loud they fill my body, though I don't make a peep. I can't stop it. Dropping onto all fours, I grip the grass, certain I'll die.

Time and space disappear. I stay trapped in the struggle.

A man's voice says something above me. I don't get it, then hear him say, "Breathe."

Can't.

He pats my back. "It's all right. I'm here."

I want to hang on to his voice, but he's too far away. The terror's crushing me. I repeat to myself, *hang on, hang on, hang on.*

The man says more I can't understand, but I feel him patting my shoulders. Not creepy-like. Nice. His words come and go. Still, I'm not sure I'll survive.

I'm not sure how long we stay like this, then little by little, I settle back into my body. I collapse to the ground, exhausted and sweaty.

He says, "You're okay now."

I'm not.

When I look up, I see hazel eyes.

"Better?" He grins. His face is younger than his short silver hair. He's wearing a black shirt with a white collar around his neck like a priest. He says, "I have panic attacks, too. They're cruel bastards."

Closing my eyes, I nod.

The guy says more I don't catch, then I hear him say, "Sometimes, I'm all right. Other times, I'm not. In fact, it got so bad once I collapsed—"

"You're not helping." My tongue feels thick.

He chuckles. "Sorry."

It's a nice laugh. Sort of familiar. He helps me sit up, then stays as I try to catch my breath. That's hard to do this close to Officer Riker's cross. I wonder if this is where he died.

Me and the priest don't talk for a while. I'm exhausted.

He follows my gaze over City Cemetery. "You're curious about the crosses?"

I nod.

"There's already been over one hundred murders this year in Remington and it's only June. That's about one death every day and a half." I don't comment, but he keeps talking. "I look forward to when there are none."

"It'll never happen."

"Why?"

"It's Paradise."

"True."

We fall silent again. This guy has such straight white teeth. Drugs have never touched him. I can't figure out his age 'cause he doesn't have one wrinkle, but that's old-man hair, for sure. I sit cross-legged and pick the grass, thinking.

"What's on your mind?" he asks.

"Where do you get the crosses?"

"I make them myself. I paint each one white, then write the name in black. We hold a vigil every December and invite all the victims' families. Some people from law enforcement and the city attend, as well. This year will be our third memorial."

I promise myself to skip Mama's ceremony when the time comes. No matter what.

"I'm Father Waldo."

We shake. "Like Where's Waldo?"

"Absolutely. I've got a red-and-white striped shirt under here right now."

The priest makes me smile inside the tiniest bit.

"And you are?" he asks.

"Copper."

"Nice to meet you, Copper. What brings you to St. Columba's?"

"That murder in the paper today."

"Yes, well. Officer Felix Riker and his family were longtime members of our parish." The priest stares at the dead man's cross.

"What was he like?"

"Interesting. Felix could be hard, but he had a gentle heart. He helped with our homeless ministry. His wife, Ann, sings in the choir and his two sons are altar boys. His death was a great loss for our church and our city."

I add all that to my mental list. "Was he on duty that night?"

"Why are you so interested in this?"

"I like those true-crime shows."

He says, "Felix wasn't on duty. Our burglar alarm had gone off about midnight and he met me here to check it out." The priest watches the church's side door, where a tiny Mary holding baby Jesus is carved above the entrance. "I feel guilty for calling him. He'd probably still be alive if it weren't for me."

"Maybe not. Cops risk their lives every day."

"That's a valid point."

"What'd you find when the alarm went off?"

"Nothing out of the ordinary."

"Has it ever gone off before?"

"Unfortunately, a lot. We've had communion silver stolen. Money from the offering plate. Things like that."

We both watch the graffiti on the wall of the church's youth rec center. Gang battlegrounds are everywhere.

I say, "Anything else weird happen that day?"

"Yes. A strange homeless woman came by that morning."

"Strange how?"

"She and her kids were panhandling, but she also seemed interested in the construction site across the street."

I read the sign on the other side of the road:

FUTURE HOME—SALVATION ARMY

The skeleton frame stands there for what will be the shelter—steel columns, ladders with long platforms—along with a cement truck, safety cones, dirt and workmen. A whizzing sound fills the air from all the power tools.

The priest says, "I'd seen her boys before. Looking back, I realize she might've been scouting the place because they were robbed the next night."

"What was stolen?"

"Several thousand dollars' worth of construction equipment."

"Did you catch her name?"

"Yes, because it was so unique. She's Bird and her two young sons are Salt and Pepper."

Those names pierce my heart, though I try to hide my surprise and irritation. "Did the police question her?"

"I'm not sure, but I told them about her." Father Where's Waldo's mouth purses tighter as he studies me. "Why are you so intrigued by all this?"

"I read about it in today's paper."

"And?"

"That's it."

"You realize you just lied to a priest."

"It's okay. I lie to everyone."

He's got a great, deep belly laugh. Loud and full of oomph, like a skinny Santa Claus. It's nice, but I know better than to trust religious folks. They use people, steal from their congregations and murder mamas.

"Wait." Father Where's Waldo peers at me closer. "Do I know you?"

"Yeah, but I'm not sure how."

We go back to studying City Cemetery. I'm thinking, then I ask him, "Have you ever lead the chapel service at Mission for Hope Shelter?"

"Yes. Once. I'm on the schedule to volunteer there more this summer."

"I thought so." I try to remember his sermon but can't.

He says, "I don't mean to pry, but do your parents know you're here?"

"Sort of." I glance at the fluffy sky.

"It's dangerous for you to be out alone."

"Duh." I point to my black eye and Diablo scar.

"What happened?"

"School fight and the Barrio Brothers."

"You're a fiery one."

"You have no idea." I think about my long red curls.

"Is there someone . . . an adult I can call for you?"

Shaking my head, I stare at Mama's name. It's hard not to feel the weight of these one-hundred crosses and the blood they've spilled.

"Wait, I know you," the priest says. "How'd I miss it? You said your name is Copper?"

"So?"

He glances toward Mama's cross, then back at me. "Copper Daniels?"

"Yeah?"

"Aren't you Corrine Noblitt's daughter?"

CHAPTER 10

Me and Father Where's Waldo stare at each other closer, while I feel a triangle between me, Mama and this priest. He seems to be searching my face for more traces of her and wondering about my wounds, no hair, and probably overall nuttiness. He scores major points for not asking.

I've got just as many questions about him, though I settle on the most important one. "How . . . do you know Mama?"

I swear his ears turn bright pink. "We went to high school together." He grins and watches the evening sky, like he sees her in heaven above. "I had such a crush on Corrine. We all did." He glances my way. "You have your mother's green eyes."

"Really?" I giggle. "I think they're more like my daddy's."

"Nope. It was the first thing I noticed about you."

"Mama always called 'em emerald green."

"She's right."

"I thought priests weren't supposed to have girlfriends."

He chuckles. "Well, I wasn't one back then. Believe me, I was a troublemaker. Getting drunk, starting fights, stealing. Plus, she was never my girlfriend, and rightly so. I was bad news."

"You sound just like her type."

"I wish." He watches her cross again.

I hesitate, then ask, "What was she like?"

"Oh," he says, then describes her in a dreamy voice. His mind seems to travel back in time to that black-haired beauty from Uncle P's framed photograph—white dress, gorgeous smile, ready to capture the world.

She caught it, all right. Just not how anyone expected:

PROSTITUTE ACCUSED OF KILLING COP

Father Where's Waldo says, "Your mother was larger than life. She sang like an angel. We starred in *The Sound of Music* in school together. She was Maria and I was Captain von Trapp. I always hoped she'd win an Oscar someday."

"Instead, she got knocked up at sixteen by a married man, ran away and fell into drugs, then . . ." I drop my handful of grass.

The priest nods. "Corrine just disappeared one day. None of us knew what happened. Of course, there were all sorts of rumors . . ."

"Did you come to her funeral?"

"I couldn't. I had a mass to do, but heard the church was packed."

"Mainly gawkers." I swallow hard. "Why'd you put Daniels on there, instead of Noblitt?"

"I was torn. Corrine Noblitt is the girl I knew back then, but she'd become Corrine Daniels. That seemed more appropriate."

"She was just Mama to me."

We're both remembering the same person, but very different people. The loud crackling in the distance is probably gunfire, even though the sun's still up. Father Where's Waldo may need to add another name and wooden cross to City Cemetery by tomorrow. The body bags never stop in Paradise.

The priest asks, "Why are you staring at me?"

"No offense, but I thought you were way older 'cause of your hair."

He laughs, sliding his fingers through his thick locks.

"Premature graying runs in my family." He stands, then helps me up. "Aren't you living with your Uncle Patrick now?"

"Not anymore. He thinks Mama killed that cop, so I don't want anything to do with him."

"You think she's innocent?"

"I know it," I lie. His eyes don't believe me. "Think she did it?"

He shrugs. "The police seem to have strong evidence."

"Do you know who the eyewitnesses were?"

"I saw the police interviewing two homeless women. No, maybe one was a man, but I'm not sure. Where will you live if you leave your uncle?"

"CPS is moving me somewhere new."

"Does your father have any relatives?"

"No."

"I want to watch his interview with Gigi Carlisle tonight."

"What?"

"She interviewed your dad about your mom's case. It's airing on the six o'clock news tonight."

"Great." I groan.

Father Where's Waldo pulls his cell phone from his pocket. "Your uncle doesn't care for me, but I still think we should call him to let him know you're safe."

"Why doesn't he like you?"

"He threatened to hurt me in high school if I so much as looked at his sister. I've always resented him for that, which isn't very priestly of me." Father Where's Waldo chuckles.

"Call him if you want, but I'm staying."

"What's his number?"

I ignore the priest, then wander up and down the rows of crosses for clues—torn clothing, a piece of Mama's long hair, anything. I don't know what I'm looking for or how I expect to find something months after the murder. I bet the cops already covered this place top to bottom. It's a long shot, but that's all I've got.

Father Where's Waldo follows behind, which bugs me, but it's his turf, so I can't stop him. At least he hasn't called my uncle yet. I glance back at the priest, wondering if he's capable of murder.

"Where was the body?" I ask.

"I don't like talking—"

"ANSWER ME!"

"Goodness. You're bossy like your mother."

"I'm mean like her, too. Start talking."

He points to an empty spot nearby. "He was lying facedown over there."

"You remember anything else?"

"They found a boot-print impression here that they think might belong to the killer, but it was unusual."

"How so?"

"I don't know. I just remember the police talking about it." Father Where's Waldo takes me by the arm, not hard, but he doesn't let go. "I'm sorry, but we need to call your uncle now."

I've watched enough TV to know just what to say, "Forgive me Father, for I have sinned." I stomp his foot as hard as I can, then run like hell. He doesn't know he's lucky I liked him enough to leave his balls and boogers alone.

Still, I wonder about that priest. Mr. and Miz Jesus taught me to trust no one. Which means I know exactly where I'm going next.

CHAPTER 11

I make my way to the Shangri-La to confront Bird, watching for her or her boys. I'm excited to see Salt and Pepper again, though I might punch her lights out. Bird put the *ick* in *sick*. I can't prove it, but she helped get Mama killed long before she died. That woman's definitely on my Enemy List.

As much as I want Eddie Loco to be the murderer, a crushed skull really doesn't sound like him. He's a gun-and-knife guy. Torturing people and drawing out their pain, though I guess crushing someone's skull fits that part. I'd like to think I only have to endure one whack attack per day, but the tightness in my chest says otherwise.

I slow my breathing and try to connect to the world around me. Tents, street-sleepers and cardboard condos. *I'm okay*, I remind myself. I zigzag around the mess, but there's no way around all the broken people.

A woman pushing a wheelchair passes by with a sleeping bag and packed duffel bag crammed where someone should be sitting. A few record albums poke out of her stack. I doubt she's got a record player in there, but who knows?

"It'th not thafe here," she lisps to me, shaking her head. "It'th not thafe."

Poor thing. She's right. There's nothing safe about Paradise. I want to feel sorry that her whole life sits on two wheels, then realize she's got more than me, so I shouldn't be all judgy.

She rambles on down the sidewalk as someone steps out from EZPAWN. Me and him spot each other, then he bolts down the block.

It's Spider, Eddie Loco's punk-ass brother. Time for a little talk. I open Tommy's pocketknife and hobble on, ready to squash that bug.

Last time I saw him, he was a squatty roly-poly. We're the same age, though his long legs say he's grown. Spider's still not skinny. He's more muscly and his curly hair's cut so short it's bumpy. His plain white T-shirt is a dis to Asian Assassin red and the new gang ruling his brother's old turf.

A couple crosses Spider's path and blocks him for a few seconds, giving me a chance to catch up to him. I huff and puff, then grab his arm and don't let go. "Why are you running from me?"

"None yo'."

His knuckles have letters written in black marker across 'em: B-R-O-T-H-E-R-S

He's such a wannabe with his fake tattoo (he was too young to be initiated). That's when I notice the black spray paint on his hands. "*You* tagged my uncle's house."

"So?" He pulls away.

"Why'd you call him a traitor?"

"I kept my end of the deal. He didn't."

"What do you mean?"

"Ask him."

"I'm asking *you* now." Spider gives me a look I can't read. I grill him some more but get nowhere and change the subject. "Heard your brother killed that cop."

"I wish, but your crack-whore mama beat him to it."

"It wasn't her."

"You're trippin'."

"Okay then, who else could've done it?"

He shrugs. "I dunno. Maybe that pillow pony."

"Pillow pony?"

"Yeah, you know. That pickle sniffer, Drago."

"What's that mean?"

"You're such a rich white girl."

"Whatever. Why's Drago hate cops so much?"

"Who doesn't? Nice blade." Spider laughs and yanks the rusty knife from me, then he takes off running down the sidewalk.

"Give me that." I chase after him, though there's no way I can outrun him. I'm limping along, irritated. I don't have time for this crap.

As I zoom by a crowded corner, I pass a tattoo parlor called the Tat Cat. The smell of trash and stink hangs in the heat. Someone's car alarm goes off and won't stop beeping. I'm sweaty, tired and more frustrated at Mama.

"Stop!" I holler.

Up ahead, One-Leg stands with a group of drinking buddies and turns to the sound of my voice. He must realize what's happening 'cause he moves into Spider's way and sticks out his metal leg. That sends the Barrio Brother tumbling to the concrete.

While Spider's splayed-out, I take back Tommy's knife and go to kick Spider, but he lunges for One-Leg. "Old man."

My friend bows up to Spider and several of One-Leg's friends surround him, ready to use their bottles as weapons. I promised Tommy's pops I'd take care of him, but looks like it's the other way around.

One-Leg's gaze doesn't leave Spider. "Go on, Copper."

I hesitate but see they've got it under control. "Thanks." I edge away, then hurry on. Grateful for One-Leg and missing Tommy more.

Everything keeps running through my mind. What "deal"

was Spider talking about? Why was he mad enough to tag my uncle's house over it? And just 'cause Mama squabbled with Officer Riker doesn't mean she murdered him.

It doesn't look great, though. Maybe Spider did it. Killing a cop would get him initiated, for sure. I still need to talk to Bird, so I head toward the Shangri-La now. Most people I walk by are carrying all their stuff or have everything in a bag or backpack. Some are lucky enough to have a shopping cart like that lispy lady.

When I reach the two-story U-shaped motel, I'm expecting the crappy sign to blink at me:

$25 PER HOUR. $50 PER NIGHT.

Instead, a fancy neon sign shines *Shangri-La* in lime green. No prices usually means pricey. The painted palm trees on the turquoise walls are long gone and the whole building's solid white now. I wouldn't call it nice, but it's not a dump anymore.

Walking through the grounds, I stare at the shimmery pool ahead with swimmers in it. That hole used to have an ankle's worth of dirty water. Flimsy lounge chairs line the deck.

I don't recognize any of the people.

The OPEN sign isn't dangling by the chain in the office anymore, either. Another neon green one shines from the squeaky-clean window up front. I heard someone tried to rob this place once and she got handcuffed by a cop who turned out to be her uncle.

I sigh and go inside, relieved it still smells like a bug bomb mixed with weed. The same fake wooden walls bring back the old gloom. At least this place hasn't changed.

Behind the counter, the scrawny loser lying in his recliner is Tank Top Teddy. I'm not sure he's moved or changed his dirty wifebeater and boxers since I left, though he's got less hair to comb over than before.

The TV usually blares his favorite show, *Cops*, but he's watching the news. It shows footage from me and Dusty's wreck earlier—he's lying on the stretcher with an oxygen mask on as they lift him into the ambulance. I'm not anywhere in the picture, so I must've already escaped. Worry wallops me since I still don't know how bad he's hurt. I want to say he deserved it, but . . .

The screen switches to Gigi Carlisle in different clothes and a different hairstyle. It's a promo about her interview with my jailbird daddy. They're sitting across from each other in a cinderblock room.

In the clip, she asks him, "Do you believe Corrine Daniels Noblitt murdered Officer Riker?"

"Absolutely." Mr. Jesus doesn't blink.

The TV voice says this *shocking* interview will air tonight. You can bet Mr. Jesus is pimping himself for a comeback after prison. I guess I groan, 'cause Tank Top looks back this way from his recliner.

"Well, well, well." He stands and smiles, showing his tobacco-stained teeth. "I see the psycho doesn't fall far from the tree. You get it from both sides."

"Takes one to know one." I edge closer to the swinging door between us. "Guess your office wasn't worthy of the remodel. Who fixed up the place?"

"The Asian Assassins. Zhi Peng Wong's boys are better to me than the Barrio Brothers ever were. Criminals."

"What are the rates now?"

"More than you can afford." His left hand runs over the nub of his right pointer finger.

"What happened?" I can't help but stare.

"Nothing." He jabs his hand into the top of his boxers.

"That nothing sure looks like something."

"Go away. I haven't missed you, your skank mom, or your stuck-up dad." Tank Top walks by, then rifles through a drawer. "Your uncle's business card's here somewhere. Can't imagine that Sir Cops A Lot will be pleased you're back. Maybe I should call him, do my civic duty." Tank Top gives me a greasy smile.

I slam the swinging door against the side of the counter to

give him a quick lesson in citizenship. I point Tommy's blade straight at Tank Top. He doesn't budge, though fear flickers across his face.

Yanking him to me, I say, "I *am* psycho. I've got nothing left, so there's nothing left to lose. Where are Salt and Pepper, jackwagon?"

"I'm not their keeper. You here about your mom?"

I don't answer.

"Lucky she croaked, so there's no jail time."

I smash my head against his chin. Pain shatters through me as Tank Top stumbles back. He shouts, gripping his ugly mug. I jab my blade at him again. "Tell. Me. Now."

"Bird was in 101 yesterday. I'm not sure if they still are." He groans and shoves me off him.

I wipe the sweat from my busted eye and head toward the exit. Dizzy.

"I'm calling your uncle!"

I answer him with my O'Dell finger without looking back. The late afternoon heat washes a new wave of weariness over me. It's only six thirty, so sunset is over three hours away. Paradise will be even worse then. I'm thirsty. My uncle definitely knows the Shangri-La was part of my pattern, so depending on where he is, I've got five to fifteen minutes to find crap-sandwich Bird, then get out of here.

The sky feels even brighter with this headache. All these motel rooms have outside doors, but that's still over a hundred places to check. I stomp by the pool and stare into the crystal-clear water. A lady lies passed out in the corner lounge chair, gripping a whiskey bottle. That's more like the place I remember.

Room 101's curtains are closed, so I can't see inside. No loud Van Halen or other rock 'n' roll blasts from the clock radio, which is what Bird usually plays. No sounds. I don't want to, but I tap on the door.

"Go away!" A man yells.

Bird invites *visitors* over at all hours, so I knock again. "Bird? You home?"

A few loud stomps bang this way, then the door swings open. An angry skinhead glares at me, howling a string of cusswords that make me blush.

I take a giant step back. "Is Bird here?"

Spit flies from his mouth. He hollers all the disgusting things he plans to do to my mother.

"Well, she's dead, so good luck with that."

His shock almost makes the door slammed in my face worth it. I try two more places downstairs, but still don't find Bird or her boys. I decide to try our old room up on the second floor and head to the outdoor stairwell. The railing burns my fingers, so I let go fast.

Stupid. I learned heat rises to the top this year in school. I shake out my T-shirt to air my pits. I followed Mama up and down these steps at least twice a day, every day, for as long as I can remember. Me and Tommy Tucker took 'em while we searched for her back in February. I bite my lip, then remember I'm mad at her and move faster.

Bird may not be here at all since it's warm enough to sleep outside at night. Plus, she's usually broke. Bird didn't manage her money smart like Mama.

Course, she's still alive, so there's that.

On the second floor, I stop at Room 207.

Sweat trickles down my back, though I've got chills staring at our home away from home. Never thought I'd come back here and didn't ever want to. If these walls could talk—gross.

The room sounds quiet. The clock ticks faster with my uncle on the way. I don't feel right barging in anymore, so I knock. "Bird? Hello?"

Nothing.

I tap again. "Salt? Pepper? Guys?"

Not a sound.

Nobody's home. It's locked.

My hope sinks. I head back toward the stairs. Nothing concrete points to Mama killing that cop, but nothing proves she's innocent, either. Some say Eddie Loco did it, though Drago could've done it, too. Both have reasons to hate cops. Not sure where to go next, I take the first step downstairs.

A young voice yells from the breezeway. "What the hell do *you* want?"

Four-year-old Pepper stands outside Room 207. His older brother, Salt, six, is beside him. The three of us squeal happy when we see each other, and I sprint back to my boys. They bury themselves against my belly and we octopus each other in our love. It's been so long since I've felt this, especially since I'm not sure Mama really loved me at all.

Guilt smacks me, so I push away the ugly thought and focus on this hug. Pepper grips me tighter. "Copper, Copper, oh man, Copper."

He's a dark shadow of a boy in a red Cookie Monster T-shirt. Pepper's 'fro's almost bigger than him. Salt is white, with blond hair so curly it's almost a 'fro but isn't. His red T-shirt has a Captain America shield on it. The boys are taller and dirtier than last time, while both their bellies still pooch out from hunger. They smell like pee and b.o.

Did I stink like that?

I'm thinking yeah.

Pepper talks a million miles a minute, so I don't even bother to keep up with his gibberish. Salt clings to me in his sweet, quiet way. I love 'em like brothers. They're my only real family left. Plus, One-Leg and Mai Wong. I kiss the top of their nappy heads and hope they don't give me lice lips again.

Pepper says, "Are you back for good?"

"Don't know. Where's your mom?"

"Not sure. Is your mommy still dead?"

"Afraid so. Let's go into the AC. I'm melting out here." I shoo 'em inside, then check over the railing to the courtyard. No Uncle Patrick.

Yet. I close the door behind us, knowing the clock's ticking faster. Happiness whooshes through me being with my buddies again, 'til I scan the room.

To Go containers litter the dresser, desk and floor. Trash lies everywhere. The sheets are stripped off the double bed and piled in a heap on the mattress.

Yuck. It hurts to think of all the hours I spent under that bed while Mama worked.

Sometimes I'm still there.

The only thing in its regular spot is the red Gideon's Bible on the nightstand. This is also where I caught my jailbird daddy naked with that Mexican teenager. She stood there underage in his dress shirt, and he was married. It's not the first affair the good book's seen in this room.

Poor Salt and Pepper have nothing but the filthy clothes on their backs. This is no way for kids to live. My sunny-yellow room has a beanbag chair, a night-light, books and photo albums. I've got so many stuffed animals and dolls that they cover my bed. I've got *stuff*.

No, I don't. I ran away from the traitor. I'm homeless again. Numbness spreads inside, though I try to act normal.

Pepper pushes me onto the desk chair and grabs my left wrist. "Where'd you get that Mickey Mouse watch?"

"Disneyland."

"You steal it?"

"No." I laugh. "My uncle bought it for me there."

"For reals?"

"Yep."

"Dang. He's the best uncle ever," Pepper says.

Salt agrees. That lumps up my throat. We did have fun at the Magic Kingdom. Uncle P laughed so hard at me while we shared a milkshake that chocolate squirted from his nose. I made him rock snot like I used to with Mama. I ignore the pain.

Salt asks, "What was your favorite ride?"

"Pirates of the Caribbean."

They both nod, super excited. Pepper says, "You don't look like you anymore."

"I don't feel like me anymore."

"I want to touch your hair."

The boys laugh and rub my head. I giggle, too.

Pepper asks, "Why'd you cut it off?"

That chokes me up so much I can't talk. Salt thumbs the Diablo scar on my cheek. He stares at me while he does it, like he understands some hurts never heal.

That's true, but answers help. I ask, "You know the church with all the crosses in the yard?"

"Yep," Pepper says.

"You go there a lot?"

"Nope."

"You remember being there the day that cop was murdered?"

"A cop was murdered?!" he shouts.

"Yes. Same night as Mama." I can't finish.

Salt adds, "Mommy talked about someone being dead. I thought she meant Corrine."

"What'd Bird say?"

"Just that Diablo made her do it."

"Do what?"

He shrugs. "She said it again yesterday when we saw your uncle at Diablo's old place."

"Yesterday? You sure?"

"Yeah. It was still morning and not too hot. He was walking into their office."

"That's weird."

"Why? He's a cop."

"Long story."

Pepper sighs. "I miss your mommy. She used to buy us Fat Taco's and make us laugh. I loved snuggling up against her coat."

I grip the chair and smile, desperate to stay ahead of the whack attack building inside me. Pepper climbs on me like a jungle gym. I should be irritated, but I love it. I've missed this so much. He takes my watch and I let him. He's beaming as he clasps it to his scrawny arm.

I ask 'em, "What are the Asian Assassins like?"

Pepper says, "Meaner than the Barrio Brothers."

Salt adds, "Zhi Peng Wong scares me worse than Diablo, but Koi's the worst."

"Why?"

"He doesn't talk."

"Why do I know Koi's name?"

They both shrug. Moving on, I check the nightstand since that's where Bird keeps her drugs, but I just find sex stuff.

Gag. I close the drawer fast.

Pepper asks, "Whatcha doing?"

"Just looking." I try the dresser built into the wall, but don't find anything useful. The boys follow me to the closet. "What's this wiring for?"

"Don't know."

I slide open the door. A big coil of reddish metal wire sits on the closet floor. It looks like what they're using at that construction site across from City Cemetery. My brain takes a picture. "I need the bathroom."

"Pee or poop?" Pepper says.

"What's it to you?"

"If you can ask questions, I can, too."

I lock myself in the bathroom, then tell Salt to do the same with the door.

"But Mommy said—"

"Just do it."

"Oooookay."

Pepper whines he wants to lock it, so they bicker.

The bathroom mirror shows my black eye is even more purple and swollen. My headache hurts worse, too. I lift my shirt. The bruises from the wreck feel so tender, and the cut on my thigh still stings.

Dusty's right. I am a Scab Face. A freak with no hair. No wonder people stare. The only way out of here is the tiny window above the toilet. That's where I've jumped from before. It seems like a lifetime ago.

Even more without Mama or Tommy.

I punch away the memories and get back to work. Lifting the tank lid to the toilet, I check back there.

Nothing.

Pepper hollers from the room, "Are you pooping your brains out, or what?"

"Or what." I flush.

"Hurry."

"Okay." I hop onto the bathtub's edge. It takes me three sharp tugs to pull down the shower curtain. It finally yanks free. This was always Mama's favorite spot to hide stolen stuff. I ease the rubber end from the rod, then stare inside the tube.

Something's there but won't budge.

I shake harder. It moves a bit but stays stuck. I help pry it out with my finger and it plops to the floor. The truth lies at my feet. A clear plastic baggie stuffed fuller than I've ever seen. Those pretty white crystals will kill you.

Meth.

CHAPTER 12

Between the drugs on the floor and the other ziplock still in this shower rod, I see Bird stole way more than Mama ever did from Diablo. Yet, he still wanted to kill Mama for it. All the real Barrio Brothers are in jail, so Bird must be scamming the Asian Assassins. I wonder if Zhi's after her now.

Plus, that metal wiring . . . she's stirring up all sorts of trouble. Is she Suspect #2?

My knuckles turn white I'm clenching my fists so hard. Bird's a thief and a liar, so she could absolutely be a cop-killer, too. She obviously doesn't care about putting her children in danger, leaving 'em alone like this.

The door handle rattles and Pepper yells, "You still pooping?"

"Be right out."

I stuff the drugs back into the rod, then replace it over the bathtub. It's not right or fair someone as awful as Bird's still breathing while Mama's got grass growing above her.

Maybe they both deserve to be dead. Ignoring that pang of guilt, I plaster on a smile and step into the room. "Want to go eat?"

"Yay!" The boys clap, jumping up and down.

I've got no cash but will figure something out. We're not safe here. I can't decide where to—

A wiry figure appears at the door. Salt and Pepper freeze. They forgot to lock it.

Bird rushes and slaps me. "Who the hell are you?"

"It's me—Copper!" Her attacks don't stop. I duck and twirl. Bird's backwards skunk hair—white with black roots—is gone. It's all bleached blonde and cut in a bob. Even her shorts and tank top match. I know those are Doc Martens 'cause Mama always wanted those boots. Bird's no movie star, but she's dressed better than most in Paradise.

'Cept she's still got a druggie meth-mouth.

I do my best to block her blows, but they keep coming. "Stop, Bird! What are you doing?" I duck and twirl. "Quit, it's me!"

Her messed-up twirly eyes say I'm in big trouble. The boys yank and tug at her, shouting to stop. She doesn't. Bird moves lightning fast. She's all over me.

Finally, they pull Bird away and the four of us are out breath. Of course, she doesn't apologize. She stumbles my way, squinting. "That really you, Copper?" I don't answer, then she adds, "I thought you was your mama. Where's your hair?"

"Who cut off Tank Top's finger?"

"Eddie Loco. Tank Top testified against the Barrio Brothers at your daddy's trial."

"For narking?"

"Yep. Nobody likes a snitch."

I say, "Where'd you get that metal wiring in the closet?"

"It was already there."

"I doubt it. Why were you at St. Columba's the day that cop was killed?"

"I wasn't."

"Father Waldo says you were, and I'm believing that priest over you."

"Oh yeah," Pepper perks up. "We cut through the church to watch that construction—"

"Shut your mouth!" Bird slaps him.

Pepper wails and scrambles onto the unmade bed. Salt consoles his little brother. The boys cling to each other, crying.

I grab this crap-sandwich woman by her scrawny neck. "You stole Mama's drugs and shot 'em up before I could return everything to Diablo and save my family. You helped get her killed."

She claws at my hands. I ignore her choking sounds and squeeze more. Bird's turning purple. She's not worth jail time, but she doesn't deserve to live either. "What were you scoping out? Where's the rest of the stolen equipment? What do you know about that cop's murder?"

Bird doesn't answer, so I let my mind go blank and enjoy her misery.

Pepper shrieks, "You're hurting her!"

Salt pulls on me. Pepper screams my name. I notice the boys bawling, then snap to and drop Bird onto the mattress.

She coughs, sputters and rolls over the sheets like a total drama queen. Their whole family's in tears. I'm not sure what to do. When Bird can finally speak, she kicks at me and misses. "You almost killed me!"

"But I didn't." I try to gather up Salt and Pepper to apologize, but they won't let me touch 'em. That hurts. I try to use my sweet voice. "Don't be afraid. I just had to talk to your mommy a sec. It's okay now."

They scoop Bird into their arms on the bed, watching me in disgust. A loud knock at the door sends us all jumping.

"Police," the voice yells outside. "Open up."

I wince, realizing I stayed too long.

Uncle P. The door isn't locked. I'm trapped.

Bird, Salt and Pepper huddle together like shrieking mice.

That woman should be behind bars or six feet under. I hope my uncle doesn't beat me in front of the boys.

A great idea hits me from nowhere. I've done this before. I scoot the desk chair closer to the bathroom, then whisper to Bird, "Let me do the talking."

She cringes and nods.

I make myself stand taller, though my voice wobbles. "Come in."

"Copper?" my uncle says.

"Yeah."

"Are you all right?"

"Uh-huh. It's open."

First I see his pistol, then that mountain of a man. He's still dressed in regular clothes, his worry brow arched high across his forehead. Uncle P rushes me. I close my eyes so I don't see the first punch.

He buries me in a giant bear hug. "God, I was so worried."

It's all for show. He stares with those puppy dog eyes. It's like Mama's watching now. I can't stand it. My uncle cups my face and studies me. "That wreck looked awful."

"I'm fine." I pull away.

"Your pupils are dilated. You might have a concussion. Do you feel dizzy? We should get you to a hospital."

"I said I'm fine." I step back. "How's Dusty?"

"Stable at the hospital. Let's go."

Pepper pushes between us. "Who's Dusty? What's a concussion? Can I go to the hospital, too? I'm hunnnnnngry."

"In a minute." I refocus on my uncle. "Why were you at the Barrio Brothers' yesterday?"

"I wasn't."

Salt says, "Nuh-uh."

Uncle P glances above my head. "It . . . involves your father."

"How so?"

"I'll explain it on the way home."

"Is that why they called you a traitor?"

"Probably."

"Why's Captain Lancaster mad at you?"

"Who told you that?"

Bird elbows me out of the way. "Y'all need to go. Now."

"I need to talk to my uncle *alone*." I nod toward the bathroom.

I watch him taking mental notes around us as he walks into the bathroom. Bird hovers behind him, squawking how we should go straight home now.

They stand together in the doorway while I take a running start. He's too big, so I rush Bird from behind, shoving her as hard as I can. She topples into him, knocking 'em both off balance. As he turns to catch her, I push 'em inside, kicking their feet out of the way. I shut the door, then jam the chair under the knob like a lock. I already know it fits perfect 'cause I've done this before, thank you very little. That man deserves a taste of his own medicine.

Bird hollers all hysterical, while he's banging on the door. Pepper wails and Salt just looks wounded. I hate leaving my boys behind, but it's not safe out there. Mama ruined my life bad enough. I don't need him messing it up worse.

The evening sky looks electric outside. Sunset lights up the golden clouds, with pinks and purples bursting above. It's prettier than a painting but means the night's ugliness isn't far behind. As I sprint down the stairwell, I hear an explosion of wood behind me. Bird shrieks. Uncle P probably just broke the door down.

Here we go again.

I disappear around the corner from the motel and onto the street. I glance at my bare wrist. I could kick myself for leaving my watch behind but limp faster. I don't run toward the railroad tracks that'd take me away from Paradise.

Instead, I go deeper into hell. The last thing I want is to

spend the night here, especially alone, but I've got to find that cop-killer. Even if it was Mama. I'm not sure where to go. My phone booth doesn't have a lock on it, and that alley's nothing but trouble. Besides, Uncle P would look there since it's part of my pattern. He lied about the Barrio Brothers, so I want even less to do with him.

Traitor.

Mission for Hope's already closed for the night. They wouldn't' let me stay there without an adult anyhow. I touch the redness on my arm. On top of everything else, I'm sunburned, too. Could I have a concussion?

In the distance, the word BUS glows from the station and brightens the darkening sky. I used to dream we'd ride away to live in a little white house with red shutters and a dog named Sugar. Play together in the California ocean.

That so didn't happen. When I finally I let myself stop to catch my breath, I double over, staring at the cracks in the sidewalk. That was close.

Too close. At the end of the block, I see the blue-and-black Goodwill sign above Paradise. I'm still panting when I hear a noise behind me and realize I know the man sitting again the building behind me.

"Corn Dog?" He's bag of bones in a business suit. His hair's not sticking out every which way anymore, it's short and slicked back. His Santa-Claus beard's gone, too, where I once saw chunks of hurl in there.

Now, he's got gray stubble across his red cheeks. "Hey, Corn Dog. It's me Copper."

His watery blue eyes stare straight through me. Someone's tried to clean him up to the point he looks almost cartoony, like he should be holding droopy daisies or something.

"I, uh," I hesitate, "I'm Corrine Daniels' girl."

His eyes flicker at Mama's name. I'd think he's dead if not for the slow rise and fall of his chest beneath that coat and tie. I toe my orange sneaker onto the sidewalk as I struggle to find the words. "I, umm ... sorry I stole your five dollars. I thought it'd help repay Diablo for Mama stealing, but ..." I can't finish.

Corn Dog doesn't so much as blink. I think he might even be sober.

"I'll pay you back, I promise. Tommy Tucker doubled my money, but I don't have any cash on me now. My uncle says he opened a savings account for me, so he probably spent it all, but I'm not sure. He's really lame." I step closer. "You look nice. Where'd you get the suit?"

Nothing.

"Did you hear about Mama? Do you know anything about that dead cop?"

Corn Dog stares into the distance.

"Well, see you around." I tell him, then step away. "I promise I'll pay you back."

I kick a pebble into the gutter and am almost of ear range when Corn Dog mumbles behind me, "Goo-will."

Whirling around, he's staring into nothing again. "What'd you say?"

No response.

"Did you say Goodwill?" I hurry back to him. "Is that where your suit came from? Why'd you say that?"

He says nothing, but stares at the store sign. It's no use. Corn Dog may not be boozing right now, but he's plenty pickled from the past.

Still, maybe I can sleep in one of their donation bins. That's not a bad idea. "Thanks, Corn Dog. See you around."

I wander down the block to the store. Me and Mama never shopped at Goodwill 'cause we were always broke, though we liked using their AC or heat, depending on the time of year. So much churns inside me as I make my way there.

I'm about to head around back to the donation bins, but it's extra dark there, so I stop at the front display window. A spotlight shines onto a nice couch and a kitchen table. Clothes hang at the other end, too.

I almost faint when I realize what the faceless mannequin is wearing.

It's Mama's rabbit fur jacket.

CHAPTER 13

I burst into tears. My stomach turns as I stumble toward Mama's coat in the display window. I'm so queasy I might hurl. Instead, I press my hand to the glass. I blubbered more than once those three days she went missing, but I stayed 100% dry-eyed at her funeral and haven't cried since.

'Til now.

It's like the wall of sad built up these past four months came tumbling down. I'm crying, mixed with shaky sobs. You'd think this would send me into another whack attack, but I actually feel better. My body seems relieved. Even with all the bad Mama did . . . with all the mad she deserves . . .

I miss her.

I do.

I miss her smoothing over my crazy curls and kissing me good night beneath the Warrior Angel. I miss her throwing back her head, howling with laughter at one of my jokes. I miss us sitting in bed between clients at the Shangri-La, watching reruns of *Happy Days* or solving cases with that old lady from *Murder, She Wrote*.

Mostly, I miss being a family.

I was hers and she was mine.

That wasn't true, but I still believed it. I think I miss the lie most of all. Me and Uncle P aren't family. Neither is my jailbird daddy. I'm nothing to no one now. Still a Nobody.

I'm not sure how long I stare at Mama's jacket before I catch my breath and ask, "Did you . . . kill that cop?"

Of course, she doesn't answer.

I hiccup and wipe my nose with the back of my hand. The orange FOR SALE tag says her coat costs $5.99. It's worth so much more to me.

"Who murdered Officer Riker?" I ask.

Wait . . . that coat might hold a clue. I don't know how it got here or how she lost it in the first place, but I found my uncle's business card in a pocket after Arlene the Coat Stealer took it. There might be more. I'll come back first thing tomorrow. Goodwill opens at 9 a.m. That's—

I stare at my bare wrist. Pepper better take good care of my watch, though I doubt it. I've probably got about twelve more hours 'til I can see Mama's jacket again. The pinkish sky says it's twilight, so the sun will set in about an hour. I'm exhausted enough to curl up right here on the sidewalk to sleep beside Mama all night like old times, but that's too dangerous.

"See you tomorrow," I tell her.

I want to talk to Corn Dog again. Is this what he was trying to tell me?

Turning, I bump into a wheelchair and squeal, then realize it's the lispy woman from earlier. "Oh." I relax. "You scared me."

"Thorry." She grins a toothless smile. Her brown hair's matted to her head, and she's wearing a giant Ring Pop ring on her left hand. The stuff piled up on her wheelchair stands taller than her—the sleeping bag, her duffel and all the record albums stuffed in between. None of it makes sense.

Nothing about Paradise does.

She follows my gaze to Mama's coat. "That'th thooooooooo pretty."

I nod.

"It'th not thafe here." She mutters what she said earlier, struggling to maneuver her wheelchair from the curb. "I twied. Naomi twied."

"Who's Naomi?"

"Me."

"Oh, hi. I'm Copper."

She gives me another crooked grin. "I don't like Paradithe."

"Me neither." I help Naomi wrangle her wheelchair onto the street.

She gives me a little wave, then rambles away. "Thee you later. I thaid it'th not thafe."

"Bye." I want to feel sorry for her, but I've got no house to go home to myself. No family. Not enough stuff to even fill a wheelchair.

Still, I cup Tommy Tucker's pocketknife with the blade closed and wander away from Goodwill, feeling something strange and different. Something I haven't known in a long time.

Maybe hope?

I'm not sure, but I want more. First, I need to make it through the night to see Mama's jacket again. That means something. Not great, but a happy connection back to us. And maybe more clues.

Hobbling along, I don't spot Corn Dog at the end of the block. I check all around, but he's gone. I even ask a few people who look safe. Nobody's seen him.

I keep going and think about Mama's funeral. Uncle P held it at his Cowboy Church and every pew was full that afternoon. Tons of folks were connected to him, or to our family. After the service, they told me stuff like, "Your mother and I had been friends since kindergarten." Or, "Corrine and I danced together on the drill team."

The rest of the congregation were just gawkers. Strangers following the murder on the news with Gigi Carlisle. Folks wanting to catch a glimpse of the girl who escaped TV preacher Angela Sanborne from *The Lord's Power Hour* and the love triangle between her, Mama and my jailbird dad. I'm sure those same people are loving today's headline:

PROSTITUTE ACCUSED OF KILLING COP

This all sounds like a made-for-TV movie, but it's my *life*. Me and Mama were so close to escaping. I found the $881.01 and a bus schedule to LA she'd hidden inside the Warrior Angel. I never even knew that hiding spot existed in the statue. No telling what else she stashed there over the years.

Guess I'll never know. That emptiness knocks inside again. I'd rather take another beating from Dusty than spend the night here in Paradise. O'Dell's house is miles away, back by Uncle P's neighborhood, and I'm too tired to walk. Plus, I'm still mad at him and Mai for not telling me they're hanging out.

My best bet is One-Leg's place over in Tent City. It's not too far and he's never home. He's always said I'm welcome there any time. Do tents even have locks? Not sure. I hobble that way to find out.

At the overpass, I'm trembling as I grip the railing tighter. Cars race by as the sun sinks lower. It should've cooled off some, but Mother Nature's not having it. A small group of vets live down the hill below on the other side of this highway. During a lull in traffic, I hurry across the road. Tommy Tucker dances through me since I chased him over this very road when I thought he'd stolen my cash.

He didn't. Not really. He took the money to save me from giving it to Diablo and getting myself killed. Tommy kept it safe and even doubled it, though I'm not sure how. I also brought Mai Wong to his tent after Eddie Loco attacked her. I laid her on one of their blood-splattered sleeping bags, then O'Dell took her to the hospital for me. That got 'em together as a couple.

I peer down at Tent City and can't believe it. This place has more than tripled in size—well over one-hundred tents and tarp huts sit on that huge dirt lot now. It looks like a crazy patchwork quilt—blues, greens, oranges, browns, whites, blacks, yellows and grays. So many colors.

Scanning the grounds, it takes me a while to spot One-Leg's place. I think it's the dark green tent beside the US flag hanging longways on that far chain-link fence. A rich dude donated this land to the city. People driving by on the highway above just see an eyesore or a menace to society, but bad luck or bad choices landed everyone here. Nobody lives in Tent City by choice.

Nobody.

Chinatown is right across the street, but it doesn't look like the one in library books that's several oceans away. That Chinatown has bright, colorful buildings and roofs that bend up into a small grin and dangly lanterns hanging from either side.

This one has tiny shacks crammed together in rows, all made from different scraps: wood, metal, sheets, tarps. It's still a total slum, and the invisible boundary line between the two worlds was always so weird to me.

Paradise, over here—safe.

Chinatown, over there—unsafe.

I don't know if that side's still off-limits since Zhi Peng Wong runs 'em both or what. There's so much I need to ask Mai. I let go of the railing. I'm not sure I can spend the night in Tommy Tucker's sleeping bag. I never stayed there before but keep making my way down the grassy slope.

Anything and everything lay outside each tent: bicycles, crates, stacks of clothes, packed trash bags, ice chests, laundry baskets and more. Some people have dogs or cats, while other folks sit alone in folding chairs. Waiting for nothing.

My knife's open and ready. Most residents ignore me as I hobble by, but one guy blocks my path. He grabs his hooter-mcgrooter and grins at me. "Want a quick date?"

His lady neighbor chunks an empty beer can and lectures him while I scuttle away. Perv. My sunny-yellow room flashes through my mind. That froofy canopy bed so wasn't me, but I loved having a roof over my head. Going to sleep knowing I wouldn't get rained on or jacked up at all.

Feeling like a regular girl.

Whatever that is.

I left all that behind for this.

At the end of the row, I stare at the chain-link fence outside One-Leg's tent. Tommy scrambled over that to escape me raging about my cash. I even shouted, *"I'm going to kill you!"*

I wince at the memory. Coming here doesn't seem so smart now. One-Leg probably never cleaned up the blood after his accident. I hesitate, then tap on the vinyl. "Anyone home? It's Copper."

Silence.

"One-Leg? Can I come in?" I listen closer.

Nothing.

I unzip the old tent, then close myself inside. Looking around, I see two sleeping bags. No blood. I've got a 50/50 chance of steering clear of Tommy's bed, but a 100% chance of heartache.

Something rustles outside. I hear the door unzip behind me. There's no place to hide, so I freeze.

A burglar steps in and we scream together.

CHAPTER 14

It's Chao-Chao, the boy with kind eyes. Shrieking, we both scoot away from each other in this small tent. He's not dressed in Asian Assassin red tonight, but in black from head to toe like a burglar. He looks as shocked to see me as I am him.

I glance at the dragon tattoo on his bare arm. "What are *you* doing here?"

There's no warmth in his eyes tonight. He looks scared.

"No." He scans the place like he's looking for something. "No, no, no." He mumbles in Chinese to himself.

"Why are you here? How do you know One-Leg? Tell me what's going on."

Chao-Chao's gaze takes another sweep around, then he squeezes my hand and whispers, "Go home, Ghost Girl. Before it's too late." He kisses me hard on the mouth, his tongue runs over my teeth, then he dives through the flap opening of the tent.

That boy tastes like peppermint and tomorrows. I stand stunned for several seconds. Nobody's ever kissed me like that. Not even Tommy. I scramble after the Asian Assassin for more.

He's already scaling the chain-link fence by the time I make it outside. Chao-Chao lands on the other side and moonlight lets me see his pearly smile. He gives me a quick wave, then sprints through the darkness back to Chinatown.

I'm not sure what to do with these butterfly feelings inside. Guilt's definitely mixed in there, but he kissed *me*. I didn't ask for it. Besides, Tommy's dead. That hurts every time to remember.

Touching my heart, I watch Chao-Chao dive into the back seat of a black Suburban parked at the end of the block. Tires screech as the car peels away and disappears into the night. It looks like the same car me and Tommy watched the Asian Assassins blaze their machine guns from during their drive-by at the Barrio Brothers' headquarters. We'd been spying on the place, looking for Mama, but watched a gangbanger die that day.

I groan. I can't decide whether to go back and search One-Leg's tent for whatever Chao-Chao couldn't find or follow him, 'cept that's not really a possibility. I press my thumb to my mouth, still tasting his minty kiss.

I'm debating what to do when a beat-up yellow Volkswagen Bug rambles up to the curb beside me. The window cranks down by hand to an old Chinese woman, who's barely taller than the steering wheel. Her hair's up in a bun, and her eyes are so filmed over she almost looks blind.

"Get iiiiiiiiiiiiiiiiiiiiiiiiiiiiiiiiiiiiiin," she says in broken English.

"No, thanks." I take a giant step back.

"Get iiiiiiiiiiiiiiiiiiiiiiiiiiiiiiiiiiiiiin," she repeats. "Mai send me."

"Mai Wong?"

The lady nods.

I hesitate, watching the Suburban speed away, then rush to the other side of the VW and climb in the back. Tiny China takes off after the Asian Assassins so fast my head snaps against my seat. She drives nutso like Dusty, so I feel around for the seatbelt.

There's not one. My breath quickens, and I lose all feeling in my fingers. My worry ramps up 'til I spot the Suburban's red brake lights, then I relax a little. Tiny China stays close enough to tail 'em, but far enough behind I don't think they'll notice us. That helps calm me more.

None of the control panels are lit up on this dashboard, so I don't know how she sees to drive. This chick really might be blind.

"You need to turn on your lights," I tell her.

She doesn't.

"I, ummm, I'm Copper Daniels."

Silence.

"Guess you already knew that."

Tiny China takes a hard left, and I brace myself against the door handle. "What's your name?"

Nothing.

"How do you know Mai?" This back seat feels like a cozy blanket, and the knots unwind inside some. We rumble over the railroad tracks, then follow the Asian Assassins by all the fancy buildings downtown. I'm glad to be leaving Paradise. I still need answers, though.

Night's officially taking over the day. A streetlamp shines onto Dusty's black skid marks from earlier. I hope he's all right in the hospital. Maybe CPS will move him from his family. I still taste Chao-Chao on my lips and wonder what that kiss meant.

This jalopy cruises along and a few minutes later, we drive by the library sitting in the darkness. I wish I could've read more of the facts from this case. There's the Burger Heaven. I yawn extra big. I've finally slowed down enough that I'm exhausted. Paradise is such a drain.

A cat wails somewhere in the night, and I think of Princess. Her Evilness is probably napping on Uncle P's couch right now. I don't miss her, but her purrs weren't so bad. I'd gotten used to 'em.

I yawn again and my eyes flutter closed . . .

I wake with a start. I don't know where I am . . . then, I hear the VW's motor and spot the back of Tiny China's bun and remember. I think I smell incense burning in here, too, but don't see any around. She's a kooky little lady. We're still tailing the Asian Assassins, though our headlights aren't on anymore.

"Turn on your lights," I say. "We're going to crash."

She ignores everything I'm saying. I recognize the grown trees and houses in this neighborhood, then realize I probably only slept a minute or two. There's the little white house with red shutters, but no dog named Sugar. Mama's and Uncle P's childhood home sits quiet. They must all be sound asleep. I want to go there someday but can't since it won't be as perfect as in my dreams.

We follow the Suburban down the road 'til it dead-ends into Eternal Peace, then turns along the iron fence.

My heart jackhammers. "Wait, are they going to the cemetery? I can't go there."

Tiny China answers me in Chinese, though I don't understand a word she's saying. I grip the edge of my seat and remind myself I'm okay. We bypass the main gates and all head around back. Cold chills clench my gut. That horrible terrible night was my last time here after dark.

I can't do this. I dig my fingernails into my palms. Tiny China parks across the street from Eternal Peace.

"You're going to lose 'em," I tell her.

The gang's Suburban keeps going, then parks near the cemetery fence. They cut their headlights.

"How'd you know they'd do that?" I watch several Asian Assassins spill from their car. I think that's Chao-Chao and I spot Drago, too. The group sneaks into the graveyard.

I can't do this, then remind myself all the bad guys are dead. Diablo and Miz Jesus. Mai Wong must've sent me here for a reason.

With shaky legs, I step from the VW. Tiny China's window

has stayed down. She watches me with eyes that can't see but still somehow know.

"Who are you?" I ask the strange woman.

"Meeeeee-chellllllle." She points to herself.

"Michele?"

"Mechele." She nods, babbling more Chinese as she drives away into the darkness. The Volkswagen backfires, then putters on. A gust of wind whooshes through me. I glance at the cemetery fence, then back at the VW—

It's gone.

Disappeared.

"What the—" I stare at the empty road. There's no sound at all. I refocus and drag my feet toward the cemetery. I promised Tommy Tucker I'd take care of his pops, and the Asian Assassins were snooping around his tent.

He needs my help. I rub Tommy's closed knife a few times, then tuck him back in my pocket. It feels like years since 'Chele the photographer brought me here this afternoon—and not in a good way.

At the fence, I hook my leg over the iron bar, then jump to the other side. It dumped rain here that horrible terrible night. Silly, but sometimes I wonder how it would've been different if I had an umbrella.

I'd just found Mama's body in the Vanderhausen Mausoleum. An hour later, I held Tommy Tucker as he took his last breath beneath the Warrior Angel. I freeze, then hear Dr. Vasquez's voice in my head, reminding me to breathe. I hobble along and count my breaths. *I'm okay*, I remind myself.

I hear a guy's voice and follow the sounds to the right.

Slowly. Eternal Peace tricks you with its beauty. Makes you think it's a special place, but it's not. It's just full of bones and dust. Nothing magical about that. The trees all look like giant monsters. A branch snaps nearby that sends the nightmare through me again.

Raining. Running. Death.

A branch scratches my arm as I fly by, shrieking. My Diablo scar's throbbing, and my lungs paralyze me. I hear footsteps thudding behind me.

It's a dark shadow. I do my best to outrun him, but I can only limp so fast. He tackles me to the ground.

Something hits the back of my head.

CHAPTER 15

When I come to, I've got a mouthful of grass and struggle under his weight. I'm pinned to the ground, shrieking. Miz Jesus did this before—

He mutters in Chinese, stands, then flips me over. "Why were you running?"

It's not Chao-Chao. Or any of the others.

I do a double take and peer closer. He's a she. "Mai Wong?"

"Shhhhhh, they'll hear us. Sorry I elbowed you." She helps me up. Her jet-black ponytail dangles over one shoulder, showing the purple shaved sides of her head.

We're standing in the Jewish Section. I try to calm myself and lean back against a headstone with a six-pointed star on it, not caring who the dead person is. I whisper, "Are you crying?"

"No." Mai wipes her cheeks.

"What's wrong? Did O'Dell upset you?"

"I don't want to talk about it. We're losing them. Come on." She zigzags through the cemetery. Worry earthquakes through me and my chest might explode, but I'm not about to be left alone here. I hurry behind her.

There's no storms like that horrible terrible night. The air is warm and sticky. I don't need an umbrella. I just keep Tommy

Tucker's blade open and ready. Moonlight spills onto Mai weaving like a ninja through these graves. I stay close, but don't see Chao-Chao or the rest of his gang. I'm still a bundle of nerves.

We're headed to the farthest part of the cemetery on the left. Not toward Tommy Tucker and the Nobody Section on the right. We're going to the far side of Eternal Peace.

It's so much worse. All these headstones look like dark shadows. The past and the present swirl through me. I stay close to Mai, then whisper, "Why'd you send me here?"

"Huh?"

"How'd you know where to send that Michele lady?"

"What are you talking about?"

I explain about Tiny China and her yellow VW bug, then hear how random it sounds. Maybe I do have a concussion.

"She sounds like my NaiNai, but that can't be. Grandmother Wong died two months ago in her sleep."

I'm not sure what to think. Cicadas sing their evening song in the darkness. I hear 'em chirp a few blocks away at Uncle P's house, too, but there's a bazillion more of 'em here. This used to be my bedtime lullaby every night. My heart yanks for the girl I used to be.

We take a sharp right toward the voices in the distance, then pass a pinwheel spinning in the breeze before a tiny grave. Teddy bears and other stuffed animals sit in front of several headstones. I spot a Raggedy Ann–shaped grave and foot marker with a lamb etched into the marble.

It's Baby Land.

This is by far the saddest part in all of Eternal Peace. Parents come here to bury their young children. Every day you'd see a mom or dad bawling their eyes out, then at night, you'd still hear their sadness wailing in the wind. Some hearts never heal.

I always thought it'd be a person's worst nightmare to outlive a child but outliving a mama's not much better.

The Asian Assassins gather at the edge of Baby Land, so me

and Mai Wong squat behind a small headstone far away for spying. I don't want to, but I already know the dates chiseled into the marble of our hiding spot:

JOSEPHINE SAMOYA
OCTOBER 2, 1987–OCTOBER 2, 1987

Josephine's birth day and death day are the same. That happens a lot in Baby Land. I glance over and find one even more specific.

NATHAN WALKINS
14 HOURS
NOVEMBER 7, 1949

Shadows move across the graveyard. I recognize Drago's voice and think Chao-Chao's the taller one standing to the side of that hole. He cradles something in his arms while the others dig.

I break into a full sweat, begging myself not to have a whack attack now. I whisper to Mai, "What are they doing?"

She shakes her head and wipes her eyes. "They shouldn't have refused."

"Who?"

She grips the back of Baby Josephine's headstone so hard I worry she'll crack it in half.

My friend's definitely crying. "Tell me what's wrong."

She gulps a mouthful of tears, staring at her combat boots.

"Please?"

I'm not sure she's going to talk, when her voice trembles, "Zhi steals Chinese babies . . . He sells 'em to white people who can't get pregnant."

That's a hard punch to the gut. "Aren't there . . . adoption agencies for that?"

"This is faster. There are people who'll pay a ton for a baby *right now*."

Squinting harder at the tiny bundle awaiting, I ask, "Is that what Chao-Chao's—"

"Yes."

My heart cracks wide open, then rains down babies. Just when you think people can't get any worse, Zhi Peng flushes the whole world into the toilet of life. "Where does your brother get 'em?"

"At first, China, but that took too long and cost too much."

"Where, then?"

She fidgets in her spot. "Other places."

"Mai."

"Some come from families in Chinatown . . . most come from breeders."

"Breeders?"

"Girls who do nothing but get pregnant for their babies to be sold."

"What? How much does Zhi pay—"

"He doesn't." She stands with a huff. "Just drop it, okay?"

I yank her back down behind the tiny grave. "You'll get us caught."

Endless questions torture me as I watch the Asian Assassins dig the small hole. How many breeders does Zhi have? How long has he been stealing babies? How much do families pay for a Chinese infant?

These dirty thoughts remind me of Mama's squeaking bed at the Shangri-La. I know the stork doesn't bring babies from heaven. "Who gets these girls preg—"

"Zhi's boys, all right? That family refused to give up their child and something went wrong. He feels real bad about it."

I doubt as bad as the parents feel over their dead child. Chao-Chao still holds the bundle. I'm not sure what to think about the boy with the kind eyes who kissed me a while ago. He's not mean like the others, but he's still here burying evidence.

The other guys climb from the hole. Chao-Chao hands something to one of 'em, then hops in himself . . . looks like they give it back to him. I'm guessing it's the baby. He sets him or her into a no-name grave to rest in peace.

Do murdered children do that for all eternity?

What about slaughtered mamas?

My breathing quickens as Chao-Chao scrambles from the grave and the diggers cover the body with dirt. Everyone works in silence as the moon shines and the cicadas sing.

I sniff, feeling the weight of that poor family's loss. "Why do this here? Aren't there cemeteries in Chinatown?"

"They want to punish the family for what happened. I cannot believe my brother—" Mai Wong races across Baby Land, back the way we just came. I try to stop her before she gets us caught and killed, but she's too fast. Mai gallops through the darkness, then she steps on a pinwheel.

It snaps.

"Who's there?" Drago shouts. I recognize his voice.

Heavy footsteps tromp this way. Mai's probably safe since her brother's their boss, though Drago won't think twice about murdering this Ghost Girl. He already warned me to stay away. I don't speak Chinese, but I'm fluent in mad.

Me and Mai have enough of a head start that we just might make it. I catch her by the arm, then tug her toward the Historic Section. It's got more hiding spots with all the fancy statues and mausoleums. Clouds cover the moon, so the cemetery's pitch black. That makes it harder to see, but my body hasn't forgotten this place. Shockwaves of scared shudder through me. I'm too scared to think.

Drago yells behind us, "Mai . . ." he shouts more in Chinese. The gang's still behind, though they're gaining on us.

We pass the back of the chapel. Several cars are parked in front and the building's lit up. It's way past visiting hours, so no one should be here. She passes me and runs toward the front of the chapel.

She says something I don't catch, but I'm not about to go back to where Diablo and Miz Jesus both tried to kill me.

I grab Mai and lead her away. "Not there."

We're both breathing heavy, moving in time together. We zig, then zag through the endless rows of graves. The air turns thicker. I don't hear voices and hope we lost the bullies, but don't dare stop. The night closes in more.

Soon, pine trees surround us at the Garden of Friends pond. We're crunching over pinecones. Mai Wong stumbles, and I pause to catch her. It's more wooded back here, so it's tougher to manage in the dark.

Six Asian Assassins step from the trees, surrounding us. One guy grabs Mai Wong while another shoves me to Drago.

I scream as that thug heaves me aside. He grips me tighter by the arms, then growls low, "You didn't listen, Ghost Girl."

CHAPTER 16

Drago pushes me deeper through the pine trees, away from Mai Wong and the others. She demands he let me go, but that Koi guy blocks her and shouts Chinese at her. Chao-Chao does his best to calm everyone down but has no luck. Koi's chewing out Mai for something. Most of the gang is more interested in their argument.

I'm not sure what to do. I'm terrified, but I come from a long line of crazy and decide to go straight-up Mama on Drago. I shove him so hard he stumbles back a step, then I whisper, "I know your little secret."

"What?"

"You tell me, *Pillow Pony. Pickle Sniffer.*"

He glances back at his buddies, then pulls us even farther from ear range. A few more pinecones crunch.

Nailed it. I grin. "They don't know. Do they?"

"Shut up." Drago draws his fist back to hit me, but I see the fear in his eyes.

Bingo.

"Hurt me and I tell all of Paradise the truth. I swear." Drago's fuming mad. He doesn't budge, but I'm still alive, so I dig deeper. "You killed that cop."

"You're whacked."

"Nuh-uh. Riker hated nonwhites and gays. That makes you a double winner."

"Your mom had her own reasons for wanting him dead."

"Like what?"

"You were there. What *do* I mean?"

"I was where?"

"Here at the cemetery. She and your uncle double-crossed us."

"What does he have to do with this?"

Koi barks in Chinese to the others. I want to finish this conversation, but all the Asian Assassins fall in line.

Including Drago. I watch the shadows move and hear the pinecones as all the gangbangers march away from the Garden of Friends. Koi shoots me a hard look as he passes by. "Go home, Ghost Girl."

The sharpness to his voice freaks me out. No wonder he's Zhi Peng Wong's second-in-command. He's not crazy like Eddie Loco in the Barrio Brothers, but something about how he watches me is freaky.

Chao-Chao steals a glance my way, then leaves with the others. His minty sweetness still lingers on my lips. He butterflies through me again, and I'm glad Mai Wong can't see this blush.

She joins me. It takes a minute or so, but those gangbangers are gone. Mai asks, "What just happened? Drago doesn't back down like that."

I tell her about him liking boys.

"Wow. I'm sure my brother doesn't know that."

"Why's he hate cops so much?"

"He got sent to juvie for burglary last year but swears he didn't do it."

I don't bring up my fears of that place. "What was Koi yelling at you about?"

Mai walks to the pond. "They know about O'Dell."

"We need to warn him."

"He already knows."

"Are you sure?"

She squats at the shore's edge and picks up pine needles. Moonlight shines milky across the water as a few ducks drift by in silence. Mai doesn't realize she's in the very spot where Tommy Tucker washed blood from my hands the night before he died.

Neither of us knew Tommy would be murdered that horrible terrible night. I wish I could scream at him, *Get out of here! Go somewhere safe! Let's go to LA!*

Instead, Eternal Peace stole another piece of my heart.

Mai Wong pulls me from my thoughts with her heavy sigh. She says, "O'Dell and I had a fight. That's why I was crying. He's tired of sneaking around and wants to meet my family."

"Most girls would want that."

"Most girls don't have brothers like Zhi. Doesn't matter now. They already told Zhi." She drops all her needles into the water where they spread out, then float away. She tugs at her red bandanna tied around her wrist.

My gut twists tighter. O'Dell's a total butt munch, but the only one allowed to hurt him is *me*. I notice she's not wearing his pretty silver necklace yet, so he still hasn't given her his surprise. I almost tell her to cheer her up, but don't want to spoil it. "Anything I can do to help?"

"Can you turn back time?"

"I was just thinking that about Tommy."

Standing, Mai sighs and brushes off her cargo shorts, then links her arm through mine. She gives me a sad smile. "Let's get out of here, Ghost Girl."

"Why do they call me that?"

"You're pasty white. Forget them, we've got bigger problems. Where are we spending the night? I can't go home."

"Me neither."

We wander from the pine trees at the Garden of Friends, then through the endless graves. An owl hoots in the distance. I look for the Asian Assassins, Barrio Brothers or nosey photographers, but just see shadows. I still feel eyes watching from every direction, like I did that horrible terrible night. I tell myself it's my imagination, but my brain and body aren't quite sure.

I say, "O'Dell lives just a few blocks from here. We could—"

"We're fighting. Remember?"

"Right. Are you sure he's okay?"

"Yeah. He texted me a while ago."

"How'd you get here?"

"He dropped me off earlier."

"Why would he leave—"

"Will you please drop it?"

"Some boyfriend," I say. He was here then and was lucky Miz Jesus just nicked his chest with her knife. He could've met the same death as Tommy.

I make myself connect to now with my friend. The grass looks so lush and green. The old me would've taken off her shoes and skipped barefoot through the cemetery.

I walk on. My skin's sticky from dried sweat. We pass several headstones with rosaries hanging on 'em. Following Mai, I tell her, "You realize you're walking straight toward Diablo's sister's grave."

"Whoa." She turns sharp the other way. "I can't stand her."

Maria Flores is the whole reason Mai Wong got raped. The Asian Assassins shot her in a drive-by a few weeks before, so Eddie Loco paid 'em back by raping my friend. "A sister for a sister" seemed to be their sick thinking. Just remembering makes my Diablo scar pulse worse.

Mai says, "Let's spend the night in that chapel. It looked safe."

"No way. Diablo and Miz Jesus both tried to kill me there.

Besides, some late-night thing's going on there, though I don't know what. People aren't supposed to be here after hours."

"Can't we still go by?"

"No."

"Fine." She fans her hand over a bush. "O'Dell doesn't like to talk about that night, but he says it was horrible."

"Terrible," I add.

We pass another pond with the Whittington mausoleum standing on its own island in the middle of the water. That's rich upon rich. I don't see any ducks tonight.

Mai touches a headstone in passing. "Chandler Morrow."

"Mama says Chandler Morrow owned sixty thousand head of cattle, more than anyone else around here in the late eighteen hundreds. One time, he rode ninety miles from Remington to Dalhart and never left his property."

"Wow."

"I'm sure it was all a big fat lie."

"Your mom wasn't *that* bad."

"Your friend Drago seems to think so. He kept saying I was here, and my family double-crossed their gang."

"I'm not sure what that means, but Drago has issues and I don't mean being gay."

"Could he have killed that cop?" I ask.

"Anything is possible."

I add him to my suspect list, then ask Mai, "What's Drago mean, anyhow?"

"One who understands the ways of the dragon."

"Creepy, like their tattoos. What about Koi?"

"Strength."

"Why do I know his name?"

"He was shot in the shoulder in a drive-by back in February."

"That's it—you told me about it in our phone booth."

"Yep."

Another fight with the Barrio Brothers. Koi was another part leading up to Mai's attack.

She says, "By the way. Chao-Chao means noisy."

I laugh. "That's not him."

"I know. It's sort of a joke."

We walk on through the graveyard. It's much more fun to think about Chao-Chao's minty kiss. I want to tell Mai about him, but she's so sad about O'Dell I don't want to flaunt any happiness.

I've got to admit this place is beautiful. I'm not sure which is worse: being young and dumb enough to think Eternal Peace was some mystical, magical place or knowing it's a death trap.

She asks me, "Where's the Warrior Angel?"

"Across the Historic Section." I point toward the main gates on the far left. "We can't sleep there, either. That's where Tommy died."

"Man, I just have one little phone booth to deal with, but you have this whole cemetery."

"What happened to you is worse."

"No. It's just a different kind of bad," she says.

Nodding, I stare up at the starry sky. The colors go from dark blue to midnight black. I take in the hugeness of it all.

That gives me an idea. "Wait, I know where we can go." I lead us to one of the few places here I don't think will freak me out too much. Hopefully.

Mai says, "Do you think of 'before' and 'after' with your mom?"

"All the time."

"Does everything seem harder?"

"So much."

"Even normal stuff seems worse." She sighs. "Walking, breathing, trying to fall asleep. Eddie Loco's with me wherever I go. It happened so fast but it's taking forever to get better. It's like he ruined me."

"Yeah. Mama's death is part of me now. I hate that. My uncle even sent me to a head-shrinker lady once a week to deal with it."

"My family just pretends none of this ever happened."

Shrubs line the Main Mausoleum, and I smell fertilizer. Mama always said if you were to fly over this giant stone building it looks like a cross. This was where we slept when it was too cold outside.

"What is this?" Mai asks.

"The Main Mausoleum. It's like a country club for dead people."

"Seriously? How many people are buried here?"

"Hundreds."

"Ugggh." She shudders.

"Are you kidding? Your brother's gang just buried a dead baby."

"Yeah."

The Main Mausoleum looks like a giant fancy church. Somebodies pay a ton of cash to live in the afterlife, while Tommy Tucker and the UNKNOWN NEGRO get nothing but weeds and a foot marker.

Me and Mai go to the side courtyard. I climb on top of a square headstone beneath one of the small stained-glass windows. The family's name is HAWTHORNE. Yeah, there's a story here, but it doesn't matter. Just know they're rich enough to have a whole neighborhood named after 'em.

I say, "We used to sneak in through this window 'til *your boyfriend* fixed the latch." I regret it the second I say it and feel Mai's mood darken.

The window's locked. The latch still works. It takes several more climbs and tries to find a window that opens. Glad to know lazy groundskeepers still work here. I help Mai through the opening, then follow behind and lock us in for the night.

Marble covers the mausoleum from floor to ceiling with

fancy names all over the walls. We pass beautiful nooks and crannies tucked in everywhere. Plus, countless drawers are built into the walls with the names of the Who's Who in Remington on 'em—WEYMOUTH, BOHANNON, KINGSLEY.

Me and Mama used to sleep upstairs, so I don't want anywhere near there. I lead Mai down the thirty-four steps into the basement. There's a hundred drawers with names on 'em here, too.

I find a sitting area with a couch and two chairs. A golden mirror hangs on the wall behind us. We curl up on either end of the sofa, with our heads meeting in the middle. It's not Paradise, Chinatown or Uncle P's house, so score one for the win.

Mai's different now. I am, too. I think about our last time together inside One-Leg's tent. We were waiting on O'Dell to take her to the hospital after her attack. I whisper, "Remember what you said when I asked if you believe in angels?"

"When?" I remind her and she says, "Oh." Her voice drops.

"No, it's good. You told me, 'My NaiNai says after we die, messengers take our spirits to the gods. It's like a trial to decide our fate.'"

She finishes, "The good have nothing to fear, but the wicked spend eternity paying for their sins."

"Right."

"I wish Eddie Loco would spend eternity paying for his sins."

"Same here. I wonder if Diablo and Miz Jesus are burning right now."

We both fall back into thought. I hope hers aren't as ugly as mine, though she seems pretty dark. Summer school and fighting with Dusty feels a lot longer ago than just this morning. I guess that'd be yesterday by now.

That newspaper headline flashes through me again:

PROSTITUTE ACCUSED OF KILLING COP

I struggle to untangle the rest of today. Mama's fur coat. Father Where's Waldo. Salt and Pepper. That crap-sandwich Bird.

Uncle P at the Barrio Brothers' headquarters. Chao-Chao snooping around One-Leg's tent and his kiss. Dead babies. The Asian Assassins and Spider. Everyone telling me to go home. Calling me Ghost Girl. No wonder my nerves feel jangled.

"Copper?" Mai whispers.

"Hmmm?"

"I'm glad you showed up tonight."

"Thanks. I still don't know who that Michele lady was."

"Me neither, but"—Mai yawns and gives me a soft pat—"love you."

"Love you, too."

"Copper?"

"Hmmm?"

". . . Nothing. Night."

There's so much more I want to say, too. It's good to have a friend again. I'm sorry for yelling at her and O'Dell, and I understand how much she's hurting even though I can't know exactly.

Before I find the right words, Mai's breathing slows and evens out. For someone who's been beat up by life as bad as me, she sure fell asleep fast. Her soft snores fill the mausoleum basement.

I'm jealous. I'm stuck with me, myself and I. Plus these whack attacks. It's weird sleeping at Eternal Peace again, but at least I'm not staring up at the Warrior Angel and all those memories.

Mama's grave is just on the other side of this building. NOBLITT is what our family plot says. It's the closest I've slept to her since she snuck out and got herself killed on February 15. I'm able to talk myself off that ledge of panic.

At some point, my exhaustion finally wins out and I stop worrying about tomorrow. I need to find that cop-killer, though I need some shut-eye first.

A loud *clunk* wakes me from a dreamless sleep. I recognize the sound and sit straight up on the couch. It's the mausoleum's front door—those are men's voices. Probably the groundskeepers opening the building for the day.

I tap Mai Wong's side of the couch. "We've got to go."

She's gone.

CHAPTER 17

"Mai?" I whisper, peering around the dark basement, even though I think the only ones here are me and hundreds of corpses buried behind the walls.

Overhead, one man says to the other, "Turn on the lights."

"You bloody do it."

While they bicker about who'll do what, I rush to another sofa farther from the steps and hide behind that. My heart thumps so loud I'm sure they'll hear me.

A minute later, the room brightens. I'm still nervous they'll come down, but they're too busy arguing about something else. I stay hidden even after the main door slams shut.

They left. I'm stiff and sore as I head toward the staircase. The velvety couch we slept on is plush enough I notice one word scratched into the fabric on the side where Mai slept: HOME

She must've decided to take her lumps for sneaking out and gone back to Chinatown. I hope her family isn't too mad and she makes up with Butt Munch O'Dell soon. Like today. He's probably even more of a sad sack than her, but he better be okay. I'll check on him and tell him about the Asian Assassins, then make him take me to Paradise. I climb the steps to the first floor.

It's morning, though the sun's not up yet, so the cemetery's still dark outside. The dew on the grass smells fresh, and a lone bird chirps nearby. I'd forgotten how perfect Eternal Peace is at first light.

My bladder's full, so I find a spot behind some bushes to take care of my morning business. I haven't missed this part one bit. Looking to the east, I can't see the Warrior Angel from here, but swear I feel him watching me. Mama's mangled body was found in the Vanderhausen Mausoleum between here and the statue.

Sweat breaks over my palms. Hold it together. I've got to find who killed that cop, but maybe I should check Baby Land first for more buried babies. I grip Tommy's closed knife and hobble across the graveyard. I'm still debating what to do when I remember Mama and the Noblitt family plot are right around the corner. Not that I expect my uncle to visit before hours, but I still take a different route. There's not a cloud in the dark sky, though storms gather inside me.

Raining. Running. Death.

O'Dell lives just a few blocks away. I've got a few choice words for him dumping his girlfriend here like that. If he really did. Mai might've been lying. His butt munch of an uncle fired him after that horrible terrible night. Like the groundskeeper could've stopped all those killings.

It's Saturday, so they won't mow over the weekend. Thanks to Pepper, I don't know what time it is, but more workmen will show up soon, so I better hurry. It feels weird to not be in my canopy bed, surrounded by lame dolls and stuffed animals. My stomach growls. I wouldn't even mind some of Uncle P's bacon and eggs. Princess the Evil Cat is probably just waking up for the day.

Staring through the black fence, I watch the empty street in the distance. Did my uncle go home last night, or is he still searching for me? I feel sort of bad for all the trouble I'm causing him, then remind myself he's a traitor to many.

That same tug-of-war between Chao-Chao and Tommy Tucker stirs up inside. The new boy with the minty lips or the one with the Hershey Bar brown eyes? Very different, but yummy guys. I hope Tommy can't read my thoughts.

Something jumps out at me. I scream and stumble back.

A possum waddles by, then disappears behind a bush. I remind myself these are all just headstones and statues. The monsters are all gone.

Still, I watch the shadows. I don't even have to look as I wander through the graves, I remember these paths so much. My black eye feels even more swollen today.

"You're not supposed to be here!" a groundskeeper yells from across the cemetery. He's grandpa old in a golf cart and putters toward me on the road. I recognize his voice as the bossy one from the mausoleum a while ago.

It's smarter to not run, so I smile extra big when he reaches me. "Really? Sorry. I thought you were open."

"All the gates are locked."

"Not the main one, or I couldn't have gotten in." I walk away. "It's fine, I'll leave and come back. Have a nice day." I limp off fast, making sure to stay among the headstones where his golf cart can't go.

"Don't I know you?" he shouts.

"I don't think so." I hear him walkie-talkie someone else. I'll be long gone by the time he figures out who I am. I'm limping as fast as I can without running. The morning sky lightens, though it's still dark.

A few minutes later, I smell the sweetness from the chapel's roses before I actually see the bushes. The bright pink flowers make a U-shape line around the building.

Careful. Those pretty blooms have thorns that'll cut you to pieces. A rainbow of colors sparkle from the giant stained-glass window in front. Most of the cars are gone from last night, 'cept for a silver Lexus SUV and a red Mercedes convertible.

What's going on? The chapel door is open to a casket in the

middle of the room with a man and two ladies bickering behind it. They're all dressed in black church clothes. People didn't talk during Mama's funeral.

Fear tidal-waves my body. Diablo sliced me on that very porch. Later inside, I thought he'd kill me for sure, then Miz Jesus sneaked in from behind and slit his throat. I thought she was my savior, but . . .

I struggle to breathe. The shorter woman steps out onto the chapel porch now, so I duck behind the Mercedes. I watch her take a cigarette from her clutch purse, then light it. She gazes across the grounds. Her blonde hair's all one length above her shoulders, with a slight curl at the ends. Those are serious diamonds around her neck. Something about her sort of calms me down.

She glances this way and does a double take. "Oh, hello."

I crouch lower.

"I promise I won't bite. Come on out here."

"Ummm, hey." I take a small step forward.

She glances at the other two in the chapel, then tiptoes her high heels toward me. LV is stamped all over her brown purse.

I ask, "What's going on inside?"

She whispers, "It's a wake."

"Who's awake?"

"No," she chuckles. "We're holding a wake for my mother, who just died. We stayed up all night . . . forget it." She sighs. "This was all Genevieve's bright idea. We had a vigil for our mother, even though we're not Jewish or Catholic."

"Why are we whispering?"

"To avoid my sister's wrath."

"Oh . . . Sorry about your mom."

"It's all right. She probably died nagging us to death." The lady's got ginormous blue eyes and takes a long drag off her cigarette. "After the funeral, I'll never have to talk to my brother or sister again." Her smile brightens for the first time. She studies my buzz cut and beat-up face, then leans closer. "Do I know you?"

"I don't think so."

"What's your name?"

"Tommy."

"Nice to meet you, Tommy." Her bracelets jangle as we shake. "I'm Lisa."

A taller, angrier version of her appears on the porch and hisses, "Liiiiiiiiiiiiiiiiiiiiiisa."

"What? I just came out for a quick smoke. Get off my back, Genevieve."

"It's time to clean up now. Come help." She goes back inside.

"Be right there." Lisa smiles and waves off her sister, then the gesture turns into the O'Dell finger. A one-way salute, full on insults.

I like this chick.

"Let's go." She hurries to the Lexus and unlocks it.

"Where to?"

"Anywhere but here." Lisa slips behind the wheel.

I follow behind, then buckle up, which is good 'cause Lisa drives like Dusty and Tiny China. We're out of here. Hints of the golden sunbeams bounce off the windshield. I shiver from the air-conditioning. Thank goodness she doesn't head toward the Historic Section and the Warrior Angel. "Genevieve is your sister?"

"Unfortunately."

"Is the other guy your brother?"

"Julian." She nods. "I'm the youngest."

Genevieve, Julian and Lisa are all movie-star beautiful. I wonder if their mom was a looker, too. This lady glances my way, then stubs out her cigarette. "What are you doing here so early?"

"Nothing."

"Sure about that, wee one?"

I nod. Sunrise shimmers across the fifty thousand headstones in a soft graveyard glow. Mama always said that meant there were fifty thousand stories here, each filled with glad, sad and mad.

Lies.

All of it.

My body and brain haven't forgotten the badness from that horrible terrible night. Or last night, but it's dialed down inside this fancy car. I say, "You mind swinging by Baby Land?"

"Ick, I try to avoid that place like the plague."

"Me, too, but I'm looking for something."

"Is it part of you not being here so early?"

I snicker. "Maybe."

We drive down the narrow roads as more blue inches across the sky. Two squirrels chase each other around a tree. Eternal Peace looks so beautiful it hurts to see what all I lost. What Mama stole.

Pinwheels spin in the morning breeze, and teddy bears sit up against the headstones of Baby Land. This section marks such a short time on this earth, but their families' heartache lives on forever.

There's Josephine Samoya's grave where me and Mai hid last night while her brother's gang buried that dead baby. There's no other fresh dirt besides the mound in the far corner. No other signs of evil.

Doesn't mean it's not there. Do I tell this rich lady what happened, so she'll call the cops?

Nope. I've got enough trouble.

Not happening.

She asks, "See anything?"

"No, all clear."

"Where to now?"

I take a deep breath and go with a detour plan. I can't believe I'm doing this, but I owe him. It's been too long. I grip the pocketknife tighter.

We're there in no time. The groundskeepers still don't water enough back in the Nobody Section, and there's way too many weeds. They're just as lazy as O'Dell.

I swallow hard. "Can you give me a minute?"

"Take as long as you need," Lisa winks.

Tremors quiver up me as I walk up to the two simple foot markers buried straight into the ground. They're my favorite graves in all of Eternal Peace:

TOMMY TUCKER UNKNOWN NEGRO

I still don't know what the UNKNOWN NEGRO's name was, when he died, or anything about him. My gut says he didn't lead a happy life, though he's King of the Nobodies in death.

I'm struggling with what to say to the boy with the Hershey Bar brown eyes. "Ummm, hey . . . Sorry I haven't been by since your funeral. It's just . . ."

Lisa's engine hums behind me. Without even looking, I feel her watching. Trying to figure this out.

Good luck with that.

I grip his knife and stare at his name. "I'm not sure what I'll do if Mama really killed that cop . . . She already took so much . . ." My mind sees the pink candy heart he gave me the day before he died. How he looked when he shoved it into my mind. The tiny letters . . . *MISS YOU.*

"I miss you, too," I whisper. Tears fill my eyes. He means so much more to me than Chao-Chao, who's sweet but . . .

I hurry away from Tommy's foot marker without a goodbye, before I fall apart. No use in lying and saying I'll be back, since who knows if that's true. We didn't talk about his pops, either.

A girl with no mama.

A father with no son.

I holler back to the UNKNOWN NEGRO. "Take care of him."

When I slip back into the Lexus, I expect twenty questions from Lisa. My smile feels extra fake. "Thanks."

She's drinking from a flask. Her leather handbag lays open to a pink pistol.

"You've got a gun?" I shout.

"Mmmm, it's okay." She nods, guzzling more. "I've got my concealed license. Had to." Another drink. "It's not safe out there."

That's just what Lispy Naomi told me last night. *"It'th not thafe here. It'th not thafe."*

Don't I know it. I buckle up, kicking myself for traipsing off with another stranger and this one's getting shnockered at dawn. Wait . . . I've got another idea. A good one. "You up for a detour with your gun?"

"I thought you'd never ask. I'll even reschedule my acupuncturist if need be." She grabs the steering wheel, still holding her flask.

Me and Lisa roll past the cemetery gates with the golden EP across 'em. The clock on the car dash says 6:37 a.m. Uncle P's house is toward the right.

We go left. There's not much traffic at this hour.

Lisa guzzles more. "I'll be so glad when the funeral is over tomorrow."

"Family stuff is hard."

"You have no idea." I nod, then she gives my bruised face a once-over. "Actually, maybe you do, wee one."

A blush heats my cheeks. I feel like Mama and Tommy are written all over me. Lisa and her pink pistol are such wannabes. She wouldn't know danger if it bit her silky butt. Man, I seem to pick the crazies.

Her eyes widen at the run-down houses in the neighborhood a few blocks from the cemetery. Just sad, unloved and almost forgotten. If this was Eternal Peace, it'd be the Nobody Section, for sure.

We park in front of a shabby mailbox that barely stands on its post. Letters, bills and magazines overflow from it. This house is about the same size as Uncle P's, but so not the same. Grass this brown might burn if the weather reaches the triple digits again, and that feels like it's a given today.

Lisa asks, "Who lives here?"

"The guy who gave me this black eye." I stare at Dusty Hamlyn's porch.

"Do I get to shoot him?"

"He's in the hospital."

"You hurt him that badly?"

"No." I snicker. "He was in a car wreck. Long story, but it's his brother Billy's fault."

"Can I shoot Billy?"

"No bullets. Just stand behind me with your gun as my muscle. Don't talk or shoot."

"Glad I didn't cancel my acupuncturist for this." She grumbles as we head toward the house.

Dusty lives on the wrong side of the cemetery and the wrong side of life. No cars are in the driveway. I wonder if Billy's Trans Am is totaled or if anyone's even home.

Me and Lisa might fall through the porch it's so rickety. I tap three times on the door, then step back in case fists come flying. I hear the *click* of Lisa's pistol behind me. She just took it off safety.

"Don't—" I say as the door swings open.

Billy Hamlyn stands there, barefoot in jeans, with ripples across his belly. A cigarette dangles from his pouty lips, and he's holding a beer can. His light brown hair curls at his shoulders. He wears a gold fish earring dangles from his left lobe. Him and O'Dell are in the same class, but . . . wow. Billy Hamlyn is a beautiful bad boy and nothing like his lame-o brother.

I hear Lisa sigh behind me, then make myself stand taller. "You Dusty's brother?"

Billy looks me up and down. "You the girl who kicked his ass, then wrecked my car?"

"I did the first, but not the second."

He gives me another slow look, then swigs more beer. "You'd be hot if you had hair and tits."

"That's none of your business."

"I'm making it my business."

"Then expect me to knock your balls up to your boogers."

"Attitude." He grins. "I like it. No wonder Dusty digs you."

What the—? Down just fell up and up turned down. Dusty doesn't . . . I don't know what to say to that, so I step aside to show Billy we're packing heat.

Lisa sort of flinches, then holds up her pink pistol. I wish she'd done it with more attitude, like Charlie's Angels, but it's too late now.

I say, "Hurt Dusty again, and we'll hurt you."

"Why don't you honeys come inside for a little scotch and sofa? I wanna—"

A gunshot rings from behind. Me and Billy shout, cringing together.

Lisa blew a hole straight through the mailbox. She probably murdered a pink final notice. Billy chases us, cussing up a blue storm. We rush back to the car. He moves in closer 'til she shoots at his bare feet, then he disappears inside his house.

Lisa's howling as we speed away. "That was awesome!"

"You're insane!"

"No, I'm Lisa Vanderhausen."

The pit in my stomach drops. "What did you say?"

"I'm . . . Lisa Vanderhausen." She glances at me and drives on down the road. "What's wrong, wee one? You look positively ill."

I whisper, "My real name's not Tommy. It's Copper. Copper Daniels. My mama's body was found . . ."

Lisa slams on the brakes. "In my family's mausoleum."

CHAPTER 18

Lisa Vanderhausen whips her Lexus to the side of the street of this low-rent neighborhood. Her family started Eternal Peace cemetery over a hundred years ago, just a few blocks from here. Their name is stamped all over with statues, artwork in the chapel and their fancy mausoleum. And not just there, all over Remington, too. We watch each other, connecting the dots between our families.

"Copper Daniels." She shakes her head, clutching her diamond necklace. "I've wondered if we'd ever meet."

All I can do is nod.

"Your father and his wife used to live next door to me. I never cared for them." Her bracelets jangle as she drains her flask.

"Now you know why."

"I watched his TV interview last night while Genevieve and Julian napped—which both are against the rules for a wake, by the way." Lisa humphs. "Your dad was smooth as ever. I'm sure he'll be on TV again after prison, back to his old tricks. He'll probably get a movie deal out of this."

"Probably."

Lisa wraps her soft hand around mine. "I'm so sorry about your mother's death."

"Thanks." Her teary eyes melt my heart a little. Lisa

Vanderhausen is nutty, but she's also nice and funny, so I'll take it. She said the real word, too. I tell her, "Sorry you got dragged into my family's mess."

"It's not your fault," she says.

"Feels like it."

"Don't live your parents' shame."

"Easier said than done. Where will your mom be buried?"

"There's only one spot left in our mausoleum. The—"

"Bottom right drawer."

Lisa understands how I know that and might rip off her necklace any second. "What's your story, wee one? Beyond your mother, I mean. Why did we drive through Baby Land, visit that grave, then shoot at that hot guy?"

"No reason."

"Copper, please. You can't con a conner."

Something about the gleam in her eye speaks to me. Death binds us, so I stop trying to BS this rich lady. It might help to get an outsider's viewpoint, so I take a chance and tell Lisa Vanderhausen everything about the past twenty-four hours. Almost.

"Selling babies?" She gasps when I'm done. "Unbelievable . . . I think your mom's friend Bird killed the cop."

"Even if she didn't, she deserves to be behind bars."

"Though Eddie Loco or Drago are close seconds."

"Right."

"Wait. What does your friend Mai Wong look like?"

I describe her to Lisa, who then says, "I saw a girl just like that last night leaving the cemetery. She might've been crying. I even asked her if everything was okay, but she didn't stop."

"What time was that?"

"I'm not sure." Lisa yawns and rubs her face. "I'm sorry. I've been up for over twenty-four hours, and didn't realize it'd be important."

"Mind dropping me off somewhere nearby?"

"Do I get to shoot them?"

"No."

She grumbles and drives but keeps the pink pistol on her lap. I make her latch the safety back on and we ride in silence. Bright beautiful colors spill over the clouds. Me and Lisa Vanderhausen are kind-of-not-really friends. Her family practically owns the city. Her brother, Julian, is a bigwig businessman. I've seen him on TV. Uncle P's dragged me to their family's museum exhibits and stuff.

Minutes later, we park in front of O'Dell's white stucco house. A slew of bicycles for his five younger brothers sits on the dead grass. It's scary to think there's more like him. I'm sure some of those bikes are hand-me-downs 'cause there's well over a dozen here. I've never met his family and don't want to, thank you very little.

He's invited me, though. His piece-of-crap truck is in the driveway, behind his mom's junky station wagon. Sounds like she has a hard time getting out of bed and stays sad a lot. He doesn't talk about his dad, who left over a year ago. O'Dell's place isn't as nice as Uncle P's, but way better than Dusty's.

Sitting in Lisa Vanderhausen's front seat, I thank her for the ride. It's an awkward goodbye, though how could it not be? I head to the porch while she waits, staring me down, I'm sure. I hope that's a video game playing inside—electronic gunshots blare in the background. I pause, then ring the doorbell.

I hear footsteps, then the door swings open. "Hells bells," O'Dell says. "What do *you* want?"

"To John Deere your ass."

"What'd I do?"

"It's what you didn't do, Butt Munch." I wave off Lisa Vanderhausen and wait 'til she's gone, then give him a major talking-to about his crappy citizenship.

All he says is, "I'd never leave Mai alone."

I sigh. "I thought she might be lying."

"But you still took the chance to yell at me."

"Of course. Then how'd she get there?"

"No clue. I didn't know where she was all night, but she texted me early this morning." O'Dell shows me his screen:

Grounded. About to lose my phone. Love you. Bye.

He sees me reading all the mushy stuff he wrote back, then stuffs his phone back into his pocket. They still haven't kissed and made up. He hasn't given her his necklace.

O'Dell says, "I want to see her. Let's go to Chinatown now."

"Take me to Goodwill in Paradise first. Mama's jacket is for sale there."

"Seriously?"

"Yeah. I'll explain on the way."

"Fine, but don't tell your uncle. Let me grab my keys."

"Give me your phone. I want to watch my jailbird daddy's interview."

He tosses it to me. "Your father is a dingle pringle."

"Good thing I'm not like him."

O'Dell leaves and his brothers' laughter, screams and tears make me wonder how loud they are when they're outside. He's shown me videos of him cannonballing 'em through the air from their trampoline. I'm sure they're the most popular neighbors on the block.

Sitting on the porch, I pull up Gigi Carlisle's video. She and my jailbird daddy sit across from each other in a cinderblock room. She's dressed up. He's wearing prison orange.

She says, "Hello, I'm Gigi Carlisle with *News Action Four*, here today at the Kyle C. Danforth Unit with the ex-Reverend Anthony Sanborne from the former mega-show, *The Lord's Power Hour*. He's in prison for embezzlement and tax evasion, while his wife and cohost, Angela Sanborne, murdered a homeless woman named Corrine Daniels Noblitt. Noblitt was also the mother of Sanborne's illegitimate daughter, who is eleven. Angela Sanborne died in a police standoff when the homeless girl was saved by her uncle, Sergeant Patrick Noblitt."

The girl.

It feels weird hearing my life talked about behind my back. That reporter doesn't know the cold, hard facts about that moment. Uncle P, O'Dell and Tommy Tucker all stood outside the Warrior Angel in the pouring rain and watched, helpless as Miz Jesus held her steely knife against my neck. Time moved faster and slower than ever before. She tried to kill me, but Tommy swooped in and her blade stabbed him first. Just as my uncle shot her between the eyes.

If he'd just been half a second faster.

If, if, if.

I miss what Gigi just said, so I rewind the recording.

She asks Mr. Jesus, "Do you think Corrine Daniels Noblitt killed Officer Felix Riker?"

"Absolutely." He doesn't even blink.

"Why?"

"I'd been in contact with Corrine that day, trying to get her clean and sober for our daughter, but saw she was out of control. She was paranoid, convinced someone was after her. She even mentioned Officer Riker by name."

"Why should we believe you? You're a convicted felon, after all."

"I lost two women I cared about that night. That changed me forever."

I wish it didn't, but that shoelace feeling ties me to him. His badness is in my blood. In my bones.

The interview ends with Mr. Jesus. "I just want to serve my time, get out and be a good father to my daughter."

Those words chill me. I'm not living with my uncle the traitor anymore, but I sure don't want to grow up with my jailbird daddy. Talk about a lose-lose. I realize I'm shaking.

O'Dell gives me a biscuit, then hurries on to his pickup.

"Thanks."

"Who was that woman who dropped you off?"

"Lisa Vanderhausen."

"How do you—scratch that. I don't want to know. You look like shit, by the way."

"Checked the mirror lately?"

We pile into his truck. There's no trash, beer cans or To Go boxes anywhere inside. Amazing what people will do for love. I catch him up on everything. Sort of. I'm not sure where Mai lives in Chinatown. I'm not even sure what her house looks like.

O'Dell stuffs a pinch of tobacco under his bottom lip and we go. He doesn't know not to drive by Eternal Peace. I've never told him about my whack attacks. I eat my breakfast and remind myself I can do this. I've been there twice in the past twenty-four hours and managed okay.

We pass Tommy Tucker in the Nobody Section. Soon after is the giant cross that's Maria Flores. I remember Diablo wailing over his sister's grave in the nights leading up to that horrible terrible night. He sobbed in Spanish like the wailing wind. *"I'm sorry, I'm sorry, I'm sorry."*

O'Dell says, "I haven't been back to the cemetery since Tommy's funeral."

"I wasn't there by choice." I look away. "What have you told Mai about that night?"

"Not much."

I glance at the black fence in my side mirror 'til we're in another neighborhood altogether. I survived again. I save the last bite of biscuit in my pocket. Just in case.

O'Dell says, "I still have nightmares about it, though."

"Really?" I watch him closer.

He grips the steering wheel tighter. "It replays like a movie. I even dream about your mom's blue tattoo sometimes. Weird stuff, like how can angel wings chase you?"

I nod.

His phone rings and my uncle's name flashes across the screen—PATRICK NOBLITT.

"You tell him I'm here and I tell him about you dating the sister of the biggest drug lord in Paradise."

O'Dell groans, then answers. "Morning . . . Hey there . . . Uh, no, I still haven't heard from Copper. Yeah, I'm sure she's okay. She resourceful." He winces, then bobs his head. "No problem. I've got a few errands to do first, then I'll go wait for her at your house . . . Okay, glad to help. Bye."

"Nice lying."

"Shut up." He pulls out Mai's necklace, then cups it in his steering-wheel hand. The beautiful black stone dangles from the silver chain for the girl he loves. Their fight's breaking his heart. Their misery is bumming me out. O'Dell seems a little less butt-munchy right now.

O'Dell says, "You should at least give your uncle a chance."

"Mind your own business."

He keeps watching me, but not talking.

"What?" I snap.

"You need to face it that your mom might actually be guilty."

I glare out the window to a lady pushing a baby stroller. That's all I've done the past four months.

On. So. Many. Levels. My old life keeps flashing by now. The Burger Heaven where me and Mama begged on the corner with our sign. The library where we went to Story Time almost every day. All the fancy people downtown who ignored us.

The digital sign at that bank says it's already eighty-five degrees. Today will be another scorcher. Next to the Church of the Living Water, a small boy sits on the edge of the water fountain that's run dry. He doesn't look homeless or scared, though I wonder why he's alone and where his parents are. Sometimes grown-ups are just crappy.

A minute later, the truck rambles over the railroad tracks into Paradise. My body tightens. I need answers today, even if Mama did it. A man sits under a tree in a folding chair with a wet towel over his face. It's already that hot.

I look for Corn Dog, One-Leg, Salt and Pepper. Any of my people.

They're not here.

O'Dell parks along the street by the Party Palace. "I want to make sure Mai's not here."

"'Cause her parents grounded her outside?"

"She's snuck out before."

"Don't I know it." I limp behind him into the alley, knowing it's useless to battle love. "All right, but we're going to Goodwill next."

"Yes, ma'am."

We move between the buildings on either side of us. It feels like I'm being watched again, but I don't see anyone staring from the apartment complex. The window with the Dallas Cowboys sticker is empty, too.

O'Dell practically dives into the phone booth, then I hear him sigh.

"Told you." I walk up to him sitting alone. "Come on. Goodwill's open now."

"Shut up." He pulls out his phone and sends Mai another text.

This is going to take forever. My mouse friend dashes from an empty plastic cup over to the Dumpster. He disappears behind the bin.

"Walter?" I whisper, then kneel close by. "Hey, where are you, little buddy? I've got something for you."

I slowly set my leftover biscuit near him, then ease back to watch. He peers out and wriggles his nose at the food. Walter studies it more, then takes a few tiny steps closer, grabs a crumb and munches on it.

"Atta boy." I beam. "How've you been? I think the real Walter would love you. He's my only kind-of-not-really friend at school."

The mouse keeps nibbling.

"I'm not sure who'll protect him from Dusty since I won't be back anymore."

O'Dell walks up behind me. "Who are you talking to?"

"Walter the mouse."

"You're such a loser."

"Says the guy still holding his girlfriend's necklace. Let's go to Goodwill."

"Fine, but then we look for Mai. Plus, I promised your uncle I'd wait for you at home."

"That's not my home."

"Ingrate." He heads back toward his pickup.

"Bye, Walter. Take care." I leave the mouse eating and hope I'll see him again. Maybe I could make him my pet. He's another reason to never go back to Uncle P's house. Princess the Evil Cat would eat him.

I'm moving double time to catch O'Dell. All my aches and pains hurt twice as bad. The Butt Munch doesn't slow one bit for me. If anything, he's moving faster. I jump over a puddle, then hear a whiz and loud crash behind me. I scream.

An old TV lies destroyed where I just stood. Looking up, I see that same window hanging open now. The Dallas Cowboys sticker shines in the morning sun.

CHAPTER 19

The busted television rests at my feet—broken glass, pieces of plastic and the long black cord. It's even got the old rabbit-ears antenna. I'm shaking. That was supposed to be my smashed head there.

"Hells bells!" O'Dell rushes to me and puts his arm around my shoulder. I count up to the fifth floor to the open window and point to the apartment on the end. "I think that's where it came from."

He takes me by the hand, and we start running. We race by the back of the Party Palace onto the crowded street. Everyone looks guilty, but none of 'em pay attention to us. Paradise is still waking up for the day. I don't see Spider or any other Barrio Brother wannabes around. No Asian Assassins.

We're out of breath as we head around the corner. O'Dell says, "Someone doesn't . . . want you . . . snooping."

"I'm onto something . . . but what?"

We sprint into the run-down apartments on the edge of the block. Inside, rows of mailboxes are built into the walls. It smells hot and mildewy. A couple waiting by the elevator glance at us with no recognition.

The steps sway rickety as we dash up 'em. There's no air-conditioning, so I'm exhausted and pitting out bad. We pass a young dad holding a baby coming downstairs. He pulls the child close to him as we zoom by him.

"Sorry," I yell back.

My lungs may explode by the time we reach the fifth floor. O'Dell charges through the hallway toward the right, and I gimp along behind him. My sides ache and my black eye hurts. Behind the different apartment doors, TVs blare and people talk. Some argue. Music plays. I hear the hum of fans. Life's happening behind all these walls.

They also might be hiding a killer. They just tried to off me. O'Dell waits for me at the apartment I think the TV fell from.

Now that we're here, I'm not sure what to do, so I hold back. I don't want to die. Most of the Barrio Brothers are in jail, but who knows what gang wannabe lives here? Maybe Spider. Instead, we knock at several neighbors' apartments, but nobody answers. Getting involved can mean death. Finally, we check the door I think is the one.

No one's here. Or they're not answering.

When O'Dell gives up, I follow him slower back down the five flights. Someone doesn't want me to find the truth about that dead cop. Or maybe it's payback from something Mama did before. Wouldn't be the first time. It might also be about Uncle P. Maye even my jailbird daddy.

Back in O'Dell's pickup, we drive. He quizzes me again about what all has happened and actually listens this go-round. Goodwill's just a few blocks away. Some folks are just now crawling into their tents after a long night of partying.

Asian Assassins are already dealing drugs on several corners. I'm so glad this isn't my life anymore, though I've missed Mai, Salt and Pepper. Nothing about this new life fits right, either. I feel like Goldilocks. Where can I go that's *just right?*

We pass St. Columba's church to find a crowd gathered

outside the white wooden crosses at City Cemetery. Sunny-yellow CAUTION tape ropes off the scene:

++++++++++++++++++++++++++++++

++++++++++++++++++++

++++++++++

It's hard to see through the gawkers as the police and EMS work the crime scene. A body lies on the grass, blocked by a wheelchair with the seat packed full of junk—a duffel bag and several record albums stick out from the pile. Lispy Naomi pushed that by me last night.

"It'th not thafe here," she said.

I think that's her on the ground. Same clothes, but I can't be sure since her head's crushed.

Just like that dead cop.

CHAPTER 20

I holler to O'Dell, "Stop, stop, stop!"

He whips his truck into the church parking lot and I'm already hobbling toward all the people at the crime scene. Their b.o. stinks worse with so many Nobodies crammed together in this heat. I push my way to the front.

That *is* Naomi. I recognize the candy Ring Pop ring on her limp hand and parts of her matted hair. I might hurl. She died in the same place, in the same way as Officer Riker. Did my snooping somehow get her killed? That dizzies me.

I want to talk to Father Where's Waldo, but he's visiting with Lydia and another policeman over there. She's in full-blown cop mode and doesn't notice me, but I still step back a row just to be sure. The priest looks shaken and sad.

Unless it's all for show and *he* murdered Naomi. Two deaths have happened on his turf in the past four months, and I know firsthand that people of God can be some of the most ungodly people.

"Excuse me." O'Dell elbows his way through the crowd to me. "Did you know her?"

"Naomi." I watch an EMT over her body. "I met her yesterday. She said it wasn't safe here."

"Why would she say that?"

I shrug. "She was a mumbler . . . She didn't make much sense."

"That falling TV seems much worse now."

"It was pretty crappy before." I feel someone watching me and almost expect 'Chele the photographer to be snapping pics of this awful moment, then realize it's Gigi Carlisle staring here from the other side of the CAUTION tape. Her camera guy's filming me.

"Let's go." I rush back to the church parking lot and O'Dell follows. The construction crew at the Salvation Army is in full motion across the street. Buzzing, clanging and building. I think about the metal wiring Bird stashed in her closet and the robbery the priest mentioned yesterday. I should check that out but can't leave here fast enough. I may cry or punch someone. Luckily, O'Dell gets us out of here quick.

I wait 'til his pickup is half a block away before I announce, "This means Mama didn't murder that cop."

"Not necessarily. It could be a copycat killer."

"You just can't believe she might be innocent."

"And you won't consider she might be guilty. Remember, I saw your mom whacked out on booze and drugs a lot. She *spit* on me that last time at the cemetery. I knew her dark side."

"Doesn't mean she's a killer."

"No, but it sure adds up."

The conversation ends. I just want to wake up somewhere else and for this all to be a bad dream.

Not happening.

O'Dell sputters a stream of tobacco into his plastic cup. "She obviously didn't kill that Naomi lady, but there's a reason why she died the same way. In the same spot. Somebody's making a statement."

"But what?" I ask myself again, looking out the window and thinking about the patterns. Trying to make sense of it all.

We pass a man staring into space, holding a tiny dog. I used to dream like that, thinking about the California ocean. To be anywhere but here. I wonder what Lispy Naomi dreamed about. What she wanted . . . beyond Paradise?

I'll never find out.

O'Dell parks in front of Goodwill and Mama's dingy rabbit coat still hangs in the main window. My heart flutters that it's still there. He opens the store door for me, and I'm shocked at his niceness after our spat.

We pass loads of every kind of hand-me-down for a house: furniture, dishes, clothes, shoes and knickknacks that do nothing but collect dust. A hot-pink sign cut out like a star says—SALE!

The price tag on Mama's coat says it's $5.99. I wish O'Dell wasn't here to watch, but don't care. My fingers smooth over the soft rabbit fur, and so many feelings collide inside—happy, glad, sad, mad. This jacket is home, just like the Warrior Angel used to be. I loved nuzzling against Mama when she wore it, drunk on her love.

O'Dell wanders off without a word. I bury my face into the fur, half hoping and half worried I'll smell her scent again—cinnamon gum, cigarettes and sweat.

It's gone from here, too. Checking the collar, I spot the tag—*Neiman Marcus.*

Yep, it's hers, all right. Mama wore this short jacket like a queen. I still can't believe I'm seeing it for real. I check all the pockets.

Empty.

Uncle P's business card fell out of here before. That was my first clue he was my family and my old life was over.

I take the coat to the cash register. The gum-smacking woman behind the counter has too much makeup and not enough sleep. Her hair's a dyejob gone bad—it's the color of straw. She holds a price gun to a bunch of teacups. She keeps clicking without looking at me. "What can I do ya' for?"

"When did this get here?"

"Oh, that one's a bee-uuute. It came yesterday. You better snap it up quick."

"Do you know who donated it?"

"Sure, Arlene. She's sorting through boxes in back." The woman nods toward the swinging door across the shop.

"Arlene?"

"Yep, she's new to the program. Been sober twenty-four hours now. Got her chip last night."

"What's her story?"

"Trying to make it one day at a time. Just like the rest of us."

"Can I talk to her?"

"Sure thing. I'll call her—Hey! You can't go back there. It's authorized personnel only."

"I just authorized myself," I holler, keeping Mama's jacket.

"That coat needs to stay here, too."

What I leave her with is the O'Dell finger high in the air. He joins me in the aisle and even gives me a low five. He may be a Butt Munch, but at least he's mine.

We push through the door to a giant room full of boxes stuffed with clothes and other junk. Outfits hang on several racks, while more stuff is stacked in piles everywhere. It'd take forever and a day to organize this mess.

I recognize Arlene the second I spot her and remind myself to breathe. It's the Coat Stealer herself. It's easy to see why I confused her for Mama when she first went missing that last morning. They've both got long, straight Cher hair, though Arlene is wearing hers up in messy bun today. I spotted her from behind on a city bus, then later walking down the street. I didn't know her name then, but that's her, all right. Arlene's got big ol' bug eyes and a honkin' nose.

She's wearing headphones and humming while digging through a box. Her tube top and cutoffs make her look like a total hoochie mama.

O'Dell hangs back as I shove Mama's jacket at her. "Tell me the truth about this coat."

Arlene flinches when she sees me, then takes off her headphones. "You."

"Yeah, me. Where'd you really find this?"

"In an unlocked car."

"You said it was in a Dumpster outside of Mission for Hope."

"Oh yeah. It was there."

"Liar." I dive at her. She shrieks, and O'Dell holds me back. I wriggle away and poke the fur at her again. "Tell me the truth, or I promise you'll eat dirt."

Arlene unfolds and refolds the same pair of jeans several times. I recognize that itchy look on her face. She's jonesing for a fix so bad she might not get another chip. "I, ummm, was still using back then. My memory's fuzzy."

"It's about to get fuzzier. Where's the guy you were with then?"

"Don't remember."

"Short, squatty, flat face and dark, kinky hair."

"No clue."

"You're as bad as Mama."

"Wait a minute." Arlene peers closer at me. "You used to have long red hair. What happened to your curls?"

"Answer the question."

"Who's your mom?"

"Corrine Daniels."

"Oh my God." Arlene drops the jeans. The color drains from her face as she backs away from me. "I-I-I've got to go." She wheels around and rushes toward the EXIT sign.

I gasp and stop. O'Dell does, too.

Arlene, the lying, cheating coat-stealer, is gone.

So are the blue angel wings tattooed across her back.

Just like Mama's.

CHAPTER 21

By the time me and O'Dell chase Arlene the Coat Stealer into the Goodwill parking lot, she's vanished. There's no breeze as we search behind the building—inside empty cars, down the alley. We even ask other folks melting in the heat nearby.

Nobody saw a thing.

Or that's what they say. I realize I'm clutching Mama's fur jacket to my heart and ease up my grip on our way back to O'Dell's pickup.

He glances at the coat. "Plan on paying for that?"

"Oh, I've already *paid*."

We move in angry silence as I rest the jacket on my lap like a blanket. Just having this near makes me feel better, and I hate my weakness but refuse to pet it in front of O'Dell. He starts the engine, turns up the AC and stares at me. We stay parked.

"Don't lecture me." I don't even look at him.

"I'm not. That was straight-up weird. That lady's tattoo looks newer, but it was your mom's design, all right."

"She's no lady."

"How long did your mom have that coat?"

"Long as I can remember."

"This all means something."

I nod, picturing the blue angel wings inked across Arlene's shoulders. Even with her boob tube on, you could tell the detailed feathers covered her whole back. Ready to take flight.

Just like Mama, who flew a little too high before she crashed and burned.

O'Dell stuffs more tobacco into his mouth. "Where'd your mom get her tattoo?"

"I never asked." I let myself rub the fur like I used to my lucky penny. So many unanswered questions.

"What'd you think of your dad's interview?"

"Pffft."

"He said your mom was talking trash about Riker the day before she died."

"Doesn't mean it happened."

"Your mom might be guilty."

"So you've said. Give it a rest."

"I just think—"

"Stop!" I slam my fist on the seat between us. "You think I don't know it? You think I don't realize she might be the killer? Every day was like being trapped on a runaway train. I tried to stop her but couldn't." My voice cracks, hot tears spilling over.

"Calm down," O'Dell says. He keeps glancing at me, then finally says, "I'm on your side, no matter what."

"Doesn't feel like it." I wipe my wet cheeks.

"Take a breath."

I do. I pet Mama's coat while we watch people drift in and out of Goodwill.

He says, "I, uhh . . . I started having panic attacks after that night."

"Really? Me, too." I stare at him.

He shrugs. "How could we not? It was pure torture. The doctor says they should go away in time, but . . ." O'Dell takes out

Mai's necklace and thumbs the black stone. I'm sure he's itching to clasp it on her and make everything right again.

I sigh. "Glad I'm not the only one with whack attacks."

"You're not. Mai has them, too, though hers sound much worse than mine."

The silence between us feels less scary. There's a deeper connection now between me, O'Dell and Mai. I like being less alone, though I hate the reason. Wish she was here.

O'Dell sighs. "Spider is the one lead you haven't really followed up on. Since he might've pushed that TV from the window, let's check out the Barrio Brothers' hangout. Look for him there."

"All right. Let's get this over with."

His hand taps mine. "Are we cool?"

"Yeah. Whatever."

As we drive through the littered streets, I stare into the distance at the tall towers and mirrored buildings of downtown. Just a few miles from Paradise. Uncle P took me to eat at the Four Seasons once. Afterward, I took him around back for dessert at the best Dumpster in town. Sure, the coconut cream pie was half-eaten, but who cares? He wouldn't let us eat it and said that his allergies were making him teary-eyed, but I don't think so.

O'Dell parks on a side street half a block down from the Barrio Brothers' abandoned hotel – The Whorton. In no time, we're heading up the sidewalk where Diablo, Eddie Loco and their thugs walked every day. This place used to be in full operation with guns, knives, girls and drugs, but not always in that order.

Now their headquarters sits empty, with broken windows throughout the five-story building. Spider bragged Eddie Loco still ran the city from prison, and I hate thinking about his hunger for my panties. I follow O'Dell under the green awning with the faded white letters: THE WHOR.

It's my first time here. We go inside. Some of the lobby windows are boarded up, and others are busted out in parts. The hotel smells like weed and mold but looks just how Mama described it. Old and fancy, with ginormous golden mirrors on the faded red-velvet walls. Huge chandeliers dangle above. Old-timey couches and chairs are scattered throughout the room into little sitting areas. A steep staircase in the center with wide velvety steps.

I feel like we've traveled back in time. I picture the grand parties that used to be here. Years before the Barrio Brothers claimed it, back when beautiful people drank fabulous drinks and Paradise truly was a paradise.

What went wrong?

O'Dell whispers, "Can we turn on the lights?"

"Sure." I flip the switch, but nothing happens. Probably no electricity. I lock the front door.

"That'll save us." O'Dell turns on his phone flashlight.

Spray-painted in black across the long wall is a list of names. It's the same tagging done to Uncle P's house. I recognize four people on here:

~~RIKER~~

NOBLITT

ZHI PENG

KOI

My gut turns at seeing my uncle's name. "Think it's a hit list?"

"Maybe. Noblitt might mean your mom, even though she went by Daniels."

I nod.

"That cop is marked out, and Mai talks about how much Zhi Peng and Koi hate the Barrio Brothers."

"I bet Spider did this. He's who tagged Uncle P's house."

Me and O'Dell sneak down the first-floor hall to the back of the hotel. The floors are littered with cookie and chip wrappers, empty beer bottles and cans. I try to ignore the cemetery quiet in here. Something flutters above us. We both holler and duck.

Pigeons fly overhead, then nest in a corner of the ceiling.

Rattled, I follow O'Dell down the dark passageway, and my worry ramps up higher.

The kitchen has all the regular stuff: stainless-steel counters, a huge double refrigerator, a freezer and deep sinks. But there's also tubes and glass beakers. It looks like a science experiment, but it's for drugs.

O'Dell opens a drawer, so I peek inside a cabinet and find an ancient jar of peanut butter. I whisper, "I only saw 'em through the windows on the first or second floors. Never any higher."

"Let's check it out."

Back in the lobby, O'Dell pauses the light on a giant brown stain on the staircase carpet. He says, "Is that blood?"

I don't answer, and we go up the velvety steps. It's a zigzaggy staircase, going left, then right, with a flat landing on each level in between. The faded red carpet on the second floor leads to rooms in both directions.

One window sits in the center across from the stairs. We gaze below to a run-down courtyard with trees and a few benches, plus a lot of overgrown grass. Diablo and Eddie Loco used to walk, talk and party down there. I shiver.

Next, we roam toward the right. O'Dell's light sweeps over the closed doors along the way with fancy designs carved into the wood. I almost expect ghosts to fly out any minute it's so spooky here.

Most rooms are locked, so we keep going 'til we find one open on the left. The solid wood's so much thicker than the doors at the Shangri-La. We go inside.

The room's extra big, like a suite. It's got faded gold carpet with red diamonds the same color as the hallway. Wallpaper is peeling from the walls. A queen-size bed with a wooden headboard is in the middle, with a big sitting area and desk in the corner. I still wouldn't want to hide under that bed, but this place is a bazillion times nicer than Room 207.

There's a giant wardrobe stands in here. I know it's a wardrobe 'cause of Narnia. I check the back just to be sure there's no secret doorway to another land. O'Dell fiddles with the lock at the room's door, clicking it back and forth.

"Stop playing around," I tell him.

"I'm not."

Out of habit, I open the nightstand drawer. A discolored black Gideon's Bible sits by itself. I want to chunk it out the window. Are these blasted books everywhere?

I lift up the grubby comforter and peer under the bed. My breath catches. It's just dust bunnies. All those times our bed squeaked above me. I hated every second under there, but at least I had Mama.

Next, I try to open the window. It's stuck, though I see it's a straight drop down into that courtyard. Too far to jump. I wander back toward O'Dell and stop at a small cabinet door built into the wall. I open it and look inside.

"Stop playing around," he says.

"What is this thing?"

"A dumbwaiter. People sent down their dirty dishes or laundry in it. Let's go."

The bathroom's back by the door, so we peek inside to an old-timey white tub with four claws for feet. It faces a mirror with a gold frame. Seriously, Mama still would've been a whore if she worked here, but at least she would've been high dollar.

Me and O'Dell decide there's nothing here, so we head back downstairs. As we turn onto the landing between the second and first floors, we freeze.

They spot us down from the lobby right as we notice they're here, too. I expected Spider and his buddies.

I'm wrong. They race up the stairwell after us.

CHAPTER 22

It's Drago and some Asian Assassins I recognize but don't know. Chao-Chao isn't with 'em, so the boy with the kind eyes can't save me now.

I hobble as fast as I can, fear rattling through me. They hurl Chinese insults our way as they gain on us. O'Dell reaches back to grab my hand and pulls me up to him. We're already sprinting through the long hallway, but I hear the gang clomping down the carpet. My insides scream. It's no use. They'll catch us any second.

In one quick motion, O'Dell scoops me into his arms and dashes ahead of the gangbangers. Glancing back, I see Drago's leading the pack, and I swear blood drips from his eyes.

O'Dell dives into the same room as before. He locks the door and latches the chain. He sets me down, then rushes to the window.

"It's too far," I tell him.

The Asian Assassins beat on the door, shouting in both English and Chinese. The booming noise jolts me to the point I'll have a whack attack any second. We're trapped.

O'Dell pushes on the window. I already know it's stuck but help him anyway.

It won't budge.

The gangbangers keep pounding. Their thuds match my drumming heart. That lock won't hold much longer.

O'Dell drags me to the dumbwaiter. "Get in."

"What about you?"

The door opens, though the chain stops it. That won't hold for much longer. Angry arms and fists wave at us.

O'Dell rushes to the entrance and kicks the door, smashing it against the Asian Assassins. More cursing explodes from the other side. He presses against there. "Go! I'll come down next."

I fold myself up and close the door behind me. It's dark. O'Dell pushes the button 'cause I start the slow move down, down, down. I'm not sure he'll fit in here. Doesn't matter if they kill him first. My body breaks out into a cold sweat.

"I'mokayI'mokayI'mokay," I keep repeating, but feel myself shutting down. This dumbthingy doesn't have enough air. I'm going to die alone. I burst into tears. My brain shrieks. I can't stop shaking. It's taking forever to get down.

Thud. I've stopped.

I push on the door.

It doesn't budge. That frightens me more. I can't open this from the inside. Everything in me wants to call out to O'Dell, but I can't tip off the Asian Assassins or anyone else. I hope my friend's okay.

Blackness closes in on me. I'm trying not to use up all the air, but I can't catch my breath. Nobody 'cept O'Dell knows I'm here. I fish out Tommy's knife and rub it like crazy. At least I'll be with him again.

A siren wails in the distance. It's the most beautiful sound ever.

The door swings open, and my favorite Butt Munch stands there. I throw myself onto him.

"Sorry," he says. "I had to kick some Asian ass."

"Seriously?"

"No. I called 9-1-1. Those jackwagons ran as soon as they heard the cops. Come on." He takes my hand.

Together, we sprint back down the velvety hallway, and I see the red-and-blue cop lights flashing through the lobby windows up front. We go the other way.

Once we burst into the alley, I'm so glad to breathe in the stinky air of Paradise. We hurry around the block to the pickup down the street.

The cops are talking to the Asian Assassins outside the Barrio Brothers' headquarters. "Talking" may be too nice of a word.

A message spray-painted in red across the back window of O'Dell's truck stops us. The paint still looks wet:

GO HOME OR DIE

He groans. "Someone really doesn't want you here."

"Gee, thanks."

"You're going to pay to wash that off my truck."

"I will."

We climb into the cab. At least Mama's coat is still here. I'm irritated how much that pleases me.

O'Dell's phone rings. It's an unfamiliar number, so he sends it straight to voicemail.

It rings right back.

He answers with a gruff "'Lo?" He sits up straighter, a blush heating his cheeks. "Oh, hey there." He nods and keeps listening, then gives me his phone. "It's for you."

I whisper, "I don't want to talk to him."

"It's not your uncle. It's Gigi Carlisle with *News Action 4*."

CHAPTER 23

My voice trembles as I put the reporter on speakerphone. "Hello?"

"Gigi Carlisle here. I'd like to ask you a few questions." Her smoky voice sounds like she snorts coffee beans and the souls of baby unicorns all day.

"I, umm, can't talk. I'm headed to summer school now."

"I'm right behind you."

Me and O'Dell turn around to see her waving at us from the news van. Her camera guy sits behind the wheel, while she's riding shotgun. "How'd you get O'Dell's number?"

"He gave it to me yesterday at your uncle's house."

His blush says it's true. I want to punch his lights out, but she distracts me, saying, "Let me tell your side of the story. I think your mom is innocent."

"You do?"

"Yes. The evidence is flimsy because of lazy police work. There were multiple partial prints on the murder weapon."

"The newspaper didn't say that."

"No, they didn't. I know more as well. Let's talk."

"My uncle told me not to."

"He gave me permission."

"Nuh-uh."

"Look." She waves a piece of paper at us through their front window.

"I still don't want to."

Her voice drops. "Patrick doesn't know you're here, does he?" I squirm in my seat, then she says, "Talk to me now, or I'm calling him. Better yet, I know he's at the crime scene around the corner at St. Columba's now. He can be here in two minutes. Your choice."

"Be right there." I hang up, then toss the phone back to the Butt Munch. "You gave her your number?"

He blushes. "She's hot and I caved. I didn't realize she was using me to get to you."

"What about your girlfriend?" I wish those words hadn't come out.

O'Dell looks so hurt. I start to speak, but he waves me off. "Don't try to apologize. You'll just make it worse."

I glance back at the reporter behind us. She might be bluffing about my uncle, but I can't take any chances. I'm pretty much screwed. "Go to the Shangri-La. Let me get rid of her and I'll meet you by the motel pool there in twenty minutes. We'll talk to Bird next."

"Got it."

"I don't want Gigi to see this." I get out and caress Mama's coat one last time, then notice a red scratch mark on the *Neiman Marcus* tag.

That's never been there. I turn the label over and see written across the back in red:

24530 Bowery

"That's Mama's handwriting." I shiver.

"What?"

I show him. "What's a bowery?"

"I'm not sure."

The van horn honks and Gigi waves.

"It's a clue," I say.

"Maybe. I'll keep it safe. Be careful with that reporter."

"Aren't you going to say I look like shit?"

"It's a given." He grins as I shut my door.

I watch O'Dell make a U-turn with hate spray-painted across his back window:

GO HOME OR DIE

I repeat the address to myself as I make my way to the news van.

The cameraman comes around and slides open the side door for me. These two keep hassling me. It smells like fast food and perfume inside. I sit in the bucket seat on the second row. Camera and video equipment fill the back. The guy gets into the driver's seat, then he fades away.

Gigi Carlisle wears her long blonde hair down and curled. Her suit's not as nice as Lisa Vanderhausen's clothes, but both these chicks know power. One comes from old money and the other from the latest scoop.

She says, "What's the message mean on the back of your friend's truck?"

"Ask him. You've got his number."

"Know who did it?"

"No clue."

She presses the red record button on her phone, then stuffs it in my face. "What do you think your mother—"

"Show me my uncle's permission slip."

Gigi hands me a piece of paper. I scan all the legal mumbo-jumbo, but that's Patrick Noblitt's signature at the bottom, all right. I can't believe how much his betrayal stings.

"Now, what do you think about your mother being blamed for Officer Riker's death?"

I stop the recording and give her a line from *Law & Order* I've always wanted to use: "This is all off the record."

Her camera dude snickers 'til she shoots him the death stare to shut him up. I'm not sure she's ever heard "no" before.

I tap on my cheek like I'm thinking. She's not the only chick with balls around here. "Tell me about your photographer, 'Chele."

"Who?" They both look at me confused.

"'Chele. Dark skin, big afro."

He says, "Is that the new receptionist?"

"Right." Gigi nods. "We really haven't met her. Why?"

"No reason. Why'd you interview my father?"

"Your family is of public interest. I thought he'd have a unique perspective on the case, and I was right."

"He's an attention whore and so are you."

"Can I quote you on that?"

She's got that same TV smile as my jailbird daddy. "Brother Sanborne didn't want my mother to have me."

"I'm glad she didn't listen to him."

"He knocked up and abandoned a sixteen-year-old girl who didn't feel like she could go home. Look what happened to her."

"It's tragic, no doubt, but look at you." She winks. "You're a fighter."

"You're trying to butter me up for your stupid story."

"True, but I also admire you. You're savvier than most adults."

"That's 'cause most adults suck." They both bust out laughing and that shocks me.

She elbows him. "Didn't I tell you she's the real deal?" After they stop their snickering, Gigi refocuses on me. "Do you like being poor?"

"I'm not." I lean back. "I've got over a thousand bucks in the bank, and my uncle set up a trust fund. Strangers keep sending him money to help raise me. I'm going to college." I've never said that out loud. I wish I hadn't started with her.

"Honnnnnnnnnnnney, I'm talking better than money,

though I can get that for you, too. I'm talking power. You've got it all. Smarts, personality, and looks."

"I'm a freak."

"Even better. The world loves an underdog." She tosses back her silky hair. "I can get you booked on every TV show in America and would guide your career. What happened to your mother is unfortunate, but I can make it so you're never dependent on anyone else ever again. Let's make something good come from all this."

Gigi's got my attention. She's straight-up using me, but who cares, if it buys my freedom? I say, "My uncle will never agree to it."

"Patrick Noblitt will do whatever I want." She shows his signature again.

I glance at Camera Dude, but he looks away while she's putting the screws on me. This snake wants an exclusive with *the girl* and to pimp me out to the world. I just might take advantage of that, but I want a few things first. "Who took Mama's photo that all the news stories are using?"

"I'm not sure. The police gave it to us."

"Who are these so-called witnesses from the murder?"

"I'm not at liberty to say."

"Bye." I slide open the door.

"Wait," she says, and I pause. "I shouldn't tell you this, but it's after-the-fact." Gigi leans in and whispers, "One of the witnesses is dead."

"Who?"

"The homicide around the corner. Naomi Rodriguez saw Officer Riker's murder."

My mind whirls. Naomi's last name was Rodriguez. The sweet, lispy woman was there when that cop was killed. She saw what happened. She knew the truth.

Now she's dead.

I must look like I might hurl, 'cause Gigi asks me, "How did you know Naomi Rodriguez?"

"You're not the only one with sources."

I feel these two staring at me. They smell a juicy story. He's itching for his video camera, and she wants to shove a microphone in my face.

Not happening. I say, "Who was the other witness?"

Gigi says, "I really can't reveal that. They're in even greater danger now."

"What's a bowery?"

"It's a farm or plantation. Why?"

Camera Dude nods. "It's also a street across town. Didn't we do a piece there a while back? It was—"

"Yes." Gigi interrupts him, then she lasers her gaze into me. "Why do you ask?"

My neck hairs tingle as I stall for an answer.

The reporter's phone rings. Her screen lights up with PATRICK NOBLITT. She giggles and turns away in her seat. "Patrick, darling, hello. I really enjoyed last night."

I hear my uncle's voice but don't catch their conversation. His traitor ways just keep growing, and I sure don't want Gigi Carlisle as my step-mommy.

"No, I haven't seen Copper." She winks at me. "I saw your friend O'Dell earlier, but not her . . . I don't know why he was in Paradise." She listens some more, then makes a kiss sound. "I'll keep you posted. See you tonight."

After she hangs up, I want to slap that movie-star smile right off her pretty face.

Gigi pushes the record button again. "Ready for that interview now?"

"Yep. Here's all I've got to say, and you can quote me on it. Bite my ass and buy me lunch." I hop from the van and slide the door shut, then race straight toward the alley. I should already be meeting O'Dell at the Shangri-La.

The van engine revs. Gigi Carlisle and Camera Dude think they'll catch me on the streets of Paradise.

Good luck with that.

Naomi Rodriguez was there the night that cop was killed. So was Mama, then Miz Jesus murdered her a few hours later at the cemetery. Naomi babbled her *It'th not thafe* nonsense outside Goodwill near Mama's coat. Was she talking to Mama or herself? Did Naomi murder Officer Riker? Who's the other eyewitness?

Plus, Mama wrote *24530 Bowery* inside her coat. Somewhere she knew it wouldn't be seen and Gigi confirmed they did a story there recently. Maybe it's an address. I should go there. O'Dell can take me, so I limp faster toward the motel.

Two crime scenes happened outside Father Where's Waldo's church. He says we know each other from Mission for Hope, but I swear I don't remember his sermons from the shelter. Part of me digs someone as nice as him had a crush on Mama, but Miz Jesus seemed nice, too. Religious doesn't equal good.

O'Dell's truck's not in the Shangri-La parking lot or at the Camelot Inn across the street. He's not waiting by the pool, either.

Butt Munch. I try to be mad at him, but don't like him roaming the streets of Paradise alone. I steady myself on a lounge chair, then hear shouting across the courtyard.

It's Tank Top. He hangs up his phone, then storms into his office. I follow him there and push past the counter's swinging side gate. He's plopping into his La-Z-Boy as I ask him, "Why'd the Asian Assassins fix up this place?"

"They know a moneymaker when they see it."

"Or is it for money laundering?"

"I'm why your uncle showed up here yesterday. Maybe I should call Sir Cops A Lot again." Tank Top turns up the volume of *Cops* to drown out my voice.

I ask again, but he keeps ignoring me, so I yank the TV cord from the outlet.

The screen dies, and he leaps up. "Why are you such a pain in the ass?"

"If the recliner-shaped ass fits, kick it. I need your phone."

I pick up the receiver to dial, but he hangs it up. "You're just like your dad. Think you're better than everyone else. Get out of here, and if you so much as touch me, I swear you'll pay."

Something about his tone makes me leave. I head up the outdoor stairwell, wishing I had Mama's coat here to calm me. I wish I'd had more time to look for clues. My nerves unravel, but I do my best to stay sharp to deal with Bird. She's a slippery one.

It's extra quiet around the motel this morning. Most folks here probably had a hard night and are still asleep. The silence adds to the eeriness. Something's not right.

Fear ripples through me as I approach Room 207. The door's torn off the hinges and is propped against the opening.

"Salt? Pepper?" I knock.

Nothing.

"Bird?"

The door's heavier than it looks, but I push it aside enough to squeeze inside.

The room's ransacked—hangers scattered across the floor, every drawer pulled open, sheets ripped off the bed. The red Gideon's Bible's torn in half and the pages strewn about. My Mickey Mouse watch is crushed. I can't even read the time. My chest tightens as I look around.

The boys aren't here.

CHAPTER 24

"Salt?" I look around. "Pepper?"

They're gone. The metal wiring's missing from the closet and the mirror's cracked in the bathroom, too. The shower rod and curtain lay on the floor. The pole's empty—Bird's drugs aren't here anymore. Evil roared through this place and stole my boys. It was probably the Asian Assassins, but it might've been Spider. No telling what trouble Bird's gotten Salt and Pepper into now.

I'm not sure where to look for 'em, but I rush outside. Hobbling down the steps, I hear TV laughter coming from one of the rooms. The heat's unbearable, and I'm so worried about my friends.

A young maid pushes her cleaning cart from a room onto the main floor's breezeway. I race to her, and point to the ceiling. "What happened to Room 207?"

"Como?" she says.

What?

"The two boys—dos niños." I point again.

She stumbles back like I punched her. "Nooooooo," she says in a heavy Spanish accent.

I keep pressing her for answers, but the maid brushes by me, babbling more Spanish. She leaves her cart and vanishes into the supply closet. I hear the lock click.

The conversation ends, but my questions are just beginning. Who killed Officer Riker? Who murdered Naomi Rodriguez? Who tried to crush me with that TV? What happened to Salt and Pepper? Where is O'Dell? Why's Arlene the Coat Stealer avoiding me? What was she doing with Mama's coat? And what's 24530 Bowery mean?

Most important, is this all tied together?

Maybe the boys went to eat at Mission for Hope or the Plasma Center (where Bird sells her juices for cash). I also want to find out more about Arlene's tattoos. Plus how I really know that priest. It's not the shelter. Armed with Tommy's closed pocketknife, we head back out into Paradise. More alone than ever.

#

I try The Tattoomb first, then Dr. Ink, but they both kick me out since I'm not eighteen.

Something about Father Where's Waldo keeps needling my brain, so I decide to switch gears for a while. I'm even jumpier by the time I reach the homeless shelter. The white sign on the redbrick building still says:

Mission for Hope

Feed their bellies, then feed their souls.

Me and Mama used to eat here all the time . . . when she'd remember to feed us. Around back is the loading dock where people drop off donations. That's where Arlene the Coat Stealer first said she "found" Mama's jacket in the Dumpster.

Liar.

I'd like to smooth my fingers over the soft fur and remind myself O'Dell promised to take good care of it. 'Course that just worries me worse. Hopefully, he's with Mai Wong now and they've got no way to reach me.

The shelter's waiting room is off-white, with a front desk, some couches and chairs. It's connected to a smaller room outside the chapel, with cubbyholes built into the walls for backpacks and bags. It's between services, so the lobby's empty, but full of too many memories. I bite my bottom lip and approach the lady in the green Mission for Hope T-shirt at the front desk.

Her black hair's cut short like a boy's. Some folks who work here are from the outside world, while others are former "clients." She's way too clear-eyed and perfect-teethed to have ever been a druggie.

"May I help you?" She smiles, but I see her sizing up my injuries.

"Have you seen a woman here today with two little boys? One white and one black?"

"We don't discuss our clients."

"Please? It's super important. Their names are Salt and Pepper."

"Sorry. It's our policy."

"What about Father Waldo? Does he lead services here?"

"He sure does. I can answer that since I'm the one who recruited him from church. He's terrific."

"Oh, good."

"Why?"

"I used to come to those services, but don't remember him."

"Well, he just started last Monday."

"You sure he didn't do it before Valentine's Day?"

"Positive. I was still at my old job then. He's so great with people."

My skin prickles as something clicks for me.

Something big.

That priest doesn't know his butt's about to be wearing my name across it. "Since you go to his church, did you know that cop who was murdered? That was so sad."

She nods her head slower and bites her lip. "Felix and I worked the homeless ministry together. I'm heartbroken for Ann and the boys."

"I bet. What was Officer Riker like?"

"Felix had . . . strong opinions about certain people, but once you got past that rough exterior, he was all right."

"What kind of strong opinions?"

"Oh . . . I don't know." The lady opens the desk drawer and fiddles with the pens and pencils but doesn't pick up any. "About people who didn't look or act like him."

"I heard he didn't like minorities or gays."

She nods.

"I also heard he didn't treat his family very nice either."

"Oh, I wouldn't say that." But that's just what her body seems to be saying.

Confirmed. Felix Riker was a total jerk. "What'd you hear about his murder?"

She looks around, then whispers to me, "I heard it was a drug deal gone bad. That prostitute who killed him was supposed to be trouble."

"She wasn't *that* bad." My palms turn sweaty.

The desk phone rings, and the woman says, "I need to get back to work. We'd love to see you here again. The next service starts at—"

"Eleven." I head toward the door.

I stomp straight toward St. Columba's but keep watch for my Enemy List. That priest lied, and I've figured out why. I knew there was something fishy about him. I'm weaving by all the tents, the sleeping bags, and the fights. A burning smell hangs in the air. My body craves a shower.

I spot someone shuffling down the street.

"One-Leg!" I holler and wave. Tommy Tucker's pops waits for me.

"Copper Girrrrrrrrrrrrrrrl," he slurs, and gives me a wobbly hug. "What brings you back to Paradise?"

"We talked yesterday." I'm getting high off his fumes, so I

untangle myself from him. "You told me to do what Mama never did."

"What's that?"

"Be happy."

"Oh . . . yeah." His beard looks damp. He's covered in sweat. I stare at the hiking boot on his metal foot and a house shoe on his real one. He's a mess.

"Thanks for saving me from Spider yesterday."

"I did?"

"Yeah, you tripped him." I look around. "Have you seen Corn Dog?"

"No. Why?"

"Long story. Listen, I caught Chao-Chao sneaking into your tent last night."

"Who?"

"One of the Asian Assassins."

"Those blasted Ching Chongs . . ." One-Leg goes off on a tirade, using every insult in the book. Enough to wash out his mouth with soap.

"What was he looking for?" I ask.

He turns stop-sign red, and his gaze darts all around. "I, uh, am not proud to admit it, but . . . I caved and did a job for Zhi Peng."

"What?"

"Flipped on Bird. She stole some of their drugs, and I told 'em where to find her stash."

"They destroyed her room just now. No one was there. Did they hurt Salt and Pepper?"

"They promised not to."

"Well, they're missing."

"Oh." He stumbles in place.

"That still doesn't explain why Chao-Chao was in your tent."

"They, uh, wanted me to dig a ditch."

"For that baby?"

He nods.

Eternal Peace ripples through me. I already survived that, so I change the subject. "Did you know Naomi Rodriguez?"

"No."

"She's the homeless—"

"I know who she is . . . was."

"So which is it—did you know her or not?"

One-Leg shakes his head, stroking his beard. I'm not sure he'll talk, then he mumbles, "I'm kind of lost without Tommy and your mom."

"Same here." Death will always bind us in the worst way possible. I worry One-Leg's added drugs to his routine. I've failed him and Tommy big-time.

He asks me, "When'd you get back to Paradise?"

"Yesterday." I sigh.

The shell of the man I once knew wanders off without a goodbye, wobbling more than usual. I'm losing him, even though he's still breathing. I glance at the morning sky, half hoping Tommy's not watching me from . . . wherever.

A man limps by with his left calf muscle so swollen and purple I can't believe he can move at all. He'll lose that leg for sure. It cramps me up just watching him.

I realize I'm standing across from the bus station. The same one my jailbird daddy used to herd underage girls into the country for Diablo and the Barrio Brothers to sell 'em for who knows what. It's just one of the many reasons Mr. Jesus belongs behind bars.

It's also where I met the Midnight Man, that mysterious stranger who was bigger and blacker than the night, with a smile brighter than the sun. Michael offered to what? Help me? Eat my soul alive?

I'm not sure, but I told him no, thank you.

Fly low, baby girl, he said in his deep, ocean voice.

Then he was gone. I never saw him or his chunky sword necklace again.

Or did I? I think about the Warrior Angel and all the strange happenings that horrible terrible night as I hobble on toward City Cemetery, trying to unravel this all. A fire truck thunders by with the siren blaring. It's not the cops, but it makes me wonder where my uncle is.

Ten minutes later, I see the walls have gone up at the new Salvation Army site. Construction's in full swing, and the shelter will be finished in no time.

Naomi's body is gone, but the sunny-yellow CAUTION tape still ropes off City Cemetery. The cops are gone, so the crowd's dwindled down. The crime tech guys keep working.

I didn't know Naomi's age, but her cross will be added here soon. I stare at Mama's marker in the far-right corner: DANIELS—27.

++++++++++++++++++++++++++++

+++++++++++++++++++

++++++++++

About a dozen church people file out from the side door of St. Columba's. Some stare at me as I go inside.

This church is much bigger than the chapel at Eternal Peace. This place probably seats five hundred. It has pretty white walls and a giant sculpture of Jesus hanging on the cross in back. He's wearing a crown of thorns, blood dripping from his forehead, watching me with that same forever stare I've seen too much of lately. Candles burn in the far corner.

Father Where's Waldo stands up front near the altar, visiting with his fan club. I'm not a member anymore, but I barrel straight toward him.

He glances my way. "I don't have time to visit, Copper. Please call the office for an appointment."

"You'll make time now."

That shocks his churchgoers, but he chuckles. "Still playing detective?"

"Still playing priest?"

Father Where's Waldo gives me an uneasy smile, then he thanks the others, who break away and leave. He waits 'til we're alone, then pulls me to the edge of a pew. "What's *that* supposed to mean?"

"It means you're a liar."

"I don't think so."

"I know so. You're as bad as Mama." My mad spills over so much that I'm shaking, but not like a whack attack. This is pure rage. "You didn't volunteer at Mission for Hope back in February."

"So? We both thought we knew each other, and I made the connection you looked like your mother. I brought this all up to you. Remember?"

"She didn't give me your wallet that day." My voice trembles. "I even asked Mama about it afterward, but she never answered. That was just another lie. Like you're telling now."

"Let me get you some water before you trigger another panic—" He turns to leave.

"Stop!" I slam my hand against the pew with a loud *thwack*.

He does.

"Look at me. I know how I know you."

Father Waldo faces me, then I blast him with the truth. "You were one of Mama's bed buddies."

CHAPTER 25

Standing in this church, I see Father Waldo in a whole new light. Like the dirty neon that used to flash at the Shangri-La: $25 PER HOUR. $50 PER NIGHT.

Father Where's Waldo waves me off. "Don't be silly."

His voice cracks, so I climb into his pain and break him wide open like he did to me. "That's why I recognized your laugh. I heard it from under the bed. You volunteered at the shelter *after* Mama died."

He shakes his head of fabulous gray hair, the color draining from his face.

"You're lying as a priest."

"You're mistaken."

"I'm not. You two sang that song from *The Sound of Music* that day. Remember? You were Captain von Trapp."

A tremor quivers up Father Where's Waldo. He sinks into the nearest pew, his shoulders slumped. "I was still drinking at the time. I adored your mother in high school, but never stood a chance back then . . . plus, being a priest can be so lonely."

I point to the collar around his neck, the same color as the tulips Uncle P leaves at Mama's grave every week. White for purity. "Isn't that, ummm, against the rules?"

His eyes water over, then a stream of tears trickles down his cheeks. He doesn't wipe 'em away. I'm not sure what to do when he drops to his knees and grabs my hands. "Please don't tell. This is my life, and I really try to help people. It was just once, I swear." He lets go. "I guess you already know that."

"Did you kill that cop or Naomi?"

"Absolutely not."

I'm not sure I believe him. "I won't tell about you and Mama," I say, wondering if I mean it.

He clinches his fists in his lap. "I'm so ashamed. It's the only time I've broken my vow of celibacy."

We don't talk for I don't know how long. I can't see the crime scene through the church's stained-glass windows, but I know the sunny-yellow CAUTION tape and crosses are still there. Death follows me wherever I go.

The priest sighs. "I've wanted to confess ever since it happened, but . . ." His unfinished words flit back to Jesus hanging on the cross.

"What all did you and Mama talk about that day? I don't remember."

"Old times, mainly. Friends from high school. It's all so bizarre. Officer Riker was a parishioner, and they say your mom killed him. Plus, Naomi Rodriguez would sit in back during church sometimes. Sweet lady. I visited with her a few times . . . Now she's dead, too."

"If Mama did it, then why'd Naomi wind up murdered?"

"I'm not sure."

"Positive?"

"I didn't kill Felix or Naomi."

I switch gears. "I heard that cop was a jerk."

Father Waldo breathes out a slow, shaky breath. "It was his way or the highway."

"Did he have a happy marriage?"

"I think so . . . Ann and the boys are wonderful, but who knows what goes on behind closed doors."

I remember the squeak of the mattress with him and Mama. They rocked the bed for a really long time.

He says, "I'm so sorry. I completely took advantage of your mother."

"Well, you paid her, and if I remember right, you gave us an extra-big tip."

Father Waldo shrinks so small in the pew that I feel like I'm playing "kick the priest" and make myself stop. "How'd you figure out who Mama was?"

"I didn't. She recognized me while I was adding another cross outside several months ago. Right before Christmas. There'd been a heavy snow."

"Where was I?"

"Playing with those two little boys across the street. The construction site was still an empty lot. You three were lost in your own little worlds. Your mom had all of you."

"Where was Bird?"

"I don't know. After that, your mom and I would wave from time to time. She showed up here late one night, maybe a month before she died. Around New Year's. She needed money and, ummm, offered me her services." He clears his throat. "I declined and gave her cash, then sent her on her way. Unfortunately, that planted the seed for my sin."

He whispers so soft I almost don't hear him: "I stayed away as long as I could. I've been sober three months now. That's been one blessing from that entire ordeal."

The priest shows me a green sobriety chip. It makes me think of Arlene's twenty-four hours of not drinking. I ask him about the Coat Stealer, but he says he doesn't know her. Father Waldo's not really paying attention. He's too busy crying to himself.

His shoulders tremble, and each tear tortures me two ways.

His shame, and hearing more lies Mama never told me. I give him a few pats. "She must've liked you some 'cause we didn't take any more of your cash."

"What do you mean?"

"She always made johns pay upfront, then she'd toss their wallet down to me during . . ." He blushes, so I continue, "I always took a little more cash. She said we deserved it, but she didn't do that with you. I think Mama was sweet on you, too."

His sad smile cuts me to the bone. I know priests can't marry, but Father Where's Waldo would've made a good husband to Mama.

If he's not a killer.

He wipes his damp cheeks. "I realize it's unfair, but I'm sort of relieved you confronted me. I still plan on telling the bishop someday . . . Until then, you're my confessor."

"You wouldn't believe all the secrets I know."

"I can only imagine. Will you please forgive me?"

His face has such a sweetness I'm not sure whether to pat him or punch him. "It's okay. Your cash probably helped feed me," I lie.

Father Where's Waldo apologizes a bazillion more times, and I forgive him just as many. He says, "I'd rather keep this between us. Your uncle hates me bad enough."

"Those are my best secrets of all."

A lady rushes through a side door near us, then she stops. "Father—oops, I'm sorry. I didn't mean to interrupt."

"It's all right, Mary Caroline. What is it?"

The lady wrings her hands and walks closer. She's not regular pretty, but something about her makes you want to take another look. "Violeta Lopez is in your office, upset. Her son is wanted for attacking a man."

"Juan?"

"Yes. The police are looking for him now. Poor thing. Eduardo's already in prison, and now this."

"Wait," I say. "Are you talking about the Barrio Brothers?"

"Yes, Eduardo and Juan Lopez."

"What are their gang names?"

"Eddie Loco and Spider."

My stomach turns. O'Dell is missing. "Who'd he attack?"

"Some homeless man. Let's see, they called him . . . One-Leg Larry?"

CHAPTER 26

I shoot up from the church pew. "Is One-Leg all right?"

The lady nods. "The police said he's at Remington Medical Center now. That's all I know."

"I've got to get to him." I scoot by Father Where's Waldo on the wooden bench.

"I'll take you." He joins me.

Mary Caroline says, "I'm sorry, Father, but Violeta is waiting in your office now. She's so upset over Eduardo and Juan. I told her you'd be right there."

"Duty calls," he tells me, though his wet eyes say he wants to talk more about Mama. He asks the lady to take me to the hospital.

I groan inside but tell her I'll meet her in the parking lot, and she leaves for her keys.

The priest grins at me. "I'll wait with you."

A blush heats my cheeks. He knows I planned on bailing. Like I want to go with some nun-sounding stranger, though I guess she can't be any worse than the other kooks I've ridden with lately.

Father Where's Waldo asks if he can say a prayer for One-Leg. I say yes and think about him and his son, who stole my heart. The priest takes me by both hands, then says, "Bless, O Lord, your servant, Larry Tucker . . ."

I don't believe anyone hears these words, but they do sort of lighten me. He sounds so much more sincere than the churchy stuff my jailbird daddy said on his TV show, but I remind myself not to trust him.

Afterward, we wander to the back of the church to wait for his secretary. I flip through a sign-in book by the door. "What's adoration?"

"We have perpetual adoration at St. Columba's, meaning there's at least one person praying here every hour of every day."

"There's no one else here now." I glance over the empty pews.

"Les Hughesman was a no-show again. I need to replace him."

Father Where's Waldo stays by my side 'til he buckles me into the front seat of Mary Caroline's Ford Focus. She's his secretary. We all say our goodbyes.

As the lady drives us through the trashy streets to the hospital, she asks, "Was Father Waldo crying?"

"Yeah, I told him something sad. Can we make a quick detour? It's nearby."

"What about your friend Mr. One-Leg?"

"It has to do with his attack and might help the police. It's super important."

"I'm not sure we should."

"Please? I'm Copper Daniels. My mama's in Father Waldo's cross garden. Corinne Daniels, age twenty-seven. She died in February."

"Oh my." The secretary gasps as the name clicks for her, I wonder if she's mentally checking off several boxes in her mind.

Homeless girl.

Dead mother.

Jailbird daddy.

I cry a few boohoo, crocodile tears to convince her. "I just feel so awful about Officer Riker. Mama was already dead, but now she's a cop-killer, too."

"You poor thing. I'm so sorry for your loss. What's the address?"

I tell her about 24530 Bowery Street. She types that into her phone, then turns the car around. At least she's a better driver than 'Chele or Dusty. I'm never sad to leave Paradise, and I hope that clue really is an address. We ramble over the railroad tracks and pass the dried-up water fountain where me and Mama used to rest, dreaming of a better life by the California ocean.

Downtown, Somebodies mill around the mirrored buildings and fancy hotels. I ask Mary Caroline, "Where'd Spider attack One-Leg, anyhow?"

"The police didn't say."

"I can't believe your boss is so nice to the Barrio Brothers. They're murderers and rapists."

"It's his job to love all God's children."

"Some more than others," I mumble.

Her blank face says she's clueless to his dirty little secret. She glances at the map on her phone. "You said this was close. We still have twenty miles to go."

"Sorry. When is Ann Riker's adoration time? I want to apologize to her for my family's sins."

"I can't say, but . . . somebody just might be at mass at seven tonight if you're around then."

"Thank you." I wipe away an invisible tear. "No wonder Father Waldo says you're the best secretary ever."

Mary Caroline might burst she's beaming so bright. She wants to Captain his von Trapp.

I ask, "What's Ann Riker look like?"

"You didn't hear this from me, but she drives a navy minivan and usually wears black. That's all I can say."

I nod and look out the window. These are neighborhoods I've

never seen before. We're nowhere near Paradise. Some blocks have small, well-kept houses, while others are completely run-down with junk in their front yards.

She says, "Almost there."

It takes a while, but when we turn on Bowery Street, Koi's black Mercedes SUV is parked in front of a house. He's facing us. I recognize his license plates. The windows are so dark I can't tell if he's in the back seat like before. That lump in my chest tightens.

Mary Caroline stops across the street just as the Mercedes drives away. If Koi's in there, I wonder if he spotted me.

He's gone. There's no flowers or trees in front of 24530 Bowery Street. It's a cream-colored house, with no porch. Just three steps lead to the door. The weeds haven't been watered. It's like the cemetery's Nobody Section.

At the house we're parked in front of, I notice a woman peering at us from behind curtains. She's got dark skin and a scarf wrapped around her head. When the lady catches me staring, she disappears inside.

Mary Caroline asks me, "Why is this house important for Mr. One-Leg?"

"I'm not sure." I unbuckle myself. "Wait here."

"No, no, no." She grabs my hand. "Father wouldn't want me to let you go. We need to leave for the hospital now."

"It's fine. Besides, I'll only be a sec. I wouldn't want you to dirty your nice shoes."

She stares at her scuffed-up flats while I bolt. I need to go around back, but I don't want to get shot. I ignore Mary Caroline tapping on her car window, and I climb the front steps of the house. There's no window in the door, so I can't peek. Mama wrote this address on the inside of her coat. Out of sight. Gigi Carlisle's camera guy said there was a story here not too long ago.

This place means something. I rap three times fast, then brace myself for any bullets.

Nothing happens.

I knock again. Louder.

No one answers.

I step down. The curtains are closed in the front window. Mary Caroline waves for me to get in the car. I give her my *one sec* finger, then trot around to the back. There's no fence around the yard, so it's easy. I can't see inside the house, except for one window that's too high to peek through.

Looking around, I drag a rickety chair from an old picnic table, then climb onto the seat and stand on my tippy-toes. A sink with black smoke marks across it sits inside, wooden cabinets line the walls. Many have been burned. It's a kitchen, but chairs are knocked over and charred. A fire ruined part of this room.

What does it mean? Why did Mama care?

"Copper?" Someone grabs my leg.

I scream and almost topple over.

Mary Caroline says, "We're leaving now. This neighborhood frightens me."

"Can I stand on your shoulders?"

"No!" She stomps off.

I follow her back to the car. The same lady across the street is peering at us again from behind her curtains. She disappears again when we make eye contact. I'd be scared, too, if strangers were skulking around my place.

Especially Koi. He's got the eyes of a killer.

Mary Caroline says to get in the car, but I ignore her, and she stays behind me as I approach the woman's house.

Fake flowers fill a pot on her porch, and a summer wreath hangs on the door. This is a home and not a house. I ring the doorbell.

No answer.

I knock. I hear stirring around inside.

"Ma'am?" I holler. "I'm Copper Daniels. You don't have to open up. I just want to ask you a few questions."

She doesn't respond, but the moving inside stops. I think she's listening.

Mary Caroline moves in closer to me. I raise my voice, "Ma'am? I'm trying to solve a mystery about my mama. She's dead." My tongue thickens and I taste metal. "She wrote down the address to the house across the street, and I'm trying to figure out why it's important. Plus, that Mercedes was just here. Do you know anything that could help me?"

Nothing.

"It was their stash house," a frail woman's voice says from behind the door.

"Whose?"

"The Barrio Brothers. They made their awful drugs there, right across from where my family has lived for over fifty years. Can't do no more porch sittin'."

"What happened?"

"Cops busted them. They had a fire, too."

"Then why would the Asian Assassins be here?"

No response.

"Did you ever see a woman with a rabbit fur coat here?"

"I didn't see nothing or nobody."

I ask her a few more questions, but she doesn't say any more. She might even be gone. Poor thing.

Mary Caroline demands we go, so we do. I don't blame that lady for not getting involved. I've got a dead mama who I wish had minded her own business.

Mary Caroline sulks on the drive to the hospital. She's irritated, so I try to make churchy small talk with her, but she's having none of it. Oh well. I tried. Staring out the window, I'm worried about One-Leg. I hope he's okay. I tell myself I made the right decision to go to Bowery Street first. It belonged to the Barrio Brothers, though I still don't know why Koi was there, or how Mama's connected to any of this. We're almost to Remington Medical. It's on the edge of Paradise, though not the side by the railroad tracks. We have to drive through everything.

We pass two women catfighting on the sidewalk. They scream, slap and claw at each other. Nothing new there 'til I realize one of 'em is Arlene the Coat Stealer. Her back is to me, so I'm staring at Mama's blue angel wings. Mary Caroline slows for traffic.

"Stop the car!" I'm already out when the secretary demands I come back.

I don't and soon realize Arlene's fighting my ex–best friend, Egypt. I race across traffic toward their fight. A car almost hits me and blasts its horn.

I wave my apologies and keep going. The church secretary screams my name loud enough for Arlene and Egypt to both stop and look this way. Arlene takes off one direction, while Egypt sprints off the other.

I'm not sure who to chase since they both look guilty, but I pick Arlene since she's got Mama secrets. She weaves in and out of the crowded sidewalk, but I'm gaining on her. I keep my sight on those blue angel wings.

When Arlene reaches the corner, she watches the cars whizzing by both ways, then glances back at me. She leaps into traffic.

I scream and reach for her.

CHAPTER 27

Part of me expects Arlene's tattoo to fly her away. Instead, tires screech and a van smashes her flat. The crash tosses her like a rag doll. I shriek as Arlene's skull cracks against the asphalt.

People swarm around the accident. The driver hops out and grabs his phone, probably calling 911. I elbow my way to the front of the crowd.

Arlene lies at my feet. She's on her side facing my way, bleeding in the middle of the street. Road rash covers her body.

Kneeling, I take her bloody hand clutching a silver twenty-four-hour sobriety chip. One shoulder's slumped enough to show a few blue feathers from her tattoo. I've got so many questions, but her glazed eyes tell me they won't get answered.

Blood oozes from Arlene's mouth. Her breathing's shaky. "Sorrrrrrrrrrrrrrry . . ."

"For what?"

She struggles to speak. "I was there."

"Where?"

"When that cop . . ."

"Died?"

She breathes out a long, slow breath.

It's her last.

That same forever stare already looks into eternity, wherever that may be. The newspaper talked about two eyewitnesses at Officer Riker's murder. I thought it was a couple, a man and woman, but were Naomi and Arlene dating? Did she kill Naomi?

All I know for sure is Arlene would rather die than tell me any of her secrets. She's taking 'em to the grave. I can't stop trembling.

Death hovers through the air. I don't know if Father Where's Waldo will count this as another homicide cross to add to City Cemetery or not, since Arlene did this herself. I stare at her blood on my hands.

The van driver kneels beside me, crying. "I'm sorry about your friend. I couldn't stop in time."

"She wasn't my friend." I stand. "It wasn't your fault. She jumped in front of you. She did it on purpose."

Onlookers crowd around and debate why Arlene did it. I tuck the sobriety chip into her front pocket, then scoot away from the craziness. One cop's already dead, and the world blames Mama for it. Naomi and maybe Arlene were there that mysterious night.

They both died today. All these secrets are tied together.

Like the wings of an angel.

CHAPTER 28

The ER waiting room at Remington Medical Center is full for one o'clock in the afternoon, though I might've stumbled into the psych ward by mistake.

Scary.

I got rid of Mary Caroline in the hospital parking lot, though it wasn't easy. She was hesitant to leave, even though she doesn't like me. Luckily, she called Father Where's Waldo to check in, and he needed something back at the church office ASAP. That sent her scrambling to lover boy, with the promise to come back to me once he was taken care of.

Whatevs.

I check in at the front desk, then take a seat in a corner. Arlene's blood is dried all over my hands, bare legs and jean shorts. The T-shirt One-Leg gave me is already red, but it's now stained darker in spots. They said he's still in surgery.

Poor guy. I swallow hard and think something I don't call a prayer: *If anyone's listening, please let One-Leg survive and be healthier than ever. I can't break my promise to Tommy to take care of his pops. Please? Thanks.*

"Miss?" A teeny nurse grins, holding a clipboard. Her black hair's in two long ponytails on either side, and her scrubs have green angled stripes, like a pixy stick. She looks barely old enough to have her driver's license. "Someone needs to complete Mr. Tucker's paperwork."

"I'm not sure what to say since he's homeless. He's got nothing." I rub my bare wrist where my watch used to be. I'm still covered in Arlene's blood.

"Let's just do the best we can." Pixy Stix sits and asks me questions. Beyond name and age, the official stuff stays blank—address, employer, insurance, and pages of forms about his health and habits that I just sort of guess. Hospitals make you tell your life story before they'll help.

When we're done, the freckles on Pixy Stick's nose crinkle as she thanks me.

"That man is my best friend's father. He means . . ." I swallow hard. "The world to me."

She pats my leg, her bright eyes beaming. "We'll do everything we can. Hey, do you want to clean up?"

"Please."

She leads me down a hallway. "Are you all right? You look like you've been in a fight."

"I'm fine."

"I'm no doctor, but I could look at you . . ."

"It doesn't hurt. I just want to wash up."

Pixy Stick tries a few more times, then gives up. This is the hospital where O'Dell brought Mai Wong after Eddie Loco ruined her. This is where one friend held the other's hand and asked her questions, trying to make her laugh so she wouldn't think about what just happened. Where two people from two different worlds fell in love. I hope she's wearing his silver necklace right now.

Pixy Stick drops me off at a big, bare handicap bathroom, and I ask her, "How old are you? 'Cause you look fifteen."

She giggles. "I get that a lot. I'm twenty-six. Why?"

"I've got this uncle. He's twenty-nine, and I don't like his girlfriend. Well, she might not be—oh, just forget it."

"It's okay. I sort of have a boyfriend right now, but . . . is your uncle nice?"

"To everyone but me."

"We'll talk. Hey, I like your orange sneakers."

She leaves me, and the mirror shows what a wreck I am—buzzed head, Diablo scar on my cheek and this black eye from Dusty. My stomach still burns where the seatbelt yanked me during our wreck. To top it all off, I've got a whopping headache from head-butting Tank Top earlier. My cut thigh from my window escape has scabbed over.

Still, it's my tortured look that reminds me of the damage Paradise has done through the years. After I wash off, some of Arlene's bloodstains soaked through my shirt, but I'm better. I go back to the ER waiting room and depresses me more. From the phone on the wall, I dial O'Dell's number.

It goes straight to voicemail.

"Where are you? Are you okay?" I ask his recording. "I'm at the hospital now with Tommy Tucker's dad. Spider attacked One-Leg. It's bad. Call the ER at Remington Medical Center. That's where you and Mai . . . just get here quick."

I hang up, knowing I should call Uncle P next. He cares about One-Leg, too, but I'm not ready to hear how I'm grounded for life, or how Gigi Carlisle's my new mommy, or more lies about him not being at the Barrio Brothers' headquarters.

At the nurse's station, I ask Pixy Stick, "Can you tell me if Dusty Hamlyn is a patient here?"

"Sure." She types away on the computer, then gives me directions to his room, with a promise to call if anything happens with One-Leg.

Fifteen minutes later, I'm in Dusty's room on the fifth floor. I hear the soft *beep-beep-beep* of the machine he's hooked up to from his bed. Dusty dozes sitting up, all tucked under the sheets. Both eyes are blackened and he's wearing a bandage across his broken nose. His face is purple and swollen like a bruised blueberry.

He glances at me, then does a double take. "Am I on drugs, or is that you, Scab Face?"

"Both."

"Why are you here?"

"A friend's . . . in surgery."

Dusty nods. "Who killed that cop?"

"Still working on it."

He sits up more, then grimaces and holds his chest where I'm sure he cracked a rib or two from our wreck. Or Billy. "You tried to shoot my brother this morning."

"No. My friend did, but she murdered your mailbox instead."

"I didn't like it anyhow."

"What'll Billy do about his car?"

Dusty shrugs and looks away.

"Why'd you steal it?"

No response.

I don't touch him, but I move close enough to rest my hands at the foot of his bed. "I'm not going to hit you anymore, but you're going leave Walter and everyone else alone from now on, too. In and out of school."

He won't look at me, but slowly nods.

"Deal?" I say.

"Deal."

"Fighting's never the answer." I hear myself and should maybe follow my own advice. "Well, I better check on my friend. See you later." I turn to leave and glance out the window, spotting an angel statue down in a courtyard. I didn't even notice that place from the lobby. I'll have to check it out later. I still can't believe Arlene—

"Hey," Dusty says. I turn around, then he nods at me. "Why'd you cut your hair?"

The soft beeping of his machine may not hide the pounding of my heart. He doesn't know I just watched someone die. I walk back to him, then blow out a slow, shaky breath. I tell him what I haven't told anyone. Not even Dr. Vasquez.

"I don't know." I bite my lip so hard the inside of my mouth bleeds. I remember the horror on my uncle's face as he burst into my room and saw all my curls lying on my bedroom floor. I'd stolen the sharpest scissors in the house and cut my hair. I bawled after the first few snips, but Mama loved those curls so much and I couldn't stop myself.

My voice sounds barely above a whisper now. "It made me feel better for all of three seconds."

Dusty nods and pulls his arms out from under the covers. He shows me slashes across the backside. The whiteness and angry red scars. I stare at him.

He must see all my questions, 'cause he says, "Remember when I missed two weeks of school in March?"

"Yeah."

He jabs his arms at me again like the answers are hacked into his skin, then tucks 'em back under the sheets. "I went to the psych ward, which is way more interesting than this place."

"Why'd you try to kill yourself?"

"I didn't, dummy."

"Then why?"

"It helps . . . sort of."

I understand. "What'll happen to you when you leave here?"

"Hopefully, juvie, but . . ." He shrugs and looks off once more.

I've seen Dusty plenty of times at school. Slugged him and been punched back. Gone to the principal's office for all our fights, but this may be the first time I've ever really noticed him. The hurt behind his hazel eyes, even as the color changes between green, brown and gold. The battleground of his face.

"Has your family visited you here at all?" I ask.

"Sure." He stares at his beeping machine.

I ball up my fists, then make myself uncurl 'em. Fighting's never the answer.

Dusty gives me a crooked grin. "Tell that pistol lady to aim higher next time."

I try to smile back but can't. I don't want Dusty to see me being a crybaby or having a whack attack. I hurry from the room with a final wave.

"Later, Scab Face," he calls out.

I take the elevator back down to the first floor. Uncle P would be glued to my hospital bed if that happened to me, even though I wouldn't want him. Dusty also went to a psych ward. He gets a razor blade or knife, or even a paper clip, and cuts the backside of his arms 'til he bleeds. I guess the pain helps take away his pain.

Downstairs, Pixy Stick says that One-Leg's still in surgery. She's watching my teary face but doesn't ask, which makes me like her even more. I say, "Will you do me a favor, please?"

"I'll try."

"Call CPS." I fill her in on Dusty. Name, address and situation at home. I end with our car wreck yesterday.

She says, "You can call them. They take anonymous tips all the time."

"We both know they'll pay more attention to a grown-up. Especially a nurse. Look up his records. I bet he's been here for other mysterious reasons."

"I'm on it."

"Thank you. Do you have a cell phone I can borrow? I want to go to the courtyard and call my uncle. I promise not to call Australia or anything."

Pixy Stick gives me her phone, along with directions to the courtyard, and I'm happy to escape the ER.

Stepping out, I feel the overwhelming heat right away, but

it's so depressing inside that I stay. Lush green plants of all sizes surround the area. Ivy covers all the walls, so you can't even see into the building. This place feels like a secret garden.

A headless angel stands in the center. Light-stoned in color, she's got a long, tight dress swishing around her, with wings stretched behind her, ready to take flight. She has a totally different vibe than the Warrior Angel, but you can tell she's got her own bad-assery. It takes me a minute to realize what else is different about her . . . not only does she have no head, but no arms, either. I wonder if she lost 'em, like someone broke her, or what.

No matter, her beauty shines through. Just being near her lifts my spirits. I read the plaque at her base:

Winged Goddess

I sit on the wooden bench beside her, then type into the internet app: *sergeant patrick noblitt remington police department.*

All the links that appear are the same dead-cop stories about Mama in the news today and a few old cases he worked. Him busting the Barrio Brothers. He'd only been on the job two weeks before Mama died, but he wasn't allowed to work the case since they were family. Pretty much, he moved to town and got labeled a traitor. My family are such winners.

I don't find any dirt on him. There's not much battery left on this phone. I want to look up about Bowery Street, but the dead cop is more important, so I move on to my next subject: *felix riker remington police department.*

As a video loads, I think about that dead cop's wife and their two sons. Do they miss him? Are they sad? Do they love and hate him for who he was to their family? I press play and Gigi Carlisle interviews that cop. She holds her microphone while he brags about some drug bust in Paradise. He doesn't say if it was the Barrio Brothers, the Asian Assassins, or another gang. He's still talking when the screen goes blank. My neck hairs rise.

The phone's dead. Doesn't matter. I heard enough. Mama

twists the invisible knife deeper into my heart again. I recognized Officer Riker's voice and know why.

He was another of her bed buddies.

CHAPTER 29

Is everyone on the planet connected to Mama, either through these streets or from her bed? The thought sickens me. I rush to plants and hurl, but nothing comes out. I cough and sputter, leaving me with a gross aftertaste. I miss my toothbrush, toothpaste and having my own faucet. I'd rather be curled up on my bed reading than dealing with all this alone. I wouldn't even kick Princess the Evil Cat out of my room.

Home.

I had a home.

Not a perfect home, but a house where I lived. Uncle P doesn't overdrink. He doesn't do drugs or have a revolving door of strangers climbing in and out of his bed. We watched movies and he made me PB&J's.

The mattress squeaked extra rough when Officer Riker visited Mama at the Shangri-La. His voice replays in my head. You'd think it'd be low and gravelly since he was a bad guy, but it always sounded sort of flat. He started seeing Mama around Christmas, but he became a regular super-fast. Like two or three times a week. I remember 'em arguing in bed once 'cause Mama threatened to tell his wife about their affair. I'm sure to get us more fast cash for LA.

Why would a man like that be with a junkie?

They also talked bad about Uncle Patrick all the time. No telling what Riker said about him back at the station. I don't think Riker knew they were brother and sister. She just liked talking trash about him, and Riker was just plain mean. He left bruises on Mama more than once. She hated him.

Bad enough to kill him?

Yes.

That fact turns my stomach again, but I manage to swallow the pain and wipe my mouth. I take one last look at the Winged Goddess in her tropical getaway, then go back into the hospital.

Pixy Stick says I can see One-Leg now but can't stay long. He has a collapsed lung.

"It'll take time to recover," she says as she takes me to his room. "He's been through a lot."

We pass more nurses and workers pushing food carts, as well as regular folks I guess are visitors. No one seems to notice the girl with the black eye, buzz cut and gimpy walk. I wonder which room Mai Wong stayed in when O'Dell held her hand and tried to fix a broken girl.

Pixy Stick's pace matches mine. "I'm, uh, breaking up with my boyfriend tonight. Tell me about your uncle."

"He might not be worth it."

"Did you tell him about me when you called?"

"No. He wasn't home."

"Does your uncle at least have a job?"

"Yeah. He's a cop."

"Really, who?"

"Patrick Noblitt."

She pauses mid-step. "Officer Noblitt is *your* uncle?" The dreamy look in her eyes says she knows him.

Of course, their paths have crossed through work. Looks like she's already planning their wedding, but that doesn't mean he's noticed her. Plus, I doubt Gigi will give him up so easy. I think Lydia likes him, too. But I've got bigger problems right now. Pixy Stick leaves me alone with One-Leg.

Tommy Tucker's pops is sound asleep in the first bed, with a curtain pulled all around his area. I hear other voices in the room, and it's not a happy conversation. One-Leg doesn't look like himself in that light blue gown, hooked up to all those tubes and machines. He winces as he breathes. His face is so swollen and bruised it's hard to tell that it's One-Leg.

I slip my hand into his. He glances at me and mumbles. His eyes close again. I bite my bottom lip. "What happened with Spider?"

One-Leg whispers something, but all I catch is "Accident."

"It wasn't an accident! Spider attacked you. You saw him chase me, then he went after you. Why? 'Cause he's a thug. Why are the Asian Assassins and Barrio Brothers so interested in you anyhow?"

"Tommy ... your mom."

His eyes close. I'm not sure if he means the drugs she stole from Diablo or what. I watch the rise and fall of his chest, then stare at the empty space where his metal leg should be. Now he's really just one-leg. He's asleep. I need to stay and take care of him, but I also need answers. Spider may still be on the run and Pixy Stick says One-Leg will be here awhile, so he's safe for now.

At the nurse's station, Pixy Stick is hanging up the phone. "Just talked to CPS. You're a good friend."

"I wouldn't say that, but thanks for helping Dusty." I grab a nearby pen and scribble a cell number on a notepad. "You want to meet my uncle? Tell him about One-Leg and Dusty. Ask him to get here right away. They both need him. I'll be back." I give her the note and hurry toward the hospital exit.

"Where are you going?" she yells.

I mumble, "To squash a bug."

I'm on my way back to where the TV almost crushed me. It's

got to be where Spider lives. The smoky smell still hangs in the air, but I'm not sure from where. That's all folks in Paradise need right now, fire destruction on top of everything else.

In passing another tattoo parlor, I pause at the Tat Cat, where the store's letters look like they've been electrocuted. I go inside. A framed sign by the door says:

We specialize in all forms of artwork, from tribal to Japanese.

If you're looking for a new tattoo or just want to rework or freshen up an existing one, then the Tat Cat is for you!

Pictures of their "artwork" cover the walls inside, and people with their masterpieces from head to toe hang out here, too. Some guy lies face forward with his shorts down on a long chair. He's getting RIKKI inked across his bare butt. I'm sure she's a real peach.

The chick lasering him has endless tattoos and so many loops and piercings on her face that she probably sets off metal detectors everywhere she goes. Her tongue has a gold stud stamped in the middle.

She pauses over Rikki's boyfriend's butt and points her laser needle at me. "No one under eighteen allowed."

I don't move. "You do any blue angel wings across a woman's entire back lately?"

"I do everything," Laser Chick says. "Now go."

I'm surprised she doesn't lisp. Rikki's boyfriend orders her to get back to work, so she tells me to get lost again and the lasering starts back up. Turning, I study the pictures on the wall behind me. Roses, crosses, names, people's privates. You name it, they ink it. I always wanted angel wings just like Mama's.

Not anymore.

The phone rings and someone in back answers it, then he pokes his tattooed face out to the laser girl. "Sam wants you to fix the eyes on his Tasmanian devil. He says they're not wild enough."

"You tell him he's a user and a loser. He never called once

after we . . ." She mumbles a few things to herself, then shouts back to the guy, "Hell hath no fury like a woman scorned."

"That's it!" I say. "You're brilliant, Laser Chick."

"Out of here. I mean it."

I rush to the exit but tell her client, "Your butt's too hairy for Rikki to ever see her name."

That does not please him.

A huge piece of this puzzle just fell into place. Nobody likes to get dumped or their heart broken. I can't believe I didn't see this before. I head on back to what I think is Spider's apartment building, right by my phone booth. What'll I do if I find him?

I'm not sure. The burning smell's stronger.

A couple passes me wearing backpacks and carrying their sleeping bags. I limp by a lady sound asleep with a pillow and blanket covering her face and body on the sidewalk. Cockroaches crawl up the wall behind her.

All with the Four Seasons Hotel standing in the distance. I turn the corner, then notice a burnt pickup, behind a fire truck on the side of the road.

"Nooooooooooooooooooooooo!" I shriek.

O'Dell's pickup is charred to a crisp. The only reason I know it's his is from the spray paint on the back window. GO HOME OR is scorched off, so the message gets straight to the point:

DIE

CHAPTER 30

It's not 'til everyone turns to stare at me that I realize I'm shrieking out loud. My knees buckle and I bury my face in my hands, howling O'Dell's name over and over. The flames have been put out on his pickup, though it still smolders. Firefighters clear away their equipment. The air . . . is that what burnt flesh smells like?

My friend is dead.

I'm dizzy with grief. I should've never let him go off alone in Paradise. I should've been nicer while I had the chance. I should've made him give his necklace to Mai the second I saw it outside my phone booth yesterday. He came back here today 'cause of me. This is all my fault.

Someone's shaking me.

"Copper." Lydia holds me by the shoulders. I notice her patrol car's parked nearby.

I sob, "O'Dell!"

"Is that the guy who mows your lawn?"

"Yes!"

"He wasn't inside."

"What?"

"The truck was empty."

I collapse in her arms and she holds me. If O'Dell's not

here . . . he might still be alive. What happened to him? Where is he? The burning smell must be his seats . . . or Mama's fur coat.

It's gone for good.

My world spins too hard and too fast. All my friends are being hurt. Is it 'cause he likes Mai? Is it from Mama or my uncle? Me snooping around?

Why's this happening?

I realize Lydia's talking, and it takes a minute to pull myself together enough to understand her. She says, "Who would hurt your friend?"

"The Asian Assassins. O'Dell's girlfriend is Mai Wong, Zhi Peng's only sister."

Lydia nods, her lips pursed.

"What's wrong?" I ask.

"A witness saw one of the Barrio Brothers dragging O'Dell from his truck."

"Spider." I grit my teeth. "He just attacked One-Leg Larry a while ago and put him in the hospital."

"Could you ID Spider?"

I nod. "I need to call Uncle Patrick. O'Dell was supposed to be at our house," my voice catches, "waiting for me."

Lydia leads me to her patrol car, gripping me tighter, and I don't pull away. I stare beyond O'Dell's burnt pickup, into the streets of Paradise. Desperate for my friend. *Please be alive. Alive and okay. I can't lose you, too.*

I'm shaky as Lydia eases me into the back seat. She locks all the doors and the window between the front and back seats. I don't blame her. She knows what an escape artist I am. But I couldn't bail if I wanted to. I'm so tired of running. I don't like this new life, but it's all I've got.

Lydia says, "Want me to stay until—"

"I want to be alone."

She smiles and hands me her phone, then leaves. Two cops

guard each side of the patrol car. I'm surrounded. My fingers tremble as I stare at the numbers. Taking a deep breath, I dial Uncle Patrick before I have a chance to change my mind.

He answers on the first ring. "Did you find Copper?"

"Come get me!" I shout.

"Copper?"

"I'm with Lydia now. O'Dell's missing, and they burned his truck. I'm not sure if he's dead or alive. Plus, Mama's coat . . ." I'm bawling so hard I can't continue.

"Slow down. Where are you?"

I tell him. He says he's nearby and will be right over. My uncle also says some nice stuff I don't quite hear, then we hang up. I lie down, then curl up and cry on the back seat of a cop car where who knows how many bad guys' butts have been, but I don't care. My tears burn hot and my body shivers. I'm surprised I don't have a whack attack. Scary thoughts keep buzzing through my brain. I can't take this anymore. I could sleep for a bazillion years.

When the door opens a few minutes later, Mama's eyes stare at me from Uncle Patrick's face. I swear his black hair is grayer at the temples. I fling myself at him. He catches me, then cradles the back of my neck while I sob all over him.

He scoots onto the back seat, and Lydia shuts the door behind us. I sob, "I'm sorry . . . I'll try harder."

He rocks me back and forth. "It's okay," he whispers. "I'm here."

He's wearing khaki shorts with a short-sleeve collared shirt and tennis shoes. He doesn't look like a detective at all. He looks like my uncle. Mama's only brother. Father to Princess the Evil Cat. He smells like spice, sweat and home.

Home.

I have a home I almost threw away. A home with food. My own bed. It's safe there, too, though Uncle Patrick might not want me anymore after all the trouble I've caused. He still might send me to juvie. O'Dell pops into my thoughts, so the waterworks start all over again. "O'Dell's gone. He's gone. I shouldn't have left him alone!"

"Shhh, it's okay. We'll find him."

"Find him alive!"

My uncle holds me and lets me cry myself out. I'm not sure how long that takes, but at some point, I finally wipe my cheeks and hiccup. "I think I'm done."

"Are you all right? Did anyone hurt you?"

I game-show-hostess all the bumps and bruises along my body.

"No, I mean—"

"No one raped me."

He nods, then wipes his palms on his shorts and stares at O'Dell's destroyed truck. "What happened? Tell me everything."

I babble and jump ahead in my story, then loop back around to fill in the blanks. I'm all over the place. My uncle seems hurt his #1 fanboy didn't tell him about liking Mai Wong. Bet he's wondering what else O'Dell hid from him.

Join the club. I explain about One-Leg saving me from Spider, then getting beat up and landing in the hospital. Now O'Dell's missing, too. I even mention Father Waldo.

Uncle Patrick's jaw locks tighter. "Waldo DeSoya officiated Officer Riker's funeral."

I see my uncle remembering Mama's high school crush but keep my promise and don't mention the priest at the Shangri-La. I finish with Arlene's angel wings tattoo. Me and Uncle P fall quiet. I can tell his brain is working overtime trying to put all these jumbled pieces together. So much of this doesn't fit or make sense.

I watch him, debating whether or not to ask him.

"What?" he says.

"Are you really on vacation to take care of me?"

He shakes his head and sighs. Uncle Patrick folds his hands on his lap, looking almost seasick. "I'm on leave without pay."

"Why?"

"Insubordination."

"What's that?"

"After your mom died, my captain gave me a direct order to stay away from your father's investigation."

"How come?"

"Because we're related through you, but the leads on the case couldn't find anything substantial on your dad. He covered his tracks well."

"What do you mean? I saw the Barrio Brothers shuffle girls into a van that he brought into the country. I caught him in bed myself with an underage Mexican girl. Mr. Jesus is a total slime."

"Exactly. Human trafficking. Drugs. He did it all, but they only found the white-collar stuff, like embezzlement from his church. I worked with the Barrio Brothers to get more evidence."

"Spider?"

He nods. "That's why Salt and Pepper saw me at their gang headquarters."

"Why's Spider calling you a traitor?"

"He wants me to do something else illegal, but I refused. I can't say any more. It's for your own protection."

I ask, "When will you be a detective again?"

"Maybe never. Depends on my captain."

"Wait. *You* broke the law to make sure my jailbird daddy went behind bars?"

"Yes. I want that bastard to pay for what he did to you and your mother. I want him off the streets forever."

I let out a shaky breath. "This sort of makes me like you more."

"Well, you really couldn't like me any less."

We watch each other as his words sink in deeper. So much pain between the three of us. Families are shoelaced together by blood and bone, but also love and laughter. I fidget in my seat. "How's Princess the Evil Cat?"

"Upset. She keeps meowing around the house, lost. She's not sure what's wrong. You're what's missing."

"I don't want to go to juvie."

"What?"

"I heard you and Miz Simpson talking about me going to juvie."

"You don't eavesdrop very well because she's considering moving *Dusty* to a detention center and wanted my opinion."

"Really?"

"Really."

My smile brightens as the weight of the world lifts from my shoulders. "Can we repaint my room? I don't like the yellow."

"Sure, but we need to fix your broken window first. I think I may nail it shut." He chuckles.

"Can we start over?"

"I'd like that."

A blush heats my face. Our lives have changed so much since Mama became yesterday's headline. I'm still not sure if she murdered that cop or not, but I need to pay more attention to my own life right now. The one I'm building with Uncle Patrick.

I'm not sure what to say, so I bury myself against him and he hugs me back. Our hearts beat in time together. It's nice. I could get use to this. Then I remember *her* and pull away. "Why are you dating Gigi Carlisle?"

"Good Lord, why would you think—" He grumbles, "What did she tell you?"

"That you two are a couple and you'll do anything she wants. Hard to argue since you signed that permission form to interview me."

"It's not like that." The veins on his forehead almost pop out.

"How is it?"

"Gigi threatened to report a lie about you."

"What?"

I'm not sure he'll tell me, but then he says, "After your mother died, she said she had proof that your mom"—he does air quotes—"*used you* for her clients." He coughs and clears his throat.

A blush burns my cheeks and I can hardly talk. "She never . . ."

"I know." He squeezes my hand.

Me and my uncle stop talking. We both stare at the spray paint on O'Dell's back window:

DIE

Uncle P says, "I hope he has insurance."

"He doesn't." I can't bear to think of a world without that butt munch, so I think about something else. "Where to now?"

"Home."

"What about One-Leg?"

"Let's get you cleaned up and fed first."

"Are the reporters still camped out in our yard?"

"Yes, but not as many."

"I, uh, think Mama may have killed that cop." I explain about Officer Riker being her customer and the trash he talked about my uncle. The bruises that cop gave her. How much she hated him.

"Bad enough to kill him?" my uncle asks me.

I nod.

"That explains why I became poison at work and why I was iced from the investigation entirely. Riker turned everyone against me."

"'Cept Lydia."

My uncle nods, watching her talking to a fireman. I'm not sure if that look is love or irritation. He says, "Hmmmm. I'm less sure that your mother killed him."

"Why?"

"There was a boot print at the crime scene. It wasn't your mom's or Riker's, and there's something unusual about the tread."

"How so?"

"There's a piece of glass or a pebble or something in the bottom that affects the footstep."

I file that away. After we finish talking, Uncle Patrick makes me repeat everything to Lydia and her partner. The cops write it down and ask smart questions, so I sort of feel better.

When we climb into our pickup, my backpack is sitting in the middle of the seat. Along with Tommy's ski hat I left at the library. Uncle Patrick's yellow umbrella rests at on the floorboard at my feet.

Still Mr. Prepared. I set all my stuff on my lap. Feels good to have it back.

He starts the engine. "I'm sorry I took your bag."

"I'm sorry I ran away."

We watch the tow truck haul O'Dell's pickup down the street, and my stomach turns sour all over again. I say, "Can we stop by St. Columba's on the way home? I want to apologize to Ann Riker for Mama. They said she'll be at mass at seven."

"I'm not sure that's a good idea."

"Please?"

The air conditioner blasts me as we drive away. I don't know if that's a yes or no, but I'll deal with it either way. I dig through my backpack, then guzzle down my bottled water. I can't wait to get back to reading about the orphan girl in *A Little Princess*.

It makes me so happy to see all this again. The clock on the dash says 6:45 p.m. The sun sinks lower in the sky, with more shadows streaking across Paradise. People huddle against buildings, along sidewalks or inside their tents. They're already exhausted from the day but are preparing to battle the night.

I'm surprised when we pass St. Columba's church since it's not on the way home. I watch the crime scene outside the silent crosses:

++++++++++++++++++++++++++++++

++++++++++++++++++++

++++++++++

Different folks leave their cars to go inside for the service. Uncle Patrick pulls into the parking lot and parks, then points to a woman alone in a minivan nearby. "That's Ann. I haven't seen her since Felix's funeral."

"Was it packed?"

"Overflowing, which is always the case with a dead officer. I still can't believe Waldo DeSoya is actually a priest."

I remember how unpriestly he was with Mama.

My uncle gives me a finger-wag. "Careful what you say to Ann Riker. Regardless of who killed her husband, she's still grieving his death. Be respectful."

"Okay."

Ann Riker walks toward the church building. Her blonde hair's just above her shoulders. She wears a long, flowy black skirt and matching top. The paper said her sons are ages ten and eight.

Boys with no daddy.

A girl with no mama.

Me and Uncle Patrick make our way to her on the sidewalk. He smiles and waves. "Ann!"

She shields her eyes, then frowns and folds her arms when she spots him. That's not the usual swooning over Prince Charming.

"Patrick" is all she says.

He gives her a side hug. "I'm sorry I haven't reached out since the news broke yesterday. Every reporter in town is on my front lawn."

"Yes. This is a bit awkward." Ann Riker shrinks deeper into herself. She's a pretty woman, eaten up with grief. A few seconds of forever pass, then her gaze lands on my bald head.

Uncle P smiles and pats my shoulder. "This is my niece, Copper."

She knows who that makes me.

I watch her, struggling with what to say now that the moment's finally here. "I'm, ummm, sorry about your husband. I hate that Mama . . ." I can't finish.

"Thank you," Ann says. "I appreciate your sympathy. I'd love to visit, but the service is about to begin." Her long skirt swishes around as she hurries toward the church.

It's now or never. In my mind, I apologize to everyone, then call out, "You knew he was cheating on you."

My uncle bristles beside me. She cringes, then slowly faces us.

I nod. "Your husband's wallet. In those first few weeks he came to visit Mama, he had no pictures. Then one showed up of the boys carving pumpkins, then another from your wedding. Why'd you do that?"

"I don't know what you're talking about." She fiddles with her wedding ring.

"Yeah, you do. He never mentioned his family once to Mama, but your photos kept showing up in his wallet. Hell hath no fury like a woman scorned."

"Copper," Uncle Patrick scolds.

I say, "You were here the night your husband died, weren't you?"

"No."

"Uh-huh." I step forward. "You're the killer, too."

CHAPTER 31

"No," Ann Riker repeats, and my uncle perks up at the conversation. She keeps fiddling with her wedding ring and shaking her head at me.

"Copper," he says again.

I stare at the dead cop's wife.

She waves off Uncle P, then clears her throat while still messing with her band. Staring at where Father Waldo said her husband was murdered. She says, "It wasn't his first time to be unfaithful. He always had a penchant for whores." She glares at me, then looks away.

"So you murdered him."

"I didn't. I swear."

"You come here in the middle of the night for that adoration prayer thing. I saw your name in the sign-in book a lot."

"My weekly adoration hour is Wednesday mornings at eight. After I drop off the kids at school."

"So? You've done it all hours of the night before."

"I have insomnia. Praying helps, but I wasn't there then."

"No, but you *were* here. I have a friend who saw you."

"I . . ." Ann looks between us several more times, then seems to crumble. She buries her face in her hands and sobs. "I was here, but I didn't kill him. I didn't."

"You keep changing your story. You weren't here, then you were, but you swear you're not the murderer. Do you own a pair of boots?"

"Copper," Uncle Patrick snaps, then pats her shoulders. "It's okay, Ann. Just tell the truth. I'll help however I can."

She watches him, teary-eyed. "The police don't know any of this. They believed me when I said I was home with the boys because I'm *always* home with the boys, while Felix was drunk, or—or . . ." Ann Riker doesn't finish, but she doesn't have to. The bite in her voice says it all.

My uncle says, "Start at the beginning, then we'll sort it out together."

It takes a while for her to speak. Now she watches her husband's cross a few feet away: FELIX RIKER—53. "He'd been drinking that night. Nothing new there. We got into a fight, then he left to be with one of his *whores*. I'd had it, so I followed him."

The sweet widow's gone, and a furious woman stands in her place. I picture her two boys sleeping in matching twin beds that night, while I was snoozing at the cemetery. Seems Mama wasn't the only one to leave her kid alone then.

Despite the heat, Ann's shivering. "He went to the Shangri-La motel first. Corinne Daniels let him into her room, but they didn't . . ." She blushes and looks off. "I could hear them arguing through the closed window. She was out of control. They both were."

My uncle nods. This matches with what we already knew about Mama that night. Uncle P had even stopped by earlier, trying to talk her into going to rehab. She kicked him out.

Ann Riker's voice breaks. "I waited and confronted Felix in the motel parking lot. Corinne showed up to tell me that my husband was one of her johns. Like I didn't already know that." Ann breathes out a shaky sigh. "She demanded money, then a fight broke out between them again. I tried to stop it, but Felix shoved her, then he slammed me against my car. She pulled him off me, and I drove away as fast as I could."

Uncle Patrick asks, "Where did you go?"

"Here." She watches the cross on the church steeple. I hear singing from inside, then Ann continues, "I sat in my car crying. I guess mustering up the courage on what to do next. Go inside to pray or go home and file for divorce. Felix showed up, blaming me for everything. He was beating on my windows and threatening me."

I say, "Was it loud?"

She nods.

"Why didn't the adoration person come out?"

"Les Hughesman didn't show. He never does."

"So the church was empty?"

"I guess. Felix snapped. He opened my car door and strangled me. I thought I'd die, but . . . your mother jumped out of the back of his car. She tore him off me, which started them brawling again. I was petrified and went straight home." Ann can't stop staring at City Cemetery. Maybe reliving that painful night.

Uncle Patrick asks, "Did you see any of the eyewitnesses the police say were there?"

"I heard somebody call out Corrine's name, but I didn't I see anyone. I just left."

"A man or a woman?"

"A woman."

I tell my uncle, "That could've been Naomi or Arlene."

Ann Riker shrugs. "I didn't know Felix was dead until the police came to the house." She wails against my uncle while he holds her. "Part of me feels he deserved it. How awful am I?"

"That's reasonable, given what you've been through." My uncle pats her.

She keeps crying. Uncle Patrick's still holding her. All while

Father Where's Waldo preaches inside. I watch Mama's cross, wondering how everything went so wrong. Each time we come to City Cemetery we're just poking at death.

Uncle Patrick turns on the charm and sweet-talks the widow into giving her statement to the police first thing tomorrow. He even promises to drive her to the station and stay with her the whole time.

She presses her body deeper into his. They talk awhile longer, then he walks her to the church door. I don't want those two hooking up. I bet her sons are losers, just like their father.

I'm still not convinced Ann Riker is innocent. Uncle Patrick needs to push her harder tomorrow during the police interview. She hugs him goodbye, clinging a little too long.

Gag.

Staring at the grass, I picture where her husband's body must've been and think about that odd boot print there. When my uncle returns, I tell him, "I don't want Ann Riker to be my stepmommy."

"Don't worry. How'd you figure out she was here that night?"

"I saw her name a bunch in that adoration book, then guessed the rest."

"You're a good liar."

"Thank you."

"That wasn't a compliment." He takes out his keys and heads toward our pickup. "Let's go home."

"We can't. There's still a killer on the loose. Plus, O'Dell, Salt and Pepper are all missing."

"I'm not working those cases, and you're not Nancy Drew."

"Felix Riker and Naomi Rodriguez both died here. Arlene the Coat Stealer has a tattoo just like Mama's, and she jumped to her death to avoid talking about it. There's so much more to this."

"Yes, and you already told Lydia everything. Let the police do their jobs."

"Excuse me?" A man interrupts us in the church parking lot.

He's wearing a hard hat and vest like the construction crew across the street at the Salvation Army. The guy introduces himself and shakes my uncle's hand, then nods at me. "I saw you talking to my boss yesterday."

"Not really. He ran me off before I could say anything."

"I, umm." The man stuffs his hands in his pockets. "I think my boss may know more than he says about our robbery."

Uncle P asks, "Why?"

He shrugs. "All the flashy new things he's buying for his mistress."

"Insurance fraud?"

"Yes, sir. I bet the police will find that stolen equipment in one of his warehouses." The guy asks me, "What did you try to tell him?"

"I know a troublemaker named Bird. Bleached-blonde hair. She's got two little boys."

"One black, one white?"

"Yep," I say. "She'd been snooping around the church back then, and I found some metal wiring like you have in her motel room. I bet she knows where your equipment was stashed or sold."

"Right. I saw my boss talking to that same woman before the robbery."

I ask my uncle, "What's Bird's scam?"

"She might be holding on to stolen goods while the boss collects the insurance money. Happens all the time. He pays her a fee, then it's easy to fake receipts like he purchased new equipment."

The other man nods.

Uncle Patrick says, "I'm actually a police officer."

"Whoa." He holds up his hands. "I don't want to lose my job."

I say, "You don't have to. I can tell the cops I saw Bird's stash in her room and Father Waldo can pinpoint her snooping around the

Salvation Army's construction site the day of the robbery. The police can squeeze the rest out of her when they find her."

"I'd appreciate any help. I want justice served but would rather my boss not find it was me." The man says he'll call the police.

We square things away with him, then head to our truck.

I hate leaving my friends, but don't know what else to do. I buckle myself into my seat. "Go by the Barrio Brothers' on the way home."

My uncle shoots me a glare.

"What? O'Dell might be there."

I rest Tommy's ski hat on my lap, rubbing the brim of the wool cap and watching the sun sink lower over Paradise. Pinks and oranges stretch across the summer sky. Sunset's still almost two hours away.

I glance at my uncle. "Is Lydia your girlfriend?"

"Why are you trying to make everyone my girlfriend?"

"'Cause they all want to be, but you're too blind to see. Do you even like girls?"

"Of course I do."

"It's okay if you don't."

"I just haven't found the right one. I'd just gotten out of a long-term relationship when I moved home, and I've been focused on you." He hems and haws. "Besides, I don't have a job right now. Those are my top priorities."

"You could've told me about your job."

He grips, then regrips the steering wheel. "I felt too ashamed."

I know that feeling. I stare outside to a man sleeping curled up on a flattened box on the sidewalk. Cardboard for his mattress. I glance back to the pretty mirrored buildings downtown.

At the corner to the Barrio Brothers' headquarters, my uncle stops at the edge of the block. Two cop cars are parked in front of the hotel, but not Lydia's. "See?" he tells me. "They're on it."

I nod, remembering me and O'Dell there just a few short hours ago and my heart stings all over again. Uncle Patrick doesn't realize this is where Gigi Carlisle grilled me today. I say, "There's one last spot I want to check for O'Dell."

"No."

"Please? It's just our phone booth, and that's on the way out of Paradise. We can swing by there, then go home. I won't ask for anything else. I swear."

"Fine, but we're not getting out."

Five minutes later, we're driving down that alley. The shattered TV still lies smashed on the ground. My uncle eases the truck around the damage, then stops. I point to the apartment window with the Dallas Cowboys star on it. "I think that's where Spider lives. I'd bet money he did this. All of it."

"I'll tell Lydia."

"How long will Eddie Loco be in jail?"

"Life. He's not going anywhere. The man committed sexual assault."

That should make me feel better but doesn't. Him and jailbird daddy still haunt me from behind bars. That's when I notice it down the alley. My whole body trembles. "What the—"

Uncle Patrick follows my gaze to my phone booth standing upright like it should. He eases our truck up to it and tells me to wait here, but I'm already gone. He hollers and follows behind me.

It's cemetery quiet.

Please don't be O'Dell.

I rip open the double glass doors, then crumble to the ground.

Mai Wong dangles from the ceiling, her red bandanna tied around her neck like a noose.

CHAPTER 32

I scream and look away, though she's already seared into my brain. Mai Wong, my beautiful broken friend, hangs like a rag doll in our phone booth. Her face has turned purple. No life shines from her eyes anymore. That red bandanna always showed her connection to the Asian Assassins.

Now, I see the color of her rage.

Eddie Loco ruined her in this very spot. I knew she was struggling like me to find a new normal but didn't realize it was this bad.

Uncle Patrick buries me against his chest. I cling to him, my tears soaking his shirt. Death stole one more person I love. She's not wearing O'Dell's necklace. At some point, my uncle breaks away, then checks Mai's pulse.

Nothing.

He says, "I need to call 9-1-1. Let's wait in my truck."

I let him lead me away, my head spinning. I'm numb.

He opens his door for me and gives me a sad smile. Someone springs from the back bed of our pickup. He clubs Uncle P over the head with the back of a pistol. I watch my uncle collapse to the ground.

Shrieking, I run for my life.

The attacker scrambles after me. I only make it a few steps before I'm snatched from behind. I struggle, fighting him with all my might. We whirl around a few times, then I claw at him and almost break free, but he throws me into a sleeper hold, hooking his arm tight around my throat, then squeezing.

Can't.

Breathe.

Blackness.

CHAPTER 33

I wake up lying in the back seat of a moving car, groggy and seasick. The leather seats are so old they crack against my cheek. I try to sit up, but my hands are tied behind me with what feels like a rope. The hitch in my chest clamps down harder, and I struggle to think. I hear guys talking in Chinese up front.

Two voices, I think. One's here in the car, like in the driver's seat, and the other . . . is on speakerphone?

I would've expected Drago to do this since he's hassled me nonstop, but the voice in the car is softer. Gentler.

It's the boy with the kind eyes. He saved me from Eddie Loco in Chinatown all those months ago. I ran straight to him back then, and he kissed me just last night.

My stomach sours when I say his name. "Chao-Chao."

The driver ends the call, then glances back at me. "Ghost Girl."

"Why are you doing this?"

"I don't want to."

"But you are."

"We *told* you to go home. This is on you."

"Is my uncle okay? Where is he?"

Chao-Chao doesn't answer. Outside the window, the sun sinks lower. Night's conquering another day.

"Where are we headed?" I ask.

He ignores me. It's hard to focus.

In passing through Remington I recognize places and things but am not sure where they belong since I'm seeing 'em upside down . . . a billboard . . . a flagpole . . . a digital sign that says 8:17 P.M. and 101°.

I watch the side of Chao-Chao's face. Eyes so dark you can see forever in 'em, and those pouty lips that tasted like mint. He's dressed in red shorts and a T-shirt now—not in black like when they buried the dead baby last night.

Maybe that's a good sign.

Hopefully. I force myself to look at him straight-on. "Did you see what happened to Mai?"

"Not until you went in there." His voice shakes. "She was one of my best friends."

"Did you kill her?"

"Of course not. She should've stayed away from that O'Dell guy."

"He made her happy."

"Then why'd she hang herself?"

We pause at a stoplight. Nothing outside gives me a clue to where we are. The signal turns green and we drive on. I'm so worried about Uncle Patrick. I need to find an escape.

"I thought you liked me." I hate how wounded I sound.

"I do," Chao-Chao says.

I tug at my wrists again, but they don't break free. This car's got four doors, but it's not the Suburban that the Asian Assassins always drive. It's locked back here, so I assume the same's true up front. My legs aren't bound, so I can kick him when he comes for me.

I need to understand what's happening. "What were you looking for in One-Leg's tent last night?"

"We wanted him to do a job for us."

"Bury that baby?"

Chao-Chao nods. "You shouldn't have come back to Paradise."

"Why?"

"Your family is in danger. You probably won't believe me, but I'm trying to help you."

"Doesn't seem like it. I won't tell anyone what I saw."

He turns on his headlights. It's just now darker than light outside. That's bad news for me. From my window, I see a flash of the black pointy top of the fence at Eternal Peace upside down.

"Wait! What are you doing?" I holler. "I can't be here at night!"

Chao-Chao eases to a stop at the main gates, then hops out of the car. I can't see him, but think I hear the rattle of a lock, then catch one of the gates swinging one way, then the other opening, too.

When he gets back in, I groan. "I feel sick. Let me up."

He watches me a few seconds, then steps around and opens my door. He's wearing combat boots. He tugs on my hands, like checking they're still holding, then he pulls me upright. The pistol's tucked into the waistband of his shorts now. I stifle a scream.

Once we're inside the graveyard, he relocks the gate behind us.

When he's back, I ask, "Where'd you get the cemetery keys?"

"I've got people." Chao-Chao snickers to himself. "Just kidding. I stole 'em from your friend."

Losing his keys is part of why O'Dell's uncle fired him after that horrible terrible night. That happened over four months ago. My thoughts reel with what this all means. It sickens me that my lips ever touched Chao-Chao's. "What do you know about O'Dell?"

"You two should've stayed away. You destroyed Mai."

"Did you hurt him?"

No response.

"Zhi Peng's the whole reason she came to Paradise in the first place. It's his fault."

"He doesn't see it that way."

"Do you know who murdered that cop?"

"No."

"Did you?"

"Of course not."

"What about Drago?"

"No . . . maybe. I'm not sure. I don't think your mom killed him. She seemed nice."

"You knew her?"

He doesn't answer. Shadows stretch across the headstones. My muscles remember every second of Diablo and Miz Jesus hunting me down here.

Raining. Running. Death.

Stop. I need to stay strong if I'm going to survive this.

Chao-Chao slows by the Warrior Angel, but we drive on by it. I look away. Doesn't matter. It's dark enough I can't see the statue's face. Or the bullet hole in his base. I struggle to control my breathing and my thoughts. I can't stop trembling.

He says, "We were here, you know."

"What do you mean?"

"The night that lady preacher almost killed you. We all were—Zhi, Koi, Drago. Everyone."

"Stop lying."

He studies me through the rearview mirror for so long I'm not sure he'll say more, then he nods toward the window. "We stood outside the chapel while it poured. Diablo tried to stab you, then that woman showed up and slit his neck."

I flinch. That's just how it happened. Diablo's blood splattered my body. I thought Miz Jesus came to save me, but . . .

Chao-Chao passes the Vanderhausen Mausoleum. A green tent's set up outside for Lisa's mom's funeral tomorrow. Inside is where Miz Jesus murdered Mama. I hope Chao-Chao doesn't notice me crying.

He says, "I tried to grab you before you ran inside that crypt. I tried to save you from seeing your mom. We stood close enough to touch, but you ducked under the caution tape and were gone."

The Asian Assassins really were here that night. I was drenched to the bone. My gut knew I'd find Mama dead, but I didn't want to believe it. I remember someone reaching for me, but figured it was O'Dell trying to stop me. I found her bloody body stuffed in that drawer. The hint of her blue angel wings showing. Her mouth caught in a shrieking O, like she died mid-scream. Mama's last moments on earth were pure hell.

I swallow a mouthful of tears. Thinking about Uncle Patrick upsets me worse. He's all I've got left. I can't stop shaking.

"You okay?" Chao-Chao asks.

"You . . . don't have to do this."

"I'm not weak."

"I didn't say you were."

"They did." He stops talking.

What would've happened if Chao-Chao had caught me that horrible terrible night, instead of Miz Jesus?

Would Tommy Tucker still be alive?

Would I be dead?

His phone rings, and he answers it in Chinese. I don't understand a word of his conversation.

The past and the present collide inside as we make our way through the Historic Section. Simple moments flash by. Me and Mama chasing fireflies together here. Us watching so many sunsets together. Chao-Chao doesn't stop at the Main Mausoleum or by her grave.

We keep going. I tug at my wrists again, but they don't budge. "Why'd you bring me here?"

"This is where we first met."

"I don't get it."

"Zhi had us watching you and your mom long before she died."

"Why?"

"My enemy's enemy is my friend."

"You still haven't said how you knew her." I ask him more questions but get nowhere.

We weave on through the graveyard. I feel terrified and lost. Trees line the pond at the Garden of Friends where the Asian Assassins surrounded me and Mai Wong last night. I can't believe I'll never see her again.

The pale moon appears beside the clouds, so I stare out over the dirt, weeds and nothingness of the Nobody Section and plan my escape. I've run tied up through this place before and can do it again. I try to tell myself Chao-Chao won't hurt me, but my gut's not so sure.

He parks at the edge of the cemetery and lets me out. I hesitate, then follow behind him, tugging at my bound wrists. I gaze into the black night 'cause it feels like we're being watched again. Are the Asian Assassins out there now?

Is 'Chele the photographer snapping pictures this sec? If so, why doesn't she help me?

I know the foot markers he's leading me to, though I'm not sure why:

TOMMY TUCKER UNKNOWN NEGRO

Chao-Chao stands there, staring at my best friend's grave. "It hurt to watch you kiss him."

His tone makes my skin crawl.

"You two kissed, then he died in your arms. Just like in the movies."

"Wh-where were you?"

"We had you surrounded by that angel statue. You, your

uncle, O'Dell, this Tommy guy and the preacher lady. Your uncle's a good shot. He popped her right between the eyes."

Chao-Chao stands close enough for me to see his teeth sparkling in the dark. I feel pukey and struggle to not collapse.

"We wanted to attack, but Diablo was dead by then and Zhi had other plans."

"What?"

"You'll see." Chao-Chao chuckles. "Guess you won't." He yanks me to him, and I cringe. Our lips almost touch. He gazes into my eyes and whispers, "Tell him you love me more."

"No." I pull away and look at the name stamped on my heart: TOMMY.

"Do it." Chao-Chao's voice grows louder. Angrier.

"No!"

His fist flies so fast into my nose I don't realize what's happening 'til blood dribbles into my mouth. I holler in pain. I'm stunned for several seconds. Of course, I can't wipe my face clean. The blood tastes like metal.

He shouts, "TELL HIM YOU LOVE ME MORE!"

I whisper, "I love him more."

"Say my name."

"I love Chao-Chao more."

"Louder."

"I LOVE CHAO-CHAO MORE!"

"Good." He pats my shoulder. "I don't like the idea of you spending eternity with him, but . . ."

I shudder again. "You said you were helping me."

"I am."

I don't understand. I feel like I'm trapped in something bigger than just Mama's murder, though I'm not sure what. He takes me back to his car and seats me up front beside him. He grins and wipes blood off my upper lip, then he gives me another minty kiss. I shout and yank away from him.

He laughs.

We don't talk as we drive through the Jewish Section's fancy graves. I spot Ilana Sakowitz. She fought off the Nazis to save her children.

My mama's not here to save me.

Nobody is. It's hard to sit with my hands tied behind my back. I keep tasting blood, and my face is killing me. Chao-Chao drives slow enough for me to escape, but I don't think I can reach the handle before he grabs me again. I can't risk it.

I'll die if I don't.

Soon, we're passing the pinwheels, teddy bears and dolls still lined up against the tiny headstones shaped like Raggedy Ann and Andy. Puppy dogs and kitty cats. Others are foot markers etched with lambs, balloons and fawns.

Baby Land.

The small mound that Chao-Chao's buddies dug last night is across the way. "How many bodies have you buried here?" I ask.

"Just that one."

"Did you get any of those breeder girls pregnant?"

He doesn't say. Chao-Chao parks on the road near that grave, staring into the darkness. "Holding that dead baby was the hardest thing I've ever done . . . 'til now."

I tremble as I whisper, "You don't have to kill me."

"I'm not."

I struggle not to bawl worse. He holds my arm so gently I almost believe him, but . . . it gives me the willies passing that Chinese baby's grave. A big hole's up ahead, with a pile of dirt beside it.

That wasn't here last night. I whimper as Chao-Chao walks us to the empty—

Moonlight shines onto O'Dell, six feet below.

CHAPTER 34

O'Dell lies squirming on the dirt, bound and gagged. His eyes go wide when he spots me, and he shakes his head, yelping something behind his bandanna I can't understand. My body jolts. Someone beat the holy hell out of him. It makes my bloody nose hurt worse.

Still tied up, I slam my shoulder into Chao-Chao. "What did you *do* to him?"

"I didn't do anything. I saved him from Spider. Right?" he shouts to O'Dell, who nods back.

"How'd you get him away?"

"Ninja skills." Chao-Chao laughs and wriggles his eyebrows. He's close enough for me to kiss again. I want to scream.

He shoves me toward the hole, but I twirl away and lurch forward on the grass instead. I'm hobbling into the darkness, back the way we came.

"Run!" I shout to no one. There's nothing I can do to save me and O'Dell but turn off my brain and turn on my legs. I'm zigzagging through Baby Land. It's hard to balance tied—

A gunshot cracks by my head as Chao-Chao jerks me back to him. He's holding the pistol high in the air. My ears ring like mad.

His breath burns hot as he whispers in my good ear, "Run again and you'll see what I did to those breeders."

I'm weeping. With his gun pressed firmly against my spine, he walks me by a foot marker with several balloons floating over it. Each step takes me closer to my death.

I remember something and decide it's worth a try. I'm probably yelling as I say, "The good have nothing to fear, but the wicked spend eternity paying for their sins."

"Impressive. Where'd you hear that?"

"Mai Wong. Her NaiNai told her that."

"Sweet Mai," he sighs. "I can't believe she's really gone."

"Why'd you kill her?"

"I *told* you, I didn't. She was my friend."

"I thought I was your friend."

"No. You're my girl."

Panic strangles my insides worse. Chao-Chao's straight-up crazy. We reach the edge of the freshly dug grave where O'Dell still lies below. He knows I failed us.

"In you go." Chao-Chao pushes me hard.

I holler, unable to break my fall, then land on O'Dell with a heavy *thud*. He grunts as his chin cuffs the side of my head. My ear rings worse.

"Sorry." I roll off him. There's barely enough room for the two of us, so we lie side-by-side like a double burial. "You okay?" I holler.

He shrugs.

"Stop talking!" Chao-Chao yells.

I've got to think fast.

Too late. Something hits me.

Dirt.

It keeps falling on us. Me and O'Dell flinch. We scream as clots land on our faces and bodies. He's burying us alive!

I shout to O'Dell, "Stand up!"

He garbles something behind his gag while we both struggle to our feet. Chao-Chao shouts for us to quit and goes back to shoveling. Me and O'Dell do our best to duck our heads, but dirt pelts us faster. We can't stop screaming.

Chao-Chao leans down and whacks O'Dell's shoulder with the shovel. A few seconds later, gunfire stops us. The Asian Assassin points the pistol straight my way. "Lie back down, or I swear I'll kill him."

Me and O'Dell fumble our way to the ground again, then go back to being buried alive. We're both screaming. I don't want to die. I wish I could at least hold O'Dell's hand. I'm not sure he knows Mai is dead. He fidgets beside me, our scareds colliding together. The moon shines above our empty screams.

This is worse than before with Miz Jesus. I at least had a chance to escape with her.

We're trapped and facing an awful death. My brain hollers, *Help me, God!*

Nothing happens.

I loud-whisper to O'Dell, "Shoot me up like a cannon, like you do your brothers on your trampoline."

He shakes his head and muddles his words.

"Shut up!" Chao-Chao raises his pistol.

"Aim straight at him," I whisper. "He won't hurt me."

Maybe. I jump up as Chao-Chao swings the shovel at me and misses. O'Dell bends his knees, and I do like on his video—curl myself up into a ball onto his feet. It's hard but we sort of balance together. Chao-Chao keeps threatening and takes another swipe at us.

"Now!" I scream.

O'Dell rockets me straight into our attacker and we topple over together. I land on Chao-Chao, then sink my teeth deep into his shoulder. He screams hard. He screams death. He cusses in Chinese. I head-butt him and the pain almost knocks me out. I can barely hear.

It takes me a few seconds to recover. As I roll away from him, Chao-Chao clenches his shoulder. He growls and dives at me, catching my sneaker. I kick him with my other foot and break free, but he grabs me again.

I knee his hooter-mcgrooter as hard as I can, then leave him struggling.

As I sprint away, I shout to O'Dell, "I'll get help!"

Chao-Chao yells, "Come back, or I'll kill him!"

That stops me for a half sec.

He'll murder us either way, so I keep going. I can't lose the bloody taste in my mouth. Sure enough, he chases me through Baby Land. The moon and clouds make the night sky look so calm and peaceful. Nothing here says *buried alive*.

I find my rhythm in running with no hands. I did this before with Miz Jesus, so I can do it again. I don't have to battle the rain this time, though I've got no open hiding spots like before.

Chao-Chao laughs in the distance. "This is how you ran from that preacher lady." He even sings the theme song from her TV show she sang to me that horrible terrible night. "What a friend we have in Jeeeeeeeeeeeeeeesus, all our sins and griefs to bear."

My heart may rip from my chest any second, but I press on. Either the cemetery's darker, or I'm just not used to this anymore. I almost smash into a tree. The air whips all around me. He'll catch up any second.

I make it to the Jewish Section. He should've caught me by now—I think he's enjoying the chase. I'm exhausted and can't outrun him forever. *Do something.*

I slow my pace, then stop and stick out my leg. A few seconds later, he topples over me and hits a headstone. I hear his *oomph* as he crashes to the grass.

I wish he'd smashed his brain open, but he didn't. This buys me time. I've got to save me and O'Dell. Uncle Patrick doesn't even know where I am. Plus, Chao-Chao locked the front gates. I'm too big to slip through the fence. The best I can do is hide and hope he doesn't shoot me or O'Dell.

That thought slows me.

I hear Chao-Chao somewhere behind me. I need to lead him farther away from my friend. We're playing cat and mouse. I let him find me, then lose him again. Anything to survive. We move deeper into the Historic Section, past all the fancy headstones and statues.

My ears ring worse as I race on, hopeless. I'm not sure where to go. I just know I'm going to die.

Chao-Chao grabs my arm and jerks me toward him. His fingernails dig into my skin, but I stomp his foot as hard as I can. He cusses and lets go. I race away all loosey-goosey. Blood's dried to my face and my nose throbs. He'll expect me to go straight back to O'Dell, so I can't yet. It'd be my pattern.

Chinese cusswords follow behind me. I've done everything I can to forget Eternal Peace, but it's in my blood. It's in my bones. From every tree branch, to each piece of marble, this place is part of me.

He's quick, but I remember I'm a Ghost Girl. The Asian Assassins are right. I've spent my whole life living among the dead. Use it. Speeding up, I disappear into the shadows.

My legs pound. I've told myself the bad guys were dead—Diablo and Miz Jesus. My jailbird daddy's behind bars, but I've got a whole new set of problems if Zhi Peng Wong and his gang really spied on me and Mama. Long before that horrible, terrible night.

Why?

Did Mama know?

Does my uncle?

I don't hear Chao-Chao behind me anymore, but I don't slow my pace. I rush to the right, then duck left through some trees. The moon sneaks behind the clouds, so everything goes black. I force myself to hobble on.

When I can see again, I realize I'm almost home to the Warrior Angel and curse myself for coming back to where my uncle shot and killed Miz Jesus. Where Tommy Tucker died. It's too dark to see the statue's face as I collapse beneath his base.

"Ow!" The sharp edge of the pillar's bullet hole cuts me.

Cuts me.

I spin around, then slide my tied wrists back and forth like a knife along the jagged side with the bullet hole. It works, but I howl. It's cutting me as it slices through the rope. Blood trickles down my wrists.

It's excruciating, but I don't stop.

Almost there.

I break free as Chao-Chao tackles me to the ground. We roll through the grass, over and over. Him, then me, then back again. He's so much stronger, but I've got hate on my side, so I hold my own. We bump into the two praying hands of Miz Elsie's grave nearby. Chao-Chao pushes against my face so hard he almost snaps my skull in half. I punch him in the gut.

He lets go, and when I hop up he trips me. I miss the headstone by half an inch. I kick him away, and jump back up and cram his face against Miz Elsie's marble. He crumples to the ground.

I look around for something to tie him up. There's the rope I just cut through, but it's frayed and ruined. He's not wearing a belt.

Me neither.

The severed rope is all I've got. My slashes burn as I loop it around his wrists once. That's the best I can do, then knot it. I wish I could tie him to a tree or grave, but there's not enough extra.

Plus, I need to get back to O'Dell. My own cuts sting and my nose still hurts so much. I grab Chao-Chao's pistol and stick it in the top of my shorts, then kick him once more.

He's totally conked out. For a split second, I think about shooting him.

No, I'm not a killer.

The clouds break away and moonlight shines on the Warrior Angel like a spotlight. The statue's got his left hand stretched out toward heaven as always, but there's something hanging from his staff on the right.

A jacket.

Mama's fur coat.

CHAPTER 35

I'm blinking 'cause I don't believe what I'm seeing—Mama's rabbit coat. I assumed it burned in O'Dell's truck.

I don't know why it's here.

I don't know what this means.

But it means *something.*

"Chao-Chao?" I rush to him on the other side of the statue, then shake him hard. Calling out his name.

He doesn't budge. I almost worry I killed him for a few seconds, then notice his chest's still moving.

I rush back to the Warrior Angel, staring at Mama's jacket dangling above. The statue's base is still over my head, so it'd be a hard climb up there. I should get back to O'Dell anyhow, but I can't stop myself from staring at the coat.

It's the only thing I've got left of her. I've always loved that jacket. So soft and warm. Plus, she wrote *24530 Bowery* inside it. I don't know if there are more clues inside or if Chao-Chao just left it to torture me. Maybe someone else did.

O'Dell needs me.

Now.

Debating, I read the statue's name—MICHAEL. My angel

book at home says Michael is the Chief Angel of the Lord and the conqueror of Satan.

He's not saving me now. I'm all we've got. O'Dell's here. He's alive. He's a total butt munch, but he's still mine. Mama's coat will have to wait.

I growl my frustration, then take one last look at Chao-Chao and limp back toward Baby Land for my friend. I take turns holding one bloody wrist while the other bleeds freely, then switch sides. It hurts so much. My ears keep ringing and my entire body aches, but I'm so glad to wipe my crusty nose. I should be celebrating since I escaped that monster, but I'm not.

I know better. Others might be lurking in the shadows.

With everything in me, I want to scream O'Dell's name to let him know I'm coming for him, 'cept he's halfway across the cemetery and I don't want to tip off any more bad guys. I've got Chao-Chao's gun to protect me and can untie O'Dell with Tommy's pocketknife. The blade is super dull, so it may take a while, but it'll work. I breathe hard and sprint on.

Thoughts of Tommy Tucker flitter through me. His sandy-blond hair and those Hershey Bar brown eyes. The sweetness of his lips. How hard I cried as he took his last breath beneath the Warrior Angel. He's the boy who stole my heart. He's the one I love.

The night twists tighter, and I'm almost crawling through the graves I'm so exhausted. It's still hard to hear, but I race on.

At the chapel, the forever light shines inside onto the giant stained-glass window up front. All the pretty colors just remind me of all the different ways I almost died.

"You're okay," I tell myself, then add more pressure to my wrists. At least the bleeding's slowed. My nose is better, too.

In the Jewish Section, I feel movement nearby and duck behind a headstone much taller than me. Gripping Chao-Chao's gun, I turn off the safety and point it toward the noise. It doesn't reassure me.

A shadow skulks through the graveyard. It's a man, though I can't tell who. He doesn't move light-footed like Chao-Chao or lumber along like Drago.

Could it be Zhi Peng or Koi?

Someone else?

I shiver. Whoever it is, he glides through the cemetery like he knows his way around here. That worries me. I almost follow the stranger, but don't want to go looking for trouble.

O'Dell.

Holding on to the gun, I sneak toward Baby Land to rescue him. A few minutes later, I finally pass the eerie balloons hovering over that foot marker . . . then, the small mound where they buried the dead baby.

I'm sprinting to the grave Chao-Chao dug. When I'm close enough that it's safe, I shout down to O'Dell, "It's me!"

The hole is empty.

CHAPTER 36

My heart leaps for a split second. O'Dell's still alive!

'Cept there's no way he climbed out on his own. He was bound and gagged. Maybe he managed to cut himself free like me.

Staring into the dark hole, I don't see any clues about what happened, but hope maybe that stranger I just saw pulled him out.

Probably not, or they'd be together. That wasn't O'Dell I just saw. I know his walk. I'm not sure where to go or what to do to find him. I clutch Chao-Chao's pistol, hobbling past all the toys, stuffed animals and trinkets in Baby Land. The high-pitched ringing in my ears won't stop.

My friend's not here. Eternal Peace is huge—fifty thousand burials, so it's possible we're making giant loops around and missing each other.

It's insane to go farther into the cemetery with Chao-Chao still out there, even though he's tied up, but I've got to find my friend. My gaze sweeps over all the headstones. A breeze makes me shiver.

Someone grabs me from behind.

I scream.

Strong hands spin me around. I jab the gun in his face, about to pull the trigger.

"It's me!" Uncle Patrick shouts.

I bury myself against him. He garbles something, then taps me.

"What?" I yell.

He takes away the pistol. "What's wrong? I've been calling out for you."

"Oh." I explain the gunshot and everything else.

"I'll call the police . . . wait, no." He doesn't have cell reception.

"How'd you find me?" I holler.

"Some strange woman woke me up in Paradise and brought me here."

"Was she tiny and Chinese?"

"No, tall and white."

"Never mind. Did you pass the Warrior Angel?"

"Yes. One of the Asian Assassins was tied up there."

"That's Chao-Chao. He's who knocked you out, then took me. Did you see Mama's coat?"

"No, but I was going fast."

I groan and gaze across a Raggedy Andy headstone. The Asian Assassins have taken over Eternal Peace. Fear bubbles up inside. I dissolve into my uncle again, letting myself feel safer, then realize we're standing right where me and Mai Wong watched that baby get buried last night.

JOSEPHINE SAMOYA

April 24, 1987–April 24, 1987

I pull myself away. "We've got to find O'Dell."

"Let's go to my truck so I can call the police. I had a signal there."

"Where'd you park?"

"Outside the Garden of Friends." He holds Chao-Chao's gun in one hand and takes me by the other. We race through all the tiny headstones.

I don't look back at the empty grave where Chao-Chao just

tried to bury me alive. I stay focused on finding O'Dell and getting help. My gaze darts over the headstones of all my Jewish buddies. That's where I spotted the stranger. Was that Uncle P?

I keep scanning the grounds for our friend, worrying we're surrounded by Asian Assassins. Red bleeds from my heart.

A siren snaps me back to my senses with my good ear. I'm not sure if it's the police or firemen. Either way, help is on the way. I swear someone's following us, but I hold on to my uncle and race faster.

As we approach the darkened chapel, my Diablo scar throbs. Something startles me nearby.

"Is someone there?" I shout to Uncle P.

"What? No." He tugs me along.

Nobody grabs us. Nothing happens, so I focus on just running. Moonlight tumbles across all the endless graves. We should be turning left toward the Garden of Friends.

Instead, I pull away from my uncle and step right. "We can't leave O'Dell. He needs us."

"The police are almost here."

"They won't find him." I step back. "I know where he is."

"Where?"

"The Vanderhausen Mausoleum."

Uncle P's eyebrows furrow. "What makes you think that?"

"He tried to stop me from seeing Mama there that night . . . it's like code for where *not* to go."

"Then why go there?"

"Patterns." I take off sprinting. "He'll do the opposite. I've done it all day." I limp back toward the Historic Section.

My uncle catches up to me in no time. He doesn't try to lecture or stop me, and he even takes my hand while I lead the way. The Main Mausoleum stands like a dark shadow in the distance. My whole body's on high alert. The cicadas are still singing, but their sweet songs can only do so much.

We've got to find O'Dell. I owe him. Plus, I'm worried about Chao-Chao. He might wake up any second. The Asian Assassins want me gone since I saw what they did last night. Could they have murdered Mai, then made it look like a suicide?

A brick-size rock of terror sits on my chest. So much hurt from Mama. So many lies. Still, I live in her and she lives in me. I want so much more from the world, but it just sees me as the cop-killer's daughter. Some freak Gigi Carlisle wants to pimp on TV.

I'm tired of living in Mama's shame. I hate feeling like I'm caught in other people's games—Mama's, the Barrio Brothers' and the Asian Assassins'. Even my jailbird daddy's.

My breath quickens. Another whack attack hovers just beneath the surface, then I remind myself again I'm a Ghost Girl—pale, freckly, with no hair. I have no past or future.

Just now. That makes me the perfect person to get us out of here alive. A bazillion stars sparkle over all the pretty bones. Death lives at the cemetery, but not as much as in my heart. Life's there, too. I just need to focus more on that for a change.

Me and Uncle Patrick breathe in time together like one person. We move through the shadows, past the tree-stump graves, mint bushes and long stone crypts above the ground.

The green tent's set up outside the Vanderhausen Mausoleum. The crypt is tiny inside. Eight bodies total. I don't want to go back there—I don't.

The door's cracked open. It was locked when Chao-Chao drove us by earlier. I wish I had his gun, but my uncle took it.

He aims it at the opening, then motions for me to keep quiet.

"O'Dell?" he whispers.

I hear a muffled sound inside with my good ear—like a yelp.

"Stay back." Uncle Patrick dashes into the mausoleum.

I'm right behind him. Up the three stone steps, then inside.

Just like before.

My uncle uses his phone as a flashlight. O'Dell lies curled

up in the corner, still bound and gagged. Bloodied and bruised. He's crying. He's sitting next to where I found Mama's body stuffed in that bottom drawer.

I rush to him. "Are you okay?"

He shouts a garbled scream and leans away from us, blocking his face with his hands. My uncle pulls down the bandanna to free O'Dell's mouth and he shouts, "Don't hurt me! Don't hurt me!"

"It's us," I tell him.

He looks between me and Uncle Patrick, then asks, "Who are you?"

CHAPTER 37

Huddled beside Uncle Patrick in this small mausoleum, O'Dell's words slap me extra hard. "Who are you?"

I ask him, "Can you see?"

"Of course I can see. You look like shit."

He's got a giant gash in his head. I want to hold him, but he acts spooked and I don't want to scare him worse. I'm not sure what to do.

Uncle Patrick asks him, "Would you like me to untie you?"

"Please."

His sharp pocketknife slices through that rope, no problem. The ties fall to the cold cement floor.

"Thanks." O'Dell smooths over the rope burns on his wrists. He won't look at us.

My uncle says, "Do you know who we are?"

"Yeah. Patrick and . . ." He rubs his head.

"Copper," I say.

"Right. I know that."

"Do you know who *you* are?"

"Of course," he chuckles. "I'm . . . I, uhhh, know that. I just can't think of it this sec. I'm O . . ."

"You're Eugene O'Dell."

"I *know*, dumb-ass. Stop calling me Butt Munch."

I'm so happy I could cry.

Uncle Patrick rests his hand on O'Dell's shoulder. "What do you remember?"

"Being in my truck in Paradise, then someone yanked me out."

"Who?"

"That guy I chased from your house." O'Dell turns to me.

"Spider," I nod. "Did he say anything?"

"Yeah . . . 'Go home.'"

"That's what they spray-painted on the back of your truck. That's what the Asian Assassins keep telling me." The red message flashes through my mind:

GO HOME OR DIE

That shuts me up fast. I don't want to be the one to tell him they burned his truck to a crisp, or that his girlfriend is dead. I bite my lip so hard it bleeds. My whole body tingles like I'm on fire.

I ask, "How'd you get out of the hole?"

"Some guy. He brought me here, or maybe I got here on my own. I don't remember." O'Dell yawns. "I'm sleepy."

"Don't." My uncle shakes him. "You might have a concussion. We should get you to a hospital."

I add, "We need to see One-Leg, too. Let's go back to your pickup."

"Nope. We're staying here. I think I've got enough reception." Uncle Patrick texts the police our location.

I should feel better since O'Dell's alive and in one piece, but I don't. He doesn't realize his world's wrecked forever. The long lists of *last times* he'll collect about Mai Wong. All the heartache ahead of him.

The seconds scream by. He pulls the silver necklace from his pocket. "I haven't given this to Mai?"

I shake my head; tears rush up my throat.

"Why not?"

I shrug, feeling my uncle's gaze tighten around us.

O'Dell struggles to his feet. "I don't like this place. I want to find Mai. Let's go."

The mausoleum door creaks open. Spider points a knife toward us that's dripping with blood.

He grabs me.

CHAPTER 38

"It's him!" O'Dell ducks behind my uncle. "That's who pulled me from the hole!"

I'm facing those two while Spider's arm loops tighter around my neck, to the point I'm almost choking. The knife jabs so deep against me it hurts to breathe. I'm staring at where I found Mama's body stuffed in that drawer. Fear paralyzes me worse.

Spider instructs my uncle to put down his gun. He does, then Spider closes the mausoleum door.

I'm a goner.

The four of us are cramped here in the dark. Uncle Patrick raises his hands in surrender, so the flashlight from his phone beams a hole onto the ceiling. He tells Spider. "Stay calm. No reason for anyone to get hurt."

"I kept my end of the deal. You didn't."

"I'm working on it."

"Too late. I killed that chink."

I ask, "What are you talking about?"

"Shut up." Spider yanks me back. My heart's battering inside.

Uncle Patrick's gaze never leaves Spider. "You don't want to go to prison, Juan."

"Don't call me that." He nods toward me. "She doesn't know, does she?"

"No."

"What if I tell her now?"

"Go ahead."

I'm not sure what they mean. Who'd Spider kill? His arm feels so sweaty I want to crawl out of my skin, but I'm too scared to move. O'Dell hides behind my uncle.

Uncle Patrick asks Spider, "What do you want?"

"Paradise. We ruled those streets 'til *she* killed Diablo." His knife's blade pokes me.

I whimper to myself. The terror rushes back. *Raining. Running. Death.*

My uncle says, "Take me."

"He wants her."

"Who?"

"Eddie Loco."

Uncle P's jaw tightens. "He's in prison."

"Is he?"

Several seconds pass. I try not to think of Eddie Loco, but remember his hungry fingers reaching for my panties.

My uncle says, "You're not taking Copper."

"Looks like I am."

Spider's breath burns hot on my neck. There's no air left in this small mausoleum. I'm not sure I can control these silent screams much longer.

Uncle Patrick's flashlight shuts off, so it's total blackness. I feel my uncle's hand pulling me toward him as Spider yanks me back. I bite that Barrio Brother as hard as I can. He shouts and his knife clatters to the stone floor. O'Dell's screaming.

Pushes and shoves, I'm trapped between it all.

I break free and kick the door open, then spot the outline of O'Dell to the side. I drag him from the brawl, tugging him outside.

I lead us to a giant headstone and we hide behind it. He can't stop sobbing. The fight grows louder.

"It's okay." I wrap my arms around him. Red-and-blue police lights swirl a few sections over, near the Warrior Angel. I think I hear voices, too, so we're going to stay put.

A gunshot cracks inside the mausoleum. I scream my uncle's name and start toward the crypt. O'Dell pulls me back.

"Don't" is all he says.

I fight him, but he doesn't let go. My Diablo scar rages against my cheek. It's another horrible terrible night. Now I'm the one crying all over O'Dell.

The seconds stretch on forever while death drifts over the warm summer breeze. An owl calls out in the distance.

A shadow bursts through the mausoleum's stone door, then I watch Spider skulk off toward Baby Land like the creepy-crawly he is.

My uncle rushes out, all in one piece. I block his path and grab him. "No! You're still in trouble at work. Let the cops do their jobs."

"I've got to catch him."

"I can't lose you, too."

That seems to snap him back to his senses. He wraps me and O'Dell in a giant bear hug, holding us tight. Looks like Eternal Peace won't steal any more of my people this time.

Uncle Patrick rests his chin on my head. "You could never lose me."

CHAPTER 39

At Remington Medical Center, we leave O'Dell sleeping in his hospital room. An ambulance brought him here and we followed. He's got a broken nose, two black eyes, a few cracked ribs and too many stiches in his noggin to count. The doctors say his head wound may affect his memory awhile longer, but he'll be back to his butt-munchy self soon.

Uncle Patrick made the doctors examine us, too. I'm banged up, but okay. The ringing in my ears has lessened. At least I'm not shouting anymore. The police found us at the cemetery, though I'm not sure if they've captured Spider or Chao-Chao yet.

Pixy Stick stops by to say hi and tell us CPS talked to Dusty earlier and he's sound asleep now. My uncle thanks her for taking care of me and they talk a bit. I think she's already planning their wedding. This one I could tolerate. Lydia, too.

I do and don't want to visit One-Leg. Doesn't matter. The head nurse says it's too late 'til my uncle flashes his police badge and goes all Johnny Law on her. She's taking us there now. I'm so proud of him for breaking the rules for me again that I just keep my mouth shut.

Walking down the hallway, I breathe in that unmistakable

smell of disinfectant. People stare at us like we've been to hell and back.

We have.

It still feels strange holding my uncle's hand, like I've got my shoes on the wrong feet, but we're so laced together. That's how it is with family. You're knotted to each other, whether you like it or not.

We pass the giant ivy-covered windows to the hospital's outdoor courtyard. A man walks in through the doors, so I spot the Winged Goddess for a split second. Even with no arms or legs, she's still holding court over all the flowers and plants.

Me and Uncle P talked more about the lady who took him to Eternal Peace. All he remembers is her name was Michele. I tell him about One-Leg on the elevator ride up to the tenth floor. Our lives have changed so much since I ran away from home almost thirty-six hours ago.

Some good.

Some not.

I keep thinking how I failed Tommy Tucker. His pops is a druggie mess now. Sure, Uncle P didn't ever let me check on him back in Paradise, but still . . .

My uncle tugs at my fingers. "We'll get through this. O'Dell will be back to himself soon."

"Mai Wong won't." I'm glad he doesn't give me a pep talk or try to play pretendsies like Mama always did. He just leaves me be.

"You sure you want to see him now?" My uncle asks.

I nod and we go.

One-Leg's in a private room now. Our friend is sitting up, awake, in his hospital gown in bed. He's still pale, but his cheeks have a little more color. We stand on either side of him. I rest my hand on the empty spot of the sheets where One-Leg's metal leg should be.

I apologize to Tommy Tucker in my mind, before ruining his father's life. "You killed that cop."

"What?" One-Leg flinches.

"You murdered Officer Riker the night Mama died."

"No."

"Yep. You saw him attack his wife and Mama in the church parking lot. I don't know if you followed 'em there or what, but the boot prints at the crime scene are yours."

He shakes his head, and I keep nodding. "Your metal leg doesn't leave as heavy a tread mark, and your other boot has a pebble or piece of glass in the sole that gives it a weird print. The priest talked about it."

Uncle Patrick nods since that's what he said earlier in the cop car. He picks up the phone from the hospital nightstand. "Let's prove her wrong, Larry. The nurses can bring your boots here now."

One-Leg's shoulders slump and I struggle to breathe. He stares out the window to the night sky where a bazillion stars twinkle back. "Me and Naomi were just sharing a drink in the dark across the street. If we'd just gone somewhere else. Wrong place, wrong time . . . story of my life." His voice sounds heartbroken.

When he looks at us again, he just shrugs. "That cop never even saw us. He knocked his wife around 'til she left, then he went straight for Corrine." One-Leg's tears turn from a tiny trickle to full-on blubbering. It's like the past four months finally burst from him and it's all gushing out now.

My friend cries some more, then he lets out a slow, ragged breath. "Riker bloodied up your mom bad. He was choking her, and I swear to God he would've killed her if it hadn't been for me."

"I believe you." I squeeze his palm, weeping to myself. I heard how that cop treated Mama in our motel room. Riker was awful, but me and Uncle P both seem to see One-Leg's new life behind bars.

Thanks to me. Uncle Patrick looks wrecked, too.

One-Leg knots the sheet around his fist, not looking at us. "I picked up a brick from that construction site, rushed there, then hit him as hard as I could. Something in me snapped . . . I couldn't stop myself—'til Corrine took the brick away." One-Leg doesn't wipe away his tears.

That explains Mama's blood and prints on the weapon. I ask him, "What about Arlene?"

"Who?"

"Arlene the Coat Stealer. She has angel wings tattooed across her back, just like Mama."

"Don't know her."

"Are you sure she wasn't there?"

"Positive."

My uncle turns to me. "What exactly did she say to you?"

"'I was there when he died.' I thought she meant that cop, but now I'm not sure."

Uncle Patrick turns back to One-Leg. "What happened after you realized Officer Riker was dead?"

"Corrine tossed the brick and hugged me, thanked me for saving her. She wanted to get straight home to Copper."

Silence fills the room. We all know what happened next. My uncle gives One-Leg a tissue from the nightstand, then asks him more cop questions.

Tommy Tucker's dad dabs his face, then blows his nose. "Why didn't I wipe off my prints?" He pulls me closer. "Your mom was already gone. The cops came up with the theory that she did it, so I just let 'em. I didn't think about the trouble this would cause. I'm sorry . . ." His howls fill the tiny room.

It hurts to watch his world fall apart.

Me and my uncle glance at each other. I hate to cause him more pain. I don't want to know the truth, but another life's at stake. I wait 'til One-Leg's cried himself out, then ask him, "What about Naomi?"

His blood pressure rises—I can tell from his beeping machine. One-Leg turns redder, then chokes out a sob. "I should've stuck with booze. I don't even remember doing it. Whatever the Asian Assassins started giving me . . ."

Uncle P says, "What do you remember?"

He picks at the edge of the tape holding down the IV at his wrist. "Me and Naomi had our stories straight and the cops believed us. Everything was fine 'til she got a guilty conscience . . . I remember passing the church when she told me, but . . ." He shrugs and stares outside again.

I say, "Do you think you killed her?"

He nods once. "She was my lady friend. We'd found each other just before Tommy died. He would've loved her. I gave her a ring and everything."

The Ring Pop.

One-Leg shakes his head, staring into the darkness. I remind myself about his PTSD and all his partying. Officer Riker was the heat of the moment. A jury could probably forgive him for protecting Mama, but Naomi ...

My uncle assures him we'll do whatever we can to help him, but he's got to tell us everything. Why he's involved with the Asian Assassins. How Bird's involved. All the secrets he knows about Mama.

One-Leg mumbles something so quiet we don't hear him. Me and my uncle both lean in. "What's that?" I say.

He whispers, "I think I need a lawyer."

CHAPTER 40

Me and Uncle Patrick do everything we can to convince One-Leg we're on his side, but it's no use. He gets so agitated that he buzzes the nurses to kick us out. We're standing near his closed door in the hallway. Even at this late hour, the hospital stays busy.

My uncle says, "I have to call my captain."

"I know."

He tilts my chin up to meet his gaze. "This isn't your fault."

"None of this would've happened if I'd just stayed home like you said."

"We'll do everything we can to help him."

I nod, almost afraid to touch Tommy's knife in my pocket. Uncle P squeezes my shoulder. He doesn't let go and I realize what he's doing. "I'm not going to run away this time. Promise."

"Pinkie promise?"

That makes me smile the teensiest bit as we lock fingers together. I wonder if he feels as beat-up by life as me. How long before I go completely crazy? My uncle faces me while stepping down the hall with his phone. He passes the janitor mopping, then stops by the stairwell door. Probably to block the exit.

I'm so tired of running, and I can't leave Tommy Tucker's pops again. I didn't do one thing to bring back Mama but made everything so much worse. One-Leg's life is ruined now, and poor Naomi might still be alive if I hadn't butted in. Maybe he'll change his mind about us after the cops show.

I can't hear Uncle Patrick's conversation, but he looks wrecked, too. Mama's brother isn't so bad.

I mean, he is. What a stuffed shirt, but he broke the law for me. I'm so glad that Michele lady brought him—

The exit door opens, then someone yanks my uncle into the stairwell. I just see an arm, then thin air.

No one else seems to notice. The staff's all hard at work. My chest squeezes and I'm frozen a few secs, then I force myself down to the nurses' station.

Racing by, I tell the older man behind the counter, "Call 9-1-1. Someone just pulled my uncle down those steps. He's Sergeant Patrick Noblitt."

"Stay here, kid." The guy chases after me.

I've got enough of a head start that I grab the mop from the bucket, rush into the stairwell, then jam it through the door handle behind me. He's too old to help, so I need to keep him safe. His worried face appears in the window as he bangs on the door.

His shouts follow me down the steps. I take Uncle Patrick's phone off the ground, then limp on. Blood speckles the concrete.

That was the tenth floor. I hear shuffling feet and muffled voices a few flights below. The blinders fall off and I feel how much my uncle means to me. He's been my rock when I've been nothing but a pain. How'd Spider figure out we came to the hospital? He must've followed us from the cemetery. I think that was him.

I hear a woman's startled scream downstairs, then Uncle P shouts, "Get back!"

I'm guessing she stepped into the stairway. Wrong place. Wrong time.

Hurrying, I see the trail of blood grows. I'm on the fifth floor now. My fingers tingle and my legs go numb, but I limp on as quietly as possible.

I'm getting closer. I don't hear talking. Is Uncle P all right? I worry he's bleeding worse. Maybe it's the bad guy. I might hurl any second. I say a prayer. It's more of a command. *You BETTER keep Uncle Patrick safe and alive. He's all I've got.*

Each step hurts. I expect a full-blown whack attack any second, but somehow I keep going. I catch voices several floors above me. Sounds like a normal conversation. I don't want anyone else hurt, so I stay quiet.

Not much farther. I'm so out of breath, but I hobble on. A door slams shut below, then . . .

Silence.

Is Uncle Patrick outside now? Did they go into the lobby? Is he safe?

All I hear is the pounding of my own heart. Fear chills me so much I can hardly breathe, though I tell myself to move faster. It's taking too long, but I finally make it to the bottom of the stairwell. I push through the exit—

I smash into the entrance instead. It gives just a little, but the attacker must've jimmied it like I did upstairs. I race to the main floor, wasting precious time. Ivy covers the giant windows. I can't see into the courtyard. It's the middle of the night, but there's still folks here, so I keep my mouth shut. I've ruined enough lives.

As I burst onto the patio, three screaming women rush by and one of 'em grabs me. "Don't! He's got a hostage!"

"Get help. I'll wait here," I say, then leave as soon as they're in the lobby.

It's a cloudless night. White lights twinkle above the Winged Goddess in the center of the courtyard. Ivy-covered walls make this the perfect torture chamber.

Uncle Patrick's got blood spilling from his side as someone drags him behind the angel statue.

The attacker meets my gaze.

CHAPTER 41

It's Chao-Chao.

The boy with the kind eyes who kissed me last night.

He shoves my uncle to the ground. Patrick groans as the Asian Assassin leaps onto the statue's bench, then yanks down several strands of lights.

The entire patio falls so dark I can't see for several seconds. I hear his shoes slap across the bricks. The doors rattle. What's he doing?

That horrible terrible night rises up inside. I drop to my knees and struggle to breathe. I'm both freezing and burning hot. My mind screams I'm going to die. Panic coils around me tighter. I can't even make out the Winged Goddess, but still beg her.

Help me.

Nothing happens.

I expect Chao-Chao to attack me, but instead I hear the crack of a gun across the way. Uncle P shrieks.

Is he dead? My thoughts repeat *...I'mokay ...I'mokay ...I'mokay.*

I'm so not all right but keep saying it 'til I feel myself again. Shaky and scared. My uncle moans in pain through the darkness.

He's alive!

Pushing myself to stand up, I move woozy across the patio.

Something slides over the bricks, then Chao-Chao cusses and fumbles around.

The gun? I hear pounding at both courtyard doors. That's it. He blocked off the other door. I grope around the statue, feeling the flowers and other greenery. I grab a loose stake along the garden's edge.

Uncle Patrick groans louder.

Squinting, I spot Chao-Chao's shadow moving as he yells, "Got it."

Does he mean the gun?

I sneak across the walkway, creeping up behind the Asian Assassin. With all my hate, I jab the pointy stake at the Asian Assassin, but just catch the back of his arm. The metal stake clatters against the bricks.

His scream splits the air as he folds onto all fours like the dog that he is.

I'm paralyzed as Chao-Chao rises and stands above me. His pearly smile sparkles in the moonlight. He grabs me and whispers softer than a kiss, "Time to die, Ghost Girl."

CHAPTER 42

The patio lights flicker above us. Chao-Chao grips me tighter. The strands go on and off like a strobe light. I spot Uncle Patrick bleeding on the ground on the other side of the headless angel. I worry he's fading fast.

The lights go on, off.

On. Off.

Chao-Chao looks so calm gripping me by the neck. I gag, leaning back. He clutches tighter. I hear Uncle Patrick groan.

It's dark, then light.

On. Off.

Loud thuds bang from the outside doors. Someone's in the stairwell. Chao-Chao laughs.

Raining. Running. Death.

Darkness closes in 'til a banging noise high above the courtyard makes me glance up. Dusty knocks at his hospital window, so many feet higher. He's shouting, then disappears into his room.

I cough and sputter. The lights continue to flash as my struggle rages on. Chao-Chao doesn't let go of me. Inching backward, I trip over one of the stakes at the foot of the statue and we tumble into the garden together.

He loses his hold. I scramble up from the ivy, then sprawl

against the Winged Goddess, feeling how crumbly she is beneath me. Chao-Chao dives at me, tearing my T-shirt. I scream. He backhands me. I crash against one of her wings.

His hand clamps over my mouth, then he snorts an angry laugh. "They said I was *weak*."

I holler, then bite him. He slaps me. I'm pressed against the statue. He chokes me again. Harder.

The lights flash on. Off.

On. Off.

I feel around for something, anything, desperate to stop this monster. A clump of statue breaks off—a stone's worth. I grab it and I smash it against his head. Chao-Chao crumbles facedown into the garden, beneath the glimmering lights.

They stay on.

He doesn't move. A giant puddle of red spreads from his forehead onto the ivy.

That makes me cry worse. Shaking, I nudge my sneaker against him.

He's dead.

CHAPTER 43

I can't stop trembling as I rush around to the other side of the Winged Goddess to Uncle Patrick. Chao-Chao's pistol lies nearby on the ground, so I grab it and kneel beside the only family I've got left.

My uncle groans. Blood oozes from his stomach and shoulder. Maybe a bullet grazed him?

I'm not sure. I hold his hand, talking through my tears. "You're *going* to be all right. You hear me?"

He's glassy-eyed and doesn't answer.

Police burst through the courtyard door and point their guns at me. I raise my hands in surrender, nodding toward Chao-Chao's body, and the cops surround him. EMS also whisks onto the patio, then heads straight here. I don't let go of Uncle P 'til they make me.

Something bangs above, so I look up. Dusty's jumping up and down from his room, pumping his fists in the air. I wipe a tear and wave back.

I move out of the way and collapse onto the brick walkway, far from Chao-Chao, while some lady cop talks to me. I watch the EMS team work on my uncle, and I answer the cops' questions while the courtyard whirls around like a dream. The lights aren't flashing anymore.

They stay on like normal, though I'm not sure how since several strands were torn down. The patio sparkles over the Winged Goddess and the destruction we just survived.

When my uncle's lying on the gurney, I rush to him and wrap my palm around his. My tears splat onto his shirt. I swallow hard. "You will *not* die. I won't let you."

He gives me a weak smile.

"They said you have to have surgery. I'll be there when you get out."

After EMS checks me out, I watch the cops break out the sunny-yellow CAUTION tape for another crime scene. They cover Chao-Chao's body.

They said I was weak, he told me.

The lady cop stays with me, and we sit on the ground with our backs to him. I'm trying not to think about what just happened. It was self-defense. I had no choice.

Right?

I might even say a prayer. A real prayer. Thanking whoever is up there for keeping Uncle Patrick alive and asking for a picture-perfect surgery. Plus, I need his boss to get unmad and let him be a detective again. O'Dell needs to go back to normal, too.

Whatever that is. I'm not sure anyone above heard me, but I do feel a little better.

Father Where's Waldo strolls into the courtyard. Even in his priest clothes, he looks almost movie-starrish beneath these magical lights.

"What are you doing here?" I ask him.

"A parishioner had an emergency here, so I heard what happened. May I join you?"

The cop leaves us, and he sits beside me on the walkway. We stare at the ivy on the windows for the longest time. When I can talk, I explain about O'Dell's amnesia and my uncle's wounds.

"I will pray for them both," he says.

It's harder to talk about One-Leg killing both Officer Riker and Naomi Rodriguez. I don't even mention breaking my promise to the boy who stole my heart. Some words are too painful to say out loud.

The priest tells me, "I know you're relieved about your mother's innocence but heartbroken over everybody else. I'm so sorry."

His eyes say he means it. He runs his hand through his silver hair, then sighs. "Life's just hard sometimes."

I nod, staring at my orange sneakers. I don't mention Mai Wong's death either since I still can't believe it. My beautiful broken friend.

Father Where's Waldo glances back to the Winged Goddess behind us. Watching the statue, I feel the wind swishing all around her dress and those wings spread wide. This chick has seen battle. She's pure energy and a total badass. Enough to inspire tattoos.

The priest says, "Isn't she lovely?"

"Who broke off her arms and head?"

"She was created that way."

"Why?"

"I'm not sure, but it just adds to her power."

"What's her name?"

"I don't think that she has one, though I remember the sculptor's name is Michele something."

"Michele?"

"Yes. Why?"

"I've met a few of those lately."

'Chele the photographer.

Tiny China in her VW Bug was Mechele.

That Michele lady who brought Uncle P to the cemetery.

They all ripple through me now. I might even feel Mama and Mai Wong, too, though I'm not sure. I just try to breathe through it all.

The priest says, "You should be proud of yourself. Nobody believed in your mom's innocence but you."

"I don't feel too proud."

"Good things can come from bad circumstances." He pulls out his green sobriety chip. Three months. "We all make mistakes. I need people to support me on my journey. You do, too."

I nod, feeling the tears burn behind my eyes. I whisper, "People leave."

"Yes, but others stay. You're not alone, Copper. You've got your uncle, you've got friends."

"I don't have friends."

"Yes, you do, and that includes me. Stop pushing people away."

Wiping my damp cheek, I say, "What if I don't want to be your friend?"

"I think you do."

He watches me so close that I look away first, then mumble, "Well, my uncle still doesn't like you."

"Maybe he will in time. Whatever differences we had back in high school, we both want what's best for you now. Your mother was very special to me. It's the least I can do for her."

I wish this priest was my real father instead of my jailbird daddy. Standing, I study the courtyard. It's destroyed. A sliver of moon shines above the Winged Goddess. "I better get to Uncle Patrick."

"May I keep you company?"

"Sure. Will you tell me more about Mama?"

"She's one of my favorite subjects."

CHAPTER 44

One week later . . .

I hold white tulips as me and Uncle Patrick walk through Eternal Peace. It's another triple-digit day, so sweat trickles down my back. July Fourth is coming up soon, so tiny US flags stick up from the grass in front of all the graves.

Somebodies are big on being patriotic.

We're headed to the NOBLITT family plot. My real last name is Noblitt, but I like Daniels better, so I'm keeping it. Uncle P's cool with it now that he understands this is who I am.

It's who Mama made me.

NOBLITT

PATRICK SAMANTHA CORRINE

I pass by my grandparents, then lay the flowers beneath Mama's name. That same mad, sad and glad collide inside me again, and I just have to let 'em be.

I can't force it. I tell my uncle, "I'm okay visiting her today, but I might not be next time."

"That's reasonable."

"That's what Dr. Vasquez said." I sigh.

"You have every right to be angry with your mother, but if

you stay stuck there too long, you only end up hurting yourself. Trust me." He gives me a side hug, holding me close, and I let him.

That's how love works. It takes practice.

He says, "I'm going to make a call."

That's code for giving me space. Uncle Patrick wanders to a shady tree nearby. I watch him scanning the grounds. I wonder how often he, too, remembers that horrible terrible night. All those hungry eyes watching us. Others trying to kill us.

My uncle says he didn't see me leave the house with 'Chele the photographer. That I just ran away. He thinks Dusty gave me a concussion at school and I imagined the rest, but I know what I know. That truth rolls through me like the California ocean.

I finished summer school last week. Principal Simpson told me, "You've shown remarkable improvement in your citizenship and grades, Miss Daniels. You may advance to sixth grade."

That's mumbo-jumbo for *I rock snot*.

I finished reading *A Little Princess* and returned the book to the school library. The orphan girl got her forever family and turned out to be super rich. I'm still waiting on that second part.

CPS moved Dusty to a temporary group home while they find him the right foster family. He probably won't be at my school next year, but I'll see him this weekend at Walter's birthday party. Maybe I'll get more than just one kind-of-not-really friend.

I thanked Dusty for calling the cops at the hospital. He's taking full credit even though others called 911, too. He just said, "You owe me, Scab Face."

O'Dell's memory is all the way back, so that's good and bad since now he's heartbroken over Mai Wong. She never got to wear his silver necklace. I'm glad he didn't see her hanging in my phone booth and wish I could erase it myself.

Uncle P said they found no foul play with Mai. I keep rewinding our final conversations. Searching for clues. I'm just adding her to the long list of things to talk about with Dr. Vasquez.

My uncle also found a new lead on Salt and Pepper, so he's following up there. I need my boys to be all right. I hope Paradise didn't swallow 'em up whole.

Or worse.

I hope Walter the mouse is okay and doesn't starve. I don't want to, but sometimes I still taste Chao-Chao's kisses on my lips. The police are looking into the babies the Asian Assassins were selling. I glance toward Baby Land and try to forget what I keep remembering.

I focus back on Mama. Her newspaper headline flashes through me again:

PROSTITUTE ACCUSED OF KILLING COP

The police didn't find her fur jacket at the Warrior Angel, but it's out there . . .

I feel it.

Holding Tommy's pocketknife, I study Mama's name carved into stone:

Corrine Daniels

A Loving Mother

October 17, 1983–February 15, 2010

Sadness blooms inside me one more time, like the petals of these tulips. I'm not sure I'll ever get used to this. Grief is a heavy brick that can crush you without someone ever raising a finger.

"I knew you didn't kill that cop," I tell Mama. I don't bring up all the other bad stuff I'm still trying to untangle about her. I stood right here after she died and left my two lucky pennies on her headstone for good luck, then told her I forgive her.

Now I say something even bigger: "I forgive me."

A tear trickles down my cheek and I leave it. "I tried so hard to save you and Tommy but couldn't. Now One-Leg and Mai Wong . . ." My voice catches, and I forget to breathe for a few seconds. I think I'm about to have another whack attack, but I'm able to trick my body into believing I'm okay.

This time.

It's way harder to convince someone else they're okay. Speaking of, One-Leg's in jail waiting for his trial. He refuses to see or talk to me and Uncle Patrick. I'm glad Mama's not a cop-killer but wonder if all this was worth it.

I can't undo what's been done, and bubble gum or cherry Slurpees won't make any of this better.

"I'll see you around," I tell Mama, and tuck Tommy's knife back into my pocket.

Across the way, a white Lexus passes by and Lisa Vanderhausen waves to me, so I wave back. She's visiting her family's mausoleum. Trying to forgive her mom, too. Maybe Father Where's Waldo is right. I'm not alone. I do have friends.

I wonder if there are Fourth of July flags in front of Tommy's foot marker back in the Nobody Section.

I won't find out today and that's all right.

One problem at a time.

We got that Chinese baby dug up and buried back in Chinatown where he belongs. Closer to his people. Now he can truly rest in peace.

Uncle Patrick notices me walking back to the truck and heads that way, too. My nose still hurts from Chao-Chao. I'm not sure if the boy with the kind eyes ever really liked me for real.

I'll never know.

I've still got a mile's worth of Mama questions that may never get answered. My uncle's still on leave without pay for insubordination. He says not to worry about it, but I can count the bills stacked up on the kitchen counter. Uncle P won't use the cash that strangers send us 'cause he says that's for my future. Princess the Evil Cat doesn't care about any of this. She just whines to whoever will listen.

My uncle opens the car door for me, and I slide onto the seat. His umbrella's still there. "Let's go to the Warrior Angel."

"Seriously?"

"Yep."

On the drive over, my uncle tells me about the chocolate chip cookies him and Mama used to bake with their mom. I like listening. Him and Father Where's Waldo both remind me that Mama wasn't all bad. She called me her Copper Penny. She smoothed over my crazy curls and kissed me good night. She even saved $881.01 to move us to California.

We pull up to the Warrior Angel. The statue stands there with his stone staff in one hand and the other stretched out toward heaven. That used to calm me, but I'm not sure what to feel anymore.

I learned at the downtown library that Michele is the girl version of the name Michael. Chief Angel of the Lord.

Conqueror of Satan.

Straight-up badass.

I wonder if the Warrior Angel and the Winged Goddess have ever met. Maybe they're even boyfriend and girlfriend. That makes me reach into my pocket for Tommy Tucker's knife.

Walking to the statue, I stare at the bullet hole in the base, then take my uncle's hand. He grins a small smile.

That bullet hole shows where he killed Miz Jesus, just as she stabbed Tommy.

That same bullet hole cut my rope ties and saved me from Chao-Chao.

Good and bad.

Like flipsides of the same coin.

So many nights I lay here in my sleeping bag and listened to the cicadas sing, felt the snow beneath me, watched the first lilac blossom grow beside Miz Elsie's two praying hands, or saw the naked trees around us each fall.

All while the Warrior Angel watched over me sleeping.

A cemetery home for a Ghost Girl.

My hand slides along the ivy vines carved into the stone

statue. It's sort of nice to be home again. Not as bad as I expected. I'm taller than when I stood here that horrible terrible night. It's not all fear and sadness.

My uncle smiles and listens to me tell a funny story about Mama for a change, then he talks about how the two of 'em played Hide-and-Seek here as kids while their dad, the head groundskeeper, worked. I feel 'em all. We're hanging out together, like a regular family.

I'm not sure why I wanted to come back today. I just did. Uncle Patrick doesn't rush me like Mama would have, either. He leaves me be.

He understands the bones and lies between us.

THE END

Now that you've finished reading *Bones and Lies Between Us*, will you please consider
writing an honest review on Amazon, Goodreads or the online sales sit of your choice? Reviews are the best way for readers to discover great new books. Many thanks.

Also, watch as Copper Daniels' journey continues in her third and final book, *Beyond the Empty Grave*. Expect books from Copper's other friends, too: Tommy 'Turdmouth' Tucker, Eugene 'Butt Munch' O'Dell and more.

Get Exclusive Copper Daniels' Material

Getting to know my readers is the best side benefit of being a writer! Join my email newsletter for a free Copper Daniels' short story, *The Moon Rises at Dawn.* You'll also receive updates on new books, exclusive deals for my readers, and connect with me personally. Don't worry, I only reach out about once a month.

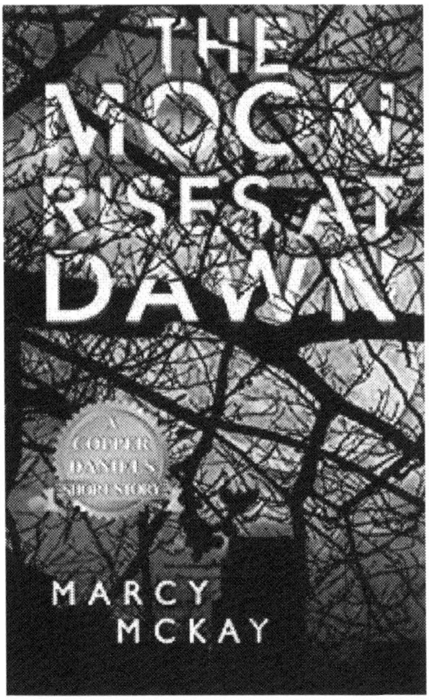

"Me and Mama wake beneath the Warrior Angel statue at the cemetery to all the screaming and craziness. A judge's body is missing from his grave. They can't have the funeral. The cops blame Mama for snatching it. I watch 'em haul her off to jail.

What about me?! I better find that body fast ...

Before I die alone on the streets."

Readers of *Room* and *The Lovely Bones* will enjoy Marcy McKay.

You can get your free short story by signing up at marcymckay.com.

Also by Marcy McKay

COPPER DANIELS SERIES

Pennies from BurgerHeaven (Book #1)

◆One Homeless Girl. Her Missing Mama. Buried Secrets.◆

"Me and Mama sleep beneath the Warrior Angel statue. It's our cemetery home ... 'til the day I wake up and she's gone.

GONE?! Now, I'm seriously freaked out and I've got to find her. But, how? Where? Has anyone seen her? She always says, *don't trust nobody but yourself.*

Wish I would've listened."

Bones and Lies Between Us (Book #2)

Four months after *Pennies from Burger Heaven* ends …

"I have a whole new life now, but it's just a different kind of bad, and it's about to get a lot worse. More secrets … more lies, all dragging me back to Paradise — the meanest, nastiest part of the city.

I don't care what the cops say, Mama didn't do it. She didn't. I'm running away to find the *real* killer.

Or, die trying."

Stars Among the Dead (Novella Prequel)

◆If I Just Could've Saved Mama from Herself.◆

"Living on the streets is hard enough, so when Mama drags me out in the middle of the night, I know we're in trouble. BIG trouble. Her so-called *secret mission* to help a "friend" is a crap-sandwich if I ever saw one and I *almost* talk Mama into going home …

Then we find that first dead body."

The Moon Rises at Dawn (Short Story Prequel)

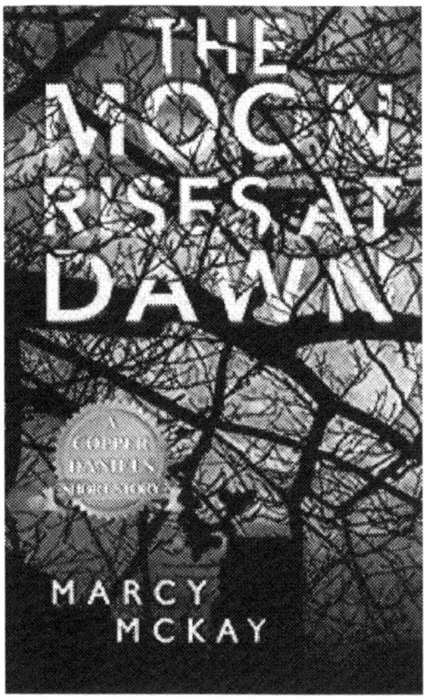

◆I Watch 'em Haul Her to Jail...◆

"Me and Mama wake beneath the Warrior Angel statue at the cemetery to all the screaming and craziness. A judge's body is missing from his grave. They can't have the funeral. The cops blame Mama for snatching it. I watch 'em haul her off to jail.

What about me?! I better find that body fast ...

Before I die alone on the streets."

BOX SET

Murder, They Wrote

Four mysteries packed full of tension, suspense, and unforgettable characters, PLUS a free bonus mystery, from the best-selling, award-winning authors of SkipJack Publishing.

Pennies from Burger Heaven Chapter 1

Me and Mama live here at the cemetery, by the Warrior Angel statue. It's our home. He always stands high on those four pedestals, with his dark wings stretched wide. That stone sword stays in his left hand, while he keeps his right out toward Burger Heaven. Asking God for help.

Who knew angels were beggars like me?

"Feeling better, Mama?" I say, then see her empty sleeping bag.

The dark green just stares back.

"Mama?" I yawn and look around to nothing but quiet graves.

She's probably gone to the bathroom. I start to lie back down 'til last night socks me in the gut. All her tears, all her crazy talk, how she got so sick. I eyeball the statue, but if he knows where she is, he's not saying.

I better go find her myself. She needed me then and she'll need me now. Especially if she's still pukey.

Climbing out of my sleeping bag, my legs feel stiff from their frosty sleep. I keep my bright blue coat zipped with the hoodie up, then rub my gloves together to get warm. My breath snakes out and my toes poke all wiggly-like through the holes in my sneakers. I can't walk in a straight line here like I do down most streets. I zigzag through all the headstones, bushes and trees. Patches of snow from last week's storm surround graves tucked into pockets of shade. Dew sparkles like diamonds on grass that's actually green on this side of the cemetery.

Everything shines brighter for the Somebodies of the world.

As I pass a turned-over vase of red roses, I set it upright. The droopy petals still smell flowery. I call out to Mama.

The birds chirp at me overhead.

Her screams from last night clatter through me again. She dropped to her knees and sobbed against my legs, "*I've got to chaaaaaaaaaaaaange.*"

I move a little faster. You can't miss Mama. She's supermodel thin and tall, with leafy-green eyes and tiny flecks of gold in 'em. Maybe she's not like a real supermodel, but she's definitely taller than me and every bit as bone skinny. She wears her jet-black hair straight down and parted in the middle. She thinks she looks like Cher. I saw the singer once on TV and didn't think so, but wasn't dumb enough to say it out loud, thank you very little. Mama doesn't have movie-star teeth, either, though she does wear a silver jacket made of real rabbit fur like they do in Hollywood. Well, it's more dingy than silver now, but I still want one just like it when I grow up.

If it was summertime, you'd see Mama's blue angel wings tattooed across her shoulders and back. She did that after I was born, inked in to protect us both. It fits her, too. She always looks ready to fly away.

The breeze swishes through the trees as I call out for her again.

Mama better get home soon 'cause O'Dell will show up for work any second, then there'll be hell to pay. We may live in the Historic Section of the cemetery, but they won't let us spend eternity here when we keel over. There'll be no flashy statues or real flowers. We'll be buried back in the Nobody Section. That used to be the only spot they allowed the Blacks, the Mexicans, the Chinamen and other No Names, too.

I pass David Marshall's grave where we took care of our morning business yesterday. His headstone is shaped like an actual tree stump. Broken trunks are supposed to be a sign for death, a life cut short, like his buried body isn't clue enough.

My gut twists. Maybe she went to the pond to feed the ducks, even though we always do that together. I'll check, but first I squat behind this elm tree. We try to switch bathrooms each time to be nice. They may be stiffers, but who wants to get peed on every day?

After I'm done, I follow a well-worn path. The big cloud above looks like someone is laughing with their mouth open wide. I can do that. I make Mama giggle so hard water squirts straight from her nose. It's funny-gross and gross-funny. You know something's hilarious when you make 'em rock snot.

We're way more than mother and daughter. We're business partners and best friends. Mama says there are over fifty thousand bodies here at Eternal Peace. When I was little she said that meant there were over fifty thousand stories, each filled with glad, mad and sad. People who made it well past their hundredth birthdays. Husbands who leave gifts on their wives' graves, while their girlfriends wait in the car. The worst are parents visiting their little ones at Baby Land. You can hear 'em crying in the wind at night. Their sadness makes you want to disapp—

That thought stops me. My world turns topsy-turvy and I have to steady myself against a grave. Scared torches my belly. Why didn't I think of it before?

The *Disappeareds.*

Rumor has it that there's a Street Killer on the loose in Paradise, murdering the Nobodies of the world. Folks will be there one second, then poof! They're gone.

Disappeared.

But, that's happening miles away from Eternal Peace. We're safe here.

Right?

"Mama!" I screech.

Ripping my lucky penny from my pocket, I pull my gloves off to rub Mr. Lincoln's beard extra hard, commanding him to find her quick. I rush through the graves. Next, we stopped at Ronald Freedmont's. My gaze darts around for her. The black iron fence loops all the way around the grounds like little, pointy soldiers. "Eternal Peace" is written in gold across the twin gates that stay locked after dark to keep the goodness in and the badness out.

What if it stopped working last night?

Biting my lip, I race faster. Salty tears try to climb up my throat, but I shove 'em down. They do me no good and I need to stay focused. Plus, Mama hates wusses. She wasn't at the pond and she's not at Ronald Freedmont's now. I lean against his too-tall grave and try to ignore the headache knocking at my brain. Mama says Ronnie here must've thought a lot of himself 'cause his name's plastered across the marble in huge, scrawly letters. A mint bush sprouts beside him. We come here every day to eat the leaves to clean our teeth. His plant grows and grows, like he waters himself with regret. That sounds like something stuck in your teeth, but it means sad, wishing you'd done different. I know all about that.

Last night, most of all. My mind whirls. Maybe she's lost, or kidnapped, or dea—

No. The Street Killer didn't get her. She's not a *Disappeared*. She's too smart for that. I'll find her any minute.

I cram the mint in my mouth, then head on, hollering her name 'til my throat croaks. The sun has started rising, a small orange flame against the sleepy blue sky. It looks more perfect than a picture. Today acts like another normal day. I sure hope so, but sprint harder, just in case.

Something jumps in front of me. I scream and stumble back, but catch myself in time. A jackrabbit hops by, springing through tiny spaces between the graves. I double over to rest and calm myself down. We've got our habits. We've got our routines. O'Dell and the other lazies are about to show up to not work all day. We're usually long gone by now and we always leave together.

What if she left without me?

Each step seems to chant *Ma-ma, Ma-ma, Ma-ma.* I should've

waited to fall asleep after her. I should've checked on her throughout the night. I should've never slept at all.

What'd she say through all her screaming and crying?

Oh yeah, she was bad-mouthing someone. "*Asshole, thinks he can trick me ... but ... I'll show him.*"

Who'd she mean? How'd he trick her? Did *showing him*get her into trouble? I trot up to a ginormous stone building. It's the Main Mausoleum at Eternal Peace and the biggest place on the grounds.

It looks like a fancy church, but a mausoleum is a cemetery house to bury Somebodies. Folks who want to stay stuck-up, even in the afterlife. We sneak inside sometimes to sleep when it's extra cold outside. I wanted to come here last night, but thought Mama was in no shape to move.

Guess I was wrong. She moved herself, all right. But where?

Creeping behind the bushes, I reach up to the window.

Locked. It won't budge. I can't believe O'Dell did his job for a change.

Yanking back my hoodie, my crazy curls spring out every which way as I zoom on from the Historic Section. I could punch O'Dell. He's such a Butt Munch. He really wants us gone. The wind moans, like it's aching for me.

The Nobody Section almost looks like nothing's back here 'til you're almost on top of it. Brown grass, tons of weeds, and most graves are just foot markers—bricks buried straight in the ground. O'Dell and his bunch never work on this side of the cemetery. Folks used to call this the Colored Section.

Mama said years ago there was this big sickness called the influenza. It was a flu that killed folks faster than the groundskeepers could dig, so they started dumping the bodies together into huge piles like trash. If the workmen then were half as worthless as O'Dell, that's not too much of a shocker.

This is our doorway in-and-out to the rest of the world. I can see from far away Mama wasn't here, but can't stop myself from checking since we passed by together last night. I walk over to my very favorite grave in all of Eternal Peace. This brick buried here on the end:

UNKNOWN NEGRO

Did they really not know his name, or did they just not care?

Anyway, he's king of the Nobodies. He's one of us.

"Where is she?" I ask him.

He's as silent as the Warrior Angel.

Maybe she's already home. Maybe we just made opposite loops and missed each other. Maybe she's there right now.

Hope fuels me as I take a different route back to check new places. Mama smells like cinnamon gum, cigarettes and sweet sweat from working so hard for us. Catch a whiff of her and you'll know a true-blue, deep-in-my-heart, looney-tunes kind of love.

All I want to do is breathe her in now and feel her hands smooth out the kinks in my hair again, while she tells me about California. We're moving there soon to start a new life. LA has palm trees and the sun shines every day of the year. We'll never be cold again.

Ever.

An invisible fist rams my gut each time she doesn't answer my calls.

Back in the Historic Section, I stop near the chapel to catch my breath. The red-bricked building has a black cross on top. They hold smaller funerals there, or when folks don't have their own church home. Naked rose bushes surround it; those thorns look ready to tear me apart. It's the one place I've never been here at the cemetery and don't want to go, but since I've had zero luck everywhere else I should check.

As I tiptoe to the porch, my hands shake like I need a fix, though I'd never do drugs 'cause it eats you from the inside out. Even worse, it gobbles up the people around you, too. I'm sweating all over, even though I see the groundskeepers and funeral people go in and out of here all the time.

I pause outside the door. Mama will spank me for sure about this, but I tug on the wooden handles anyway.

Locked.

I'm equal sad and glad 'cause I didn't want to go in there, but Mama's still missing. I should've known she wouldn't be in the chapel and race away.

I know I'm closer to home when I catch a whiff of her hurl from last night near the Vanderhausen Mausoleum. The Main Mausoleum wasn't good enough for 'em, so they built their own cemetery house. They're the snobbiest snobs. My eyes burn from the stench. I cover my mouth and keep going, wishing the wind would change direction.

The Warrior Angel stands stone still as usual. Our sleeping bags haven't budged a bit. My heart feels lost in my own body, like it doesn't know what to do without Mama. I flop in front of the statue and bury my face in my gloves. This can't be happening.

But, it is.

I make myself take three extra-slow breaths. All the folks who've gone missing were in Paradise, and that's over an hour's walk away. Besides, I still don't know for sure who's missing. That one lady was gone a while, but showed up after a bender. Everyone else are just rumors.

So far.

I sure don't want to break the rules and go out alone, but Mama sort of gave me no choice. We went straight to the Burger Heaven from here yesterday, so I guess I'll try there first. As long as I don't have to go to Paradise. It's hell on a good day, but there's no good days.

I don't have a stone sword like the Warrior Angel and I sure don't need God, but Mr. Lincoln's mojo better come back fast. I roll up our sleeping bags, then tuck 'em back in their spots—inside the lilac bush beside Miz Elsie. Her grave is shaped like two praying hands. I grab the cardboard sign Mama keeps remaking for us:

NEED MONEY FOR FOOD

GOD BLESS

She adds that last part out loud as people pass by 'cause that pulls at their heart strings, then that pulls at their purse strings. You've got to do what you've got to do.

I fold the sign and stuff it into the front of my coat. It's like my belly reads it 'cause it growls, extra long and loud.

"Shut up," I say, but it doesn't listen. Some of my body parts have minds of their own.

Stretching up to the Warrior Angel, I pat his feet goodbye and maybe for luck since Mr. Lincoln's broken. My fingers glide over the grapes and vines chiseled around his pedestal.

Even now, he doesn't give me a second look. I get that pretty much everywhere we go. My legs shake, still not sure about disobeying Mama, but a family of one isn't much of a family. The sun stretches more color across the sky now, kicking the morning in the butt with pinks, purples and oranges. Mama loves days like this. I hate that we're not watching it together.

Dang. O'Dell's tires squeal against the pavement up ahead and his truck's hauling this way. Here comes one of his drive-by ass chewings. He's just fifteen, but works full time and hassles us double time. He usually drives a white Eternal Peace pickup, but that's his truck since he's just getting to work. It's a total piece of crap and about the same color.

I stop in my tracks, remembering what O'Dell told Mama yesterday. "You two better leave today for good ... or else."

Beyond the Empty Grave (Copper Daniels Book #3)

My life was getting a little less crappy when a body that should be buried … isn't. Someone who's supposed to be dead … is alive.

That leads me on a dangerous trail of more secrets and lies … all tied back to my mysterious family. I'm not sure where this heartache will end, but my biggest worry beyond the empty grave is …

Will I live long enough to find out?

Look for *Beyond the Empty Grave* in 2020.

About the Author

Marcy McKay has survived both a house fire and raising two teenagers, though she's not sure which was worse. She's a life coach, as well as an award-winning author. Her debut novel, *Pennies from Burger Heaven* has 260+ Amazon reviews, is a 2016 Shelf Unbound Winner, as well as a 2016 USA Best Book Awards finalist for General Fiction. Marcy and her husband live on the rim of Palo Duro Canyon with a neurotic pug, while their grown kids are off making this world a better place.

Connect with her at marcymckay.com.

Acknowledgements

I've been both shocked and humbled at the incredible response to Copper Daniels. She's 100% pure fiction, but still my hero. It took a lot of blood, sweat and tears to bring you *Bones and Lies Between Us*. After *Pennies from Burger Heaven* was published in 2015, I was already struggling with the sequel (Second Book Syndrome is *real*, people). Then, my family had a house fire in 2017 and we lost our home. That entire experience changed me in every way from where I live to who I am as person and made me deal with some issues I didn't even realize were problems. It's also a perfect example of how the worst thing you thought could ever happen turned out to be the best gift ever. Yay for happy endings!

First and foremost, I want to thank my weekly critique group — Jennifer Archer, Linda Castillo, Anita Howard and April Redmon. From the moment I told you about my idea of a little homeless girl waking up alone in the cemetery, you've been my champions. I appreciate your belief in me when I've struggled to believe in myself. You make the writing process so much more fun!

Thank you also to SkipJack Publishing for giving my books a home. I admire my fellow authors and appreciate you including me into the fold: Pamela Fagan Hutchins, Ken Oder, and R.L. Nolen. SkipJack's assistant, Bobbye Marrs, deserves a crown for always taking care of everything for me with a smile.

To Mom, Greg and Molly. You always wondered how I could

spend so many happy hours alone in my bedroom growing up — I was in there making up *stories* y'all! Now, I'm writing them down. To my father, the late Roy Mason, who taught me the only difference between fact and fiction is what you heap on it.

To my family — Mark, Mason and Luke. You three make this world so much bigger and brighter for me. You are the reason I try to be a better person and pay it forward. I love each of you endlessly.

To the McKays + everyone else in my inner circle — thank you for standing beside me during life's ups and downs. I'm indebted to you for showing me that home isn't the roof over your head. Home is where the heart is.

I'm saving the best for last — to all my readers. There simply are no words to convey how much you mean to me. I'm honored at your willingness to step inside my head and join me on these journeys. I'm forever grateful. Thank you.

Discussion Questions

As you talk about *Bones and Lies Between Us*, please remember there are over 2.5 million homeless children in the U.S. today. That's one in every 30 children ...

1. Do you think Copper's anger at her mother is justified? Why or why not?

2. Why does Copper try to convince herself that her uncle is abusive?

3. What do you think Copper's whack attacks mean for her emotional health? Why does she have such a strong need for control?

4. What do you believe Tommy Tucker's pocketknife represents for Copper?

5. Copper and Mai Wong both experienced traumatic events. How does each girl respond differently to her pain?

6. What roles do the mystical creatures play for Copper on her journey, or are these women simply a byproduct of a concussion or stress?

7. Forgiveness is a central theme in *Bones and Lies.* What makes Copper finally forgive herself?

8. One-Leg Larry suffers from both PTSD and addiction. Does this war veteran deserve punishment, or did the system fail him?

9. Addiction and mental illness affect more than just the homeless. What should be done to improve treatment for these often-undiagnosed diseases?

10. Although *Bones and Lies*is told through the eyes of child, a dark, gritty world is portrayed through Paradise (the wrong side of the tracks in Remington, Texas). Which descriptions of Paradise resonated with you most?

11. After reading *Bones and Lies*, has your view of the homeless changed? Why or why not?

The Story Behind the Story

Every summer, my brother, sister and I visited our grandmother in the one-high school town where our dad grew up —Belton, Texas. She always took us by the local cemetery to visit "our people." We'd clear away the weeds, then walk the beautiful property. She spoke of everyone there (above and below the ground) with such love that I began to see cemeteries as mystical, magical places.

Fast-forward to 2008. I was driving out to Llano Cemetery, the historic cemetery in my hometown of Amarillo, Texas. It's a place I've visited countless times over the years since my father is buried there, my maternal grandparents and all my husband's family, too. As I drove past the wrought-iron gates that autumn afternoon, I heard a voice whispering in my ear (that's normal for writers).

At first, it reminded me of a story I'd heard from the local magazine publishers about a story they'd run years before. A homeless woman lived at that very cemetery. She'd sneak in each night since most people thoughts ghosts and hobgoblins roamed there after dark, so she felt safer.

When I went home and started writing down her story, I realized, ... this isn't an adult ... it's a young girl. She's ten, maybe eleven...homeless and alone. Her mama's missing, too. *Where the hell's her mama?*This child is smart and sassy, but also hungry and scared. That's the day Copper Daniels was born.

The rest is history.

Other Fiction from SkipJack Publishing

PAMELA FAGAN HUTCHINS

Act One (Prequel, Ensemble Novella)
Saving Grace (Katie #1)
Leaving Annalise (Katie #2)
Finding Harmony (Katie #3)
Heaven to Betsy (Emily #1)
Earth to Emily (Emily #2)
Hell to Pay (Emily #3)
Going for Kona (Michele #1)
Fighting for Anna (Michele #2)
Searching for Dime Box (Michele #3)
Buckle Bunny (Maggie Prequel Novella)
Shock Jock (Maggie Prequel Short Story)
Live Wire (Maggie #1)
Sick Puppy (Maggie #2)
Dead Pile (Maggie #3)
Bombshell (Ava #1)
Stunner (Ava #2)
Knockout (Ava #3)
Switchback (Patrick Flint #1)
Snake Oil (Patrick Flint #2): 2020
Sawbones (Patrick Flint #3): 2020
The Essential Guide to the What Doesn't Kill You Series

REBECCA (R.L.) NOLEN

Deadly Thyme

The Dry

KEN ODER

The Closing

Old Wounds to the Heart

The Judas Murders

Audio, e-book, and paperback versions of most titles available.

Nonfiction from SkipJack Publishing

PAMELA FAGAN HUTCHINS

The Clark Kent Chronicles

Hot Flashes and Half Ironmans

How to Screw Up Your Kids

How to Screw Up Your Marriage

Puppalicious and Beyond

What Kind of Loser Indie Publishes, and How Can I Be One, Too?

HELEN COLIN

My Dream of Freedom: From Holocaust to My Beloved America

Made in the USA
Columbia, SC
23 December 2019

85674846R00198